HIDDEN MOTIVES

"Is it possible you're revising your opinion of me, Vicky? We must meet again."

I shook my head vehemently and Jasper's face hardened.

"Then you still think my honor is in question."

"No! But now I've told the family you want to buy the Hall, too, and they hate you twice as much."

"What? You little idiot! What possessed you to give away our private business?" He grasped me fiercely by my arms. "I have the answer. Marry me, now."

I stared at him, aghast, then struggled to be free of his imprisoning hands. "Marry—you! You must be mad. Make an alliance so you can get your hands on *my* Hall!"

"I should have known that that pile of stone always comes first with you. You should rename it Vengeance Hall. Listen to me, Vicky—"

"No! It's you who wants revenge. You're just using me in all this," I said with a sudden flash of insight.

He groaned, pressing me against him. "If only you knew...." His lips came down on mine, and then he strode to his horse and rode away without looking back.

A BITTER LEGACY

JEAN DAVIDSON

LEISURE BOOKS NEW YORK CITY

A LEISURE BOOK®

December 1993

Published by

Dorchester Publishing Co., Inc.
276 Fifth Avenue
New York, NY 10001

If you purchased this book without a cover you should be aware that this book is stolen property. It was reported as "unsold and destroyed" to the publisher and neither the author nor the publisher has received any payment for this "stripped book."

Copyright © 1993 by Jean Davidson

All rights reserved. No part of this book may be reproduced or transmitted in any form or by any electronic or mechanical means, including photocopying, recording or by any information storage and retrieval system, without the written permission of the Publisher, except where permitted by law.

The name "Leisure Books" and the stylized "L" with design are trademarks of Dorchester Publishing Co., Inc.

Printed in the United States of America.

*My first 'proper' book—
for Brian, with love*

Chapter One

"He has been gathered up to heaven and rests at peace in the arms of a Greater One." I murmured the words on the headstone to myself once more, to reassure myself that finally he was truly dead. For it wasn't grief I felt—no sense of duty could induce that in me—but a wild surge of anger.

I read on, "Albert Victor Lansdowne, aged seventy-five years, 1797–1872." The words had been chiseled in fine script on pale, and as yet unweathered, marble. A single wreath, the leaves already brown and sodden, lay on the fresh grave.

Again anger boiled in me. Why should Albert Victor Lansdowne be gathered up and be at peace in heaven when he'd caused so much pain and suffering while he was alive, especially to my mother? I reached out and touched the smooth cold stone. Solid enough. I wasn't dreaming. It was true, he was dead and could no longer harm the living. Perhaps at last I would be able to let my anger go, now that my dream lay within my grasp.

The wind turned into a sudden squall, increasing the fine sea mist that shrouded the graveyard and which had already coated my thick cape with a sheen of droplets. I pulled the cape closer around my shoulders, more for comfort than warmth. I knew I should leave, but I was irrationally reluctant to go. It was as if I was afraid that when I turned away, the grave would vanish and Albert Lansdowne would be alive again.

I looked around for shelter, but there was none. The small Saxon church on the cliff top was protected only by a low dry-stone wall, and the few trees were stunted bushes, hunching away from the prevailing wind. It was typical of Albert Lansdowne, I thought, to request to be buried far from his own house, in this remote and inhospitable spot.

I'd refused to visit the grave the day before with my mother, because I knew my anger and hatred would upset her. Despite everything, she grieved for the father she hadn't seen for twenty years, since just after my birth. She was waiting for me in the village and, at the thought of her quiet patience, my anger burned anew. Beneath

A Bitter Legacy

my cape, I clenched and unclenched my fists.

At last I turned away, then froze. A man stood in the lych-gate, watching me. I was a stranger here, but the last thing I wanted was to be observed at the Lansdowne grave. So far, since my mother and I had arrived in England a few days before, I had escaped notice. I did not know what awaited me, or whether anyone would try to stop me receiving what was rightfully mine. I wanted it so much that I lived in perpetual fear of someone snatching it from me. I was also in a new country, and I didn't know who to trust. And although this man could not possibly know me or my purpose, I would still be careful.

I averted my face as I walked toward him, hoping to slip by him quickly. To my surprise, he barred my way, forcing me to look at him. I was further shocked to discover that his face was at once both strange and yet familiar.

"You're paying your last respects," he stated rather than asked.

"Sir, I don't know you," I replied. "Let me pass."

"Ah, but *I* know *you*, Miss Victoria Hunter."

My heart thudded with apprehension, but I tried to think coolly. Could we have met before? On the boat perhaps during our crossing? Yet he was not the sort of man one would forget. All the same, I studied him more fully. He wore a thick coat of dark navy wool, black leather riding boots, and was hatless, his hair dark, thick, and slightly wavy, spangled with moisture. His eyes were deep-set, as gray and cold, it seemed to me, as the North Sea, beneath his straight brows. He was not so much handsome as arresting.

"You have the advantage of me, which no doubt pleases you. But I don't know you," I said.

He took my reluctant hand in his warm, dry one and raised it to his lips. "You misunderstand me. We're distantly related by marriage. Perhaps you've heard of me. I'm Jasper Thornley."

I was momentarily relieved. Surely a distant relative could pose no threat to me. I searched my memory for recollection of his name. My mother had received pitifully few letters from her family during our years of exile in America—virtually all the twenty years of my life—but friends had corresponded regularly with her.

"Yes," I said slowly, searching his face for guile, but found none. "I do remember the name, but wasn't there something . . . I remember. Albert Lansdowne forbade you entry to the Hall, no doubt for some minor misdemeanor. So why are you here? Surely you can have no more love for him than I have."

His face abruptly became stony, impassive. "I wanted to see his last resting place." Why did I think he was lying? "And I shall attend the reading of the will tomorrow."

I stared at him in amazement. He must know

A Bitter Legacy

that nothing had been left to him in the will. Then suddenly I remembered that my grandfather, Albert Lansdowne, had hated this nephew of his by marriage, but then, as far as I knew, Albert Lansdowne had hated nearly everyone. That could only recommend my cousin, Jasper Thornley, to me.

"I can see the question clearly in your eyes, and, no, I have no expectations from the will," Jasper Thornley went on with the shadow of a smile. "But you do."

Now I was totally alert, but I could not resist saying it once more, out loud, flinging my triumph to the skies. "It's all to be left to me—everything. The Hall, the mines, the lands will be kept in a trusteeship until I reach the age of twenty-one next year, and after that I can do whatever I please."

It had been the only letter my mother had received from her father in twenty years, a curt and unyielding missive as if from a stranger, informing her of his extraordinary decision. But there had been no explanation. She'd been deeply disappointed at the lack of affection from him or any attempt to resolve their quarrel. That had concerned her more, while I had seethed with victorious delight. My prayers had been heard and answered!

"And have you decided how you wish to dispose of the house and lands?" he asked. "Has anyone else discussed the matter with you?"

"Dispose of? But I intend to accept my inheritance and live in Lansdowne Hall."

He frowned. He looked . . . Yes, he looked baffled and oddly disappointed. "Live in that bleak house so far from civilization? With a family you've never even met?"

"I'll get used to it," I objected. "Holmby Village is nearby. As for my family, I shall be telling them to live elsewhere." I couldn't wait to see their faces when I ordered them out.

He tilted his head, curious. "A tiny village when you've been used to Boston, America? Used to the company of other young ladies and visiting shops, concerts, and galleries? And to forego the company of your family, too? You must have some special reason."

"Of course! I've always dreamed of living at Lansdowne Hall." I decided to say no more. I had already betrayed too much of my feelings. What was it about this man that compelled me to speak the truth, even though it made me appear in a bad light to him? But how could I explain to a stranger that at last, with my inheritance, I could right all the wrongs to my mother, after the long years of hardship she'd suffered alone in a foreign country when her unforgiving father, Albert Lansdowne, had refused to help her. At last, through my good fortune, we'd be returned to our rightful place.

But, as part of the family, however much on the edge, he must know all this. So why didn't

A Bitter Legacy

he look at me more sympathetically?

Instead, his expression was hardening, and his next words shook me. "Then I must warn you. You will meet opposition. It is one thing to dream of the Hall, another to possess it. I know, to my cost."

"Then you wanted it, too. So you must understand how I feel."

He hesitated for a moment, then said, "Yes, that's it. I wanted to find out your price for the Hall. Perhaps you would consider selling it to me."

I couldn't stop myself from laughing. "Sell it! Never."

His eyes grew flinty, his mouth set in a firm line, and I saw a new aspect of this man. He had determination and resolve, just like me. And he had just decided that he was now my opponent.

"Then I must warn you, if you persist in your idea, and refuse to listen to the warning of those who know, I cannot answer for the consequences. I ask you to reconsider. Sell to me."

A tendril of mist passed between us, seeming to distort his features, and I shivered. For the first time I was aware of how alone we were and of my vulnerability. "My—my mother is expecting me. I must go," I said, my voice faltering as if something was instead compelling me to stay and be near him. Then I found a shred of my old familiar anger to strengthen me and spoke up more bravely, "And you remember, cousin, that I shall sell to no one, and I shall live nowhere else!"

The house in which my mother had insisted on renting rooms in the fishing village of Seadale, not far from Staithes on the wild northeast coast, had thick stone walls, built to withstand powerful winter gales over the centuries. It was so old that none of the floors or walls stood at right angles to each other any longer, and the floorboards creaked alarmingly. Nevertheless, it was cheerful and homely.

As I had expected, none of the Lansdownes had yet greeted us or had offered to arrange for our accommodations. My mother, of course, did not find any fault with this, as she had brought us to Seadale so she could visit her father's grave. But she was disturbed at being so close to the heaving expanse of the sea. We could hear it clawing restlessly night and day, and it made her anxious. The previous night she'd begged me to sit with her until she'd fallen asleep, but she still had passed a restless night, she had told me earlier this morning.

When I entered the parlor of our lodgings, she smiled affectionately, bringing a reflection of her former beauty to her face. But the smattering of gray in her hair, once the same as my own bright reddish-brown curls, gave it a faded look, and her features had softened and blurred with worry over the years. My joy at being able to restore her to her rightful position at Lansdowne Hall burned strongly inside me again.

"I've ordered tea," she said. "Come and thaw out by the fire. What possessed you to go out in weather like this? I'd forgotten just how damp the Yorkshire sea frets can be."

Before I could answer, Mrs. Cowperthwaite brought in the tray, banging it down and muttering with disapproval that we were having tea half an hour late, and probably begrudging that we were having it at all. My mother merely smiled softly, and I was angry on her behalf yet again. How people abused and had always abused her! But I intended to set that right now, and would wipe the anxiety from her face and make her beautiful again.

When she'd handed me my teacup, I told her, "I went up to the churchyard. I wanted to go alone."

She became very still. "I wish you'd accompanied me yesterday." she chided gently.

"I wasn't sure what my reaction would be and I didn't want to spoil your visit. You know how I feel about *him*. I was surprised at the simple headstone. I'd've thought he would have ordered something more flamboyant, in keeping with what he thought was his position in the world."

"Vicky, you mustn't speak about your grandfather like that," she said firmly.

"Hardly surprising, though, after all I've watched you endure because of him. He cut you off from your family and friends, condemned you to poverty and—"

"Please, Vicky! Has your life been so bad? Besides, we're still in mourning and mustn't speak ill of the dead."

"Why not? What can he do to harm us now?" As I spoke, however, there came an extra strong gust of wind, as if mocking me. I shrugged it off rather than betray my uneasiness.

"From respect, Vicky dear, respect for the head of our family who, whatever his . . . shortcomings, deserves our sincere grief."

There were tears in her eyes, and I relented. I hadn't seen her cry since we'd received the news of *his* death—I hated calling him Grandfather—but I knew from her puffy eyes in the mornings that she cried, alone, during the night.

"Now, I won't hear any more about it. What did you think of the inscription?" she asked resolutely.

We agreed, at last, that it was appropriate, and then Mrs. Cowperthwaite brought us more hot water for the tea, sniffed, and left.

"She doesn't like us," I said.

Mother laughed. "Of course she does. It's just her way. People are like that round here, but underneath they're friendly. You'll soon get used to it."

A Bitter Legacy

I hoped I would. I wouldn't let anything stand between me and my full enjoyment of my inheritance. That thought reminded me of Jasper Thornley, and I put down my unfinished buttered teacake.

"What's the matter? You usually have such a good appetite. I hope you haven't caught a cold."

"I'm not ill, Mama. No, today I met someone at the graveyard. He told me he was Jasper Thornley. I remembered that he is your nephew by marriage, but I don't know how he recognized me."

That thought had been bothering me ever since I'd left the graveyard and was free from the influence of those compelling gray eyes. I'd walked briskly down the hill, my spine tingling as if he were watching me. When I dared to look back, though, he was gone. For a moment I wondered if I'd imagined the whole encounter, then my common sense had reasserted itself. All the same, I'd almost run the rest of the way down the rutted lane, splashing through puddles, ignoring the twigs and thorns that caught at my clothes, in case he came after me and somehow managed to persuade me to change my mind.

How had he known me? The question still nagged. Had he skillfully led the conversation away from that natural question, or had we simply been intent on other matters? More disturbingly, it led to another question. Had he deliberately followed me, or was it a chance meeting? If he was following me, for how long had he been doing so, and why? However, I remembered that he had looked familiar to me. But for now I contented myself with the thought that though I favored my father much more than I did the Lansdownes, he had seen some family resemblance in me, and added that to his knowledge that I was in England, and that I had visited my grandfather's grave.

However, I could not entirely dismiss my doubts about him, even though my mother's next words made me bury them in the back of my mind for now.

"I remember young Jasper. I always liked him, but, of course, they said he was wild. A bad influence, I think that was it. It was so long ago. What did you think of him?" she asked.

"His manner was overbearing. He certainly wasn't troubled by grief. He said he was coming to the reading of the will, too."

A faraway look entered her eyes. "I shall look forward to seeing him again. His Aunt Leonie, my stepmother, was beautiful and always wore such fine clothes. There used to be a portrait of her over the fireplace in the drawing room. She had expressive gray eyes and ivory skin. Her death was so sudden. It was then that Papa—" She stopped abruptly, and I recalled Jasper's fine gray eyes, which had impressed me deeply.

And, as always, I listened avidly to anything

A Bitter Legacy

she had to say about the past, about our family, and especially about the Hall. I knew every inch of it now in my imagination and soon, soon, it would be mine.

"Did he spend a lot of time at the Hall when he was a boy?" I asked.

"Leo, his father, was close to his sister, Leonie, but my father tried to discourage Jasper from visiting us. He was fearless and such a reckless rider. I think Father feared he would be a bad influence on my brother, William. They used to ride out together over the moors." As usual, when she talked about her youth, her face glowed, and she lost some of her forty-four years. "Did Jasper say something to trouble you?" she asked. "To make you lose your appetite?"

I shook my head quickly. There was no need to add to her burdens. "Nothing can ever trouble us again. Within the week we'll be at the Hall, in our rightful place, and you'll never again have to endure—" I broke off, unwilling to dredge up old sorrows. "Everything will be all right."

"Oh, Vicky." She sighed. "You're so clear in your mind about what you want. I fear that you'll be disappointed."

"Never," I said firmly.

She frowned. "I wonder if there's still friction between him and the other members of the family? I hope there won't be any unpleasantness tomorrow."

Privately, I didn't mind if there was. "Their feuds need not involve us. Only tell me more about Jasper's Aunt Leonie. Did everyone hate it when *Grandfather* Albert brought a beautiful new bride home with him?" I asked, finally for my mother's sake acknowledging the old man's relationship to me.

"Everyone loved Leonie. She was the peacemaker in the household and helped us all forget our grief at my mother's death. Then Leonie's own death nearly broke my father's heart, but he had their daughter, little Adele, to remember her by, and did he spoil that child!" She laughed softly. "But where was I? Oh, yes, Jasper came regularly to visit his aunt, bringing messages from his father to mine." She frowned. "But I'm not sure what that was about."

"What did he do to anger Grandfather, though? Or did Grandfather just decide to dislike him?"

"Now, Vicky! I'm sure whatever it was was just some boyish prank. After that, Leonie had little contact with her family. You must remember that the grownups did not share their thoughts with their children. We lived in a world of nursery and schoolroom, with nannies, governesses, and tutors to care for us. You have had a quite different upbringing, sharing my hardships."

"I wouldn't have had it any other way," I replied fervently and truthfully.

A worried frown creased her face, and her

fingers interlaced tightly. "This will be the first time . . ." she said quietly, but didn't have to finish her statement that this would be the first time she'd faced the remnants of her family in twenty years. It would be my first time, too, as I didn't remember any of them, being barely out of the cradle when we'd left.

"Perhaps it's a good thing Jasper will be there. He may be a friend to us," she added encouragingly.

I couldn't tell her what he'd threatened. It would only distress her, but neither could I let her cherish false hopes. "No, he didn't give me the impression he'd be on our side. We'll be alone."

She sighed. "I hope you're wrong. There must be someone who—"

"We don't need anyone now. They'll be the ones needing us. As for Jasper, I suspect his motives."

The oil lamp suddenly flared and smoked, sending shadows dancing crazily in the far corners of the room. To hide my fear, the fear engendered by Jasper's opposition, that all I'd hoped for and dreamed of would be stripped from me in some way, I jumped to my feet and rang the bell loudly.

"Drat that woman!" I exclaimed. "Can't she even trim the lamps properly?"

"Vicky! You must learn to be more patient, understanding. I fear for you sometimes. You are so unbending. I sometimes think . . . I don't know."

There was something she wanted to say, but I could see her holding back, for fear of offending me. She could see how tautly I was strung. That added to my other fears, and all the strength of purpose and elation I had built up, the sure knowledge of a happy and secure future, melted away and foreboding spoke to me from the shadowed corners of the room.

Mother and I were the last to arrive at the solicitor Mr. John Pontefract's office in Whitby. One of the oldest established firms in town, his office was on the first floor, providing us glimpses from the window of the estuary and fishing boats, and the steep hill on the far side of the river. There the cottages of the old town clustered together almost on top of one another, their red pantiled roofs and tall chimneys giving them a quaint appeal, while high above on the rocky headland stood the gaunt ruins of the Abbey. It was another dull gray day of driving rain, and I was glad of the small coal fire in Mr. Pontefract's grate.

I had avoided examining the other occupants of the room, who had greeted my mother coldly, indifferently, or with curiosity when we had entered the office. But now I had to acknowledge their presence and abandon the haughty distant look I'd adopted. I was going to be presented, for the first time, to my family. But it was not a joyful occasion, and my mother's nervousness at seeing them again after so many years was clear. But she held her head high, and I was proud of her.

With what I was to learn was his usual bluff manner, Mr. Pontefract began the introductions. "This is your Great-uncle Samuel."

"Victoria." My grandfather's younger brother and sole surviving sibling acknowledged me with a stiff inclination of his head. His thick side whiskers were gray, and his hooded blue eyes were blurred with age, his hands knobbed with arthritis. He was clearly disinclined to talk to me, deliberately moving away to stand by the fire, warming his hands and studying the landscape painting on the wall.

"Your stepaunt Adele."

She wore a startling outfit in magenta, with contrasting ribs of silk and velvet, her cuffs richly decorated with buttons and lace. Her hat, perched on the front of her silvery, slightly old-fashioned chignon, was a gathering of net, feathers, and beads. She wore a black armband in mourning. She was only four years older than I, but contrived to seem much more adult, perhaps by virtue of her widow- and motherhood. She was stunningly beautiful, inherited, no doubt, from her mother, Leonie Lansdowne, née Thornley, Jasper's aunt.

"Little Vicky," she said, taking my hand in

her cool fingers for a moment. "Such terrible weather for your first visit to England. Do you remember anything about your childhood here? I remember you in your frilly bib and bonnet."

"Nothing at all," I said, disliking the way she was claiming maturity over me. "And the New England weather is not so different, apart from the extremes of winter."

Adele laughed daintily, which I assumed she had practiced often, as it sounded so contrived. "Listen to her accent, so American. You'd never guess she was English at all. And how was your crossing?"

"I enjoyed every moment, though it was long and uneventful, with only one storm to speak of. There were huge icebergs, too, quite spectacular, bigger than cathedrals—"

"A storm. Weren't you seasick?" Adele stopped my flow of words, and I realized that she hadn't been asking me questions because she was interested in the answers, but because she was after something else. To show me up? I shook my head, and she continued, "I suffer dreadfully from the *mal de mer*, even on a river, but then I suffer all the delicate ladies' complaints."

I found that hard to believe. Despite her fair skin, she looked robust enough to me.

"Your dress is fashionable at least," she said, looking me up and down. "I didn't think you'd be able to get the latest modes in America."

A Bitter Legacy

She said the last word as if it were distasteful.

My best defence, to laugh, came easily, though for a moment I felt homesick for Boston's graceful streets and vivid fall colors. "But these are Boston's *last* season clothes. We haven't been able to open our trunks yet."

"Oh, I can't get used to the funny way you speak. No one will believe you're related to an English family."

"Hardly surprising, as I've never visited before. And whose fault is that?"

"Victoria," came my mother's warning voice.

"I daresay you'll learn English ways," Adele said, but, although she still smiled, now it was the smile of a cobra, seeking the right target for its deadly strike. "Though once a colonial, always a colonial, they say."

"I wouldn't want to be otherwise," I told her. "I feel sorry for those who lack the confidence to be proud of their origins."

The cobra in Adele withdrew slightly, biding its time to draw blood.

Mr. Pontefract seized the opportunity. "Your first cousins, George and Sophie, son and daughter of your deceased Great-uncle Robert."

No brother and sister could be so unalike, I thought. There was only the faintest resemblance around the mouth to indicate they were related, the full and wide Lansdowne lips, but Sophie didn't have the straight nose that we'd all inherited. Hers had a crooked bump in the middle.

As if following my train of thought, George said, "You have the Lansdowne coloring all right. That hair and those eyes are unmistakable. Alexandra, why are you hiding there?" He seized my mother's hand and drew her forward. "You're to be congratulated on your lovely daughter. An asset to our family." Then he turned back to me. "Vicky, I've been longing to meet you, but not under such sad circumstances. I promise I had intended to come visit you in America. I didn't expect such a beauty. Isn't she lovely, Sophie?"

George's warm welcoming smile was reflected in his brown eyes, as he gave me a cousinly kiss on the cheek. His skin glowed with good health, and he was good-looking, his brown curls neat. In contrast, Sophie was a pale, whispering moth, her voice barely audible, her eyes cast down submissively.

George began to question my mother about our journey, and so I moved on to the last remaining person, standing apart from the others, and Mr. Pontefract said hurriedly, "This is your cousin by marriage, Jasper Thornley."

I'd been aware of him all the time, standing silently apart from the others, his clothes more somber, especially against George's fashionably bright checked trousers, yet more stylish. Adele, too, had constantly flicked her diamond-hard eyes in his direction. He seemed from a different world than the others—harder, leaner, more purposeful. But then, there wasn't a drop of Lansdowne blood in his veins, though I fancied the difference was due to something more than that.

Jasper took my hand, his fingers warm and firm around mine, and I was about to refer to our first meeting, and to ask him how he recognized me, when he spoke first. "This must be a momentous occasion for you, Miss Hunter. Not one you'd choose for first meetings."

George overheard and misinterpreted his words. "And it's your last meeting with her, Thornley, indeed with any of us. Mr. Pontefract insisted you be here, some legal folderol, but you have no right. I have not forgotten. None of us have."

With that, he turned his back on us, copied by Sophie, but not before she fixed us with a look of fearful fascination. The look in Jasper's eyes, by contrast, held a glint of white-hot rage, but he held it in check.

"I think you will find your long-lost family rather different from what you had expected," he said quietly, so that only I could hear him. My mother was talking with Mr. Pontefract, the Lansdownes were grouped together, casting dark glances at us, Adele's mouth turned down at the corners with displeasure.

"On the contrary, Mr. Thornley, they are

exactly as I had expected," I said crisply. "I'm only disappointed there are only these remaining four."

Immediately, he understood. "You wanted to take the whole family on?"

"Of course. Perhaps you do not know, Mr. Thornley, but my history has not been the same as that of the rest of my privileged," I spat the word out, "family. They have plenty to answer for."

"I'm aware of that, too. Be sure of that," he said, his voice heavy with meaning.

Now Mr. Pontefract claimed our attention. "It is time to read the will. Unfortunately, Miss Hunter, your Aunt Caroline is not, er, well enough to attend."

There was a short, awkward silence. My mother's sister, Caroline, had been in a home for gentlewomen for her nerves for many, many years. My mother grieved for her and wanted to visit her as soon as it could be arranged.

"Get on with it, man," Great-uncle Samuel said testily. "Read the will."

We all crowded closer, while Mr. Pontefract sat down behind his desk, cleared his throat, and picked up the relevant papers. As he read the opening phrases, I thought of my Great-uncle Samuel, stepaunt Adele, cousins George and Sophie, living at the Hall, kept in obedience by my grandfather's threats to disinherit them, waiting out his lingering illness of the past two years in expectation. And now their hopes were going to be thwarted. Everything was to be mine, mine, and therefore my mother's. It was going to give me great satisfaction to tell each one of my family to move out and find homes elsewhere—even George, who surely could not be as friendly as he appeared. I still placed my faith in no one.

I allowed myself a small smile of joy, which was spoiled by the way Jasper looked at me knowingly, as if he could see into my heart and didn't like what he saw there. Well, I felt the same way about him. What was he but a scavenger, after whatever tidbits he could find?

"And now I come to the reading of the will proper. There are bequests for some of the servants, but I'll attend at the Hall to read those. This will was drawn up six months ago, and supersedes all others.

" 'I do hereby bequeath, in the absence of a male heir, due to the tragic loss of my son, William, in 1861, and the lack of issue from my demented daughter, Caroline, over whom I pray the Lord keep watch, Lansdowne Hall, its contents, and parkland to Victoria Ann Hunter. The two mines and the freight railway and shipping berth I bequeath to George Lansdowne—' "

We all gasped. I felt dizzy and the room spun. What good was the Hall without the income from the mines, rail, and berth to pay for its upkeep? What madness was this of my grandfather's, to split the fortune and property? I imagined I could hear him laughing hollowly from his grave. Even in death he had contrived to cause dismay and dissension in the family he'd ruled tyrannically for all these years.

Then steady gray eyes locked onto mine. For some reason, Jasper was giving me the strength to hold in check my horror at this blow. Now was not the time to betray any weakness. Then my mother was at my side, pressing my arm to support and comfort me, too.

"The will states quite categorically that income from the businesses cannot be used for the upkeep of the Hall," Mr. Pontefract continued. "But the annuities et cetera can be paid from it. Finally, Albert Lansdowne has nominated Samuel, Adele, and me as trustees till Victoria reaches twenty-one next year."

Adele! I hadn't expected that additional blow. She threw me a quick sharp glance, and my blood boiled. Why her of all people? Provision was made for Caroline's continued upkeep; Adele was left a reasonable annuity and two mares in the stables; and Sophie was awarded an annuity, all to be provided from what was now George's vast income. The one that should have been mine.

"I warned him that this was not a sensible way to dispose of his property and income, but Albert was determined on this course of action and, as you know, once his mind was made up nothing could change it. It can't be contested, either. I'm sorry, Miss Hunter, but he made sure of that." Mr. Pontefract straightened the papers on his desk, and I realized that he was quite human after all. "I've arranged for a decanter of sherry to be brought in, so that we may drink to his memory."

Great-uncle Samuel, Adele, and Sophie were gathered around George, congratulating him, while I managed to fix a bland smile on my face, though I felt like scowling and shaking my fist, once more, at my grandfather. Jasper was murmuring to Mr. Pontefract, who was shaking his head.

"Vicky, I'm sorry," my mother said. "I know how much you were looking forward to living at the Hall, even though I've had my doubts."

"I should be comforting you, Mama. Anyway, all is not lost yet. I'm determined you should spend your remaining years in the house where you were born."

A smile flashed across her face. "I hope I have many remaining years and much to do in them, daughter."

"Of course. I only meant . . ." I trailed off, aware that silence had fallen and George was approaching us.

"I can't tell you what a revelation this has been for all of us, especially me. Grandfather was a dark horse all right." He smiled guilelessly. "Now, I know it's too early for you to plan ahead, but I promise you that when you decide to sell the Hall, if you come to me first, I'll give you a better than fair price. It's up to me to do all I can to help you and to keep the Hall in the family."

Everyone fell silent, waiting for my answer. This time I avoided Jasper's sardonic gaze.

"Thanks, George, but I don't want to sell."

"Foolish child," Great-uncle Samuel spoke up crustily. "How can you afford to live there or run the house? You could hardly make above a few hundred pounds of income a year from the woodlands and other produce. Even grazing rights in the parkland or a flock of sheep will not increase your income to the level required. I should know. I've been handling the accounts all these years. What would a young girl like you know about figures and money? Know how to spend it, that's all. Albert was a sick man to have made such a will."

His voice quavered slightly at the end, but I hardened my heart. "I'll find a way," I answered with quiet determination, "And be assured, Great-uncle Samuel, that I will give you all plenty of time to find yourselves somewhere else to live. I wouldn't want any of you to suffer any *hardship!*"

The taste of revenge was sweet. I hadn't meant to tell them so soon, but I couldn't resist it. Now I looked at Jasper, and saw his cool, knowing smile which was directed at me, and it affected

A Bitter Legacy

me much more than the gasps of protest from my relatives.

"Alexandra, can't you keep your wayward daughter in order?" Great-uncle Samuel barked. "Children should not threaten their elders and betters."

"Victoria is a thoughtful and loving daughter, Uncle Samuel," my mother replied equably.

He dismissed her with a sniff, not deigning to look at her, which made me seethe with anger.

"Thank goodness Grandfather had the sense to make me a trustee." I heard Adele saying, her eyes sparkling with enmity. "At least the Hall won't go to rack and ruin for another six months, till your birthday next spring, with my keeping an eye on things."

Her cuts smarted, but I didn't let it show. I was rapidly resolving that she would be the first to go.

"I'll learn all I need to know from my mother," I said shortly. "After all, she lived in the Hall for as long as you have."

"Vicky," George said, "I know I spoke too soon. This has been a shock—for me, for you, for all of us, and that's making you say things you don't mean. There's plenty of time for you to plan your future, and I shouldn't have spoken of your selling yet, though I do think it's the right course of action. Meanwhile, remember I do want to do everything I can to help you and for all of us to be friends. Sophie, too. Isn't that so?"

Sophie, her eyes still downcast, murmured agreement.

"Thank you, George. You mean to be kind and I don't want to quarrel with you, but I shall not change my mind—ever," I answered firmly.

Everyone seemed to burst out talking at once, and then Jasper, silent till now, suddenly took charge. "A toast," he said, "to the future, and to the truth and justice it's sure to bring."

Silence reigned as only I and Mr. Pontefract raised our glasses. I realized, with a heavy thud of my heart, that while the Lansdownes disliked and despised my mother and me, they really hated Jasper.

"Although the Lansdownes are renowned for their fighting spirit, I suggest this is not the time for a family squabble over the contents of the will," Jasper went on. "Albert has made sure he will not easily be forgotten. Each of us will have cause to remember him well. Now, I shall accompany Victoria and her mother to their lodgings."

George burst out angrily, "Why did you come, Thornley? You know you're not wanted."

Jasper's smile was thin-lipped. "Do you think I care whether you want me here? I go where I please. Wasn't that what William always said?"

Silence again, but this one crawled with meanings I couldn't understand and was broken, surprisingly, by Sophie. "We should let Jasper alone. I'm sure he means no harm."

"On the contrary," Jasper said, "I think your brother knows I mean you every harm."

In the hubbub that followed, I couldn't help admiring Jasper's turn of phrase, then Mr. Pontefract cleared his throat and unwillingly the Lansdownes came to heel, to conclude our business.

My mother, to my surprise, accepted Jasper's offer to accompany us to our lodgings in Seadale. One by one, we made our way down the outer stone steps along the arched alleyway to the street. The rain had washed mud and debris into the gutters, and every time a horse or cart went by, the pavements were awash with more filthy water. While Jasper went down the hill to hire a carriage, my mother and I waited in the covered alleyway. George had tried to dissuade my mother from allowing Jasper to go with us. But, when she had refused to budge, he'd shrugged, grinned, and said, "Like mother, like daughter, I suppose. Ah, we shall have some fun together," and then went off after the others.

While my mother watched for Jasper, I saw my newly met relatives walk the few yards to their own personal carriage, with a fancy *L* painted on the side in gold, pulled by their own horses. Or mine, I suddenly realized, and couldn't resist a smirk of pleasure. They were getting into *my* carriage and expecting to be pulled by *my* horses. Except that they would be fed and maintained by *George's* money.

I ground my teeth in frustration. Why had Albert Lansdowne done this? What purpose could he have had? When he cared so much about his family name and fortune, why divide and weaken it? I could feel his devious plotting beginning to manipulate me, and I hated it.

Soon we were inside our carriage, dry if not particularly warm or comfortable. I sat with my back to the horse and driver, while Jasper sat beside my mother, and then I realized why she'd wanted him to travel with us. She wanted to talk about the past, and he was happy to indulge her reminiscences, which inevitably brought them to his current circumstances. He revealed that he was living in the south of France with his father, had neither a wife nor fiancée, and that he had only recently returned to England.

At least their conversation, and I knew this was deliberate on my mother's part—how well she knew me—distracted me from the shock of having my dream overturned. When we arrived, my mother excused herself, explaining that she needed to rest. "Will you thank Jasper and see him out?" she requested of me.

Alone at last, we stood in the tiny, shadowed entranceway between the stout wooden door and thick curtain to the living room.

A Bitter Legacy

"What do you make of your family, Victoria?" Jasper asked.

"I know I wouldn't have missed the reunion for anything."

"Mmm. Such a pretty and innocent face you have, but I believe that's only skin deep. I believe you have a troubled spirit."

"One that will be troubled no more. This is the day that fulfills my dreams. At last my mother will live the way she should have all these years," I answered.

"Your mother—or you?" he challenged me.

"You don't think I'd've gone through this ordeal for my own sake, do you? When I think of all she's endured without complaint . . . Even now, she won't hear a word spoken against her father."

"Your grandfather, too, don't forget, and who has left you a considerable property which will provide you with a dowry larger than most girls could wish for—when you sell."

I ignored his last remark. "And look at the way he did it. To cause maximum pain, as always. I'm glad of one thing above all else, that I never had to meet him face-to-face."

"I see they teach you to speak your mind in America!"

"And I intend to speak it now. How did you know who I was yesterday in the graveyard?" I demanded.

His jaw tightened, but he was not dismayed.

Jean Davidson

"My father keeps me well-informed with news, and he showed me a photograph of you."

"Were you following me? Did you think to catch me off guard—easy prey, as it were?" I pressed him.

Emotion suffused his face, but he controlled it, though now the tiny entranceway seemed impossibly tiny and confining. I was imprisoned here with a man who would be my master. Except I wouldn't let him.

He didn't answer my question, but said instead, "The offer I made yesterday still stands. It's the only answer to your dilemma."

"I can overcome this minor setback on my own. Besides, George will offer me a good price—"

Suddenly, he gripped my upper arms. "You will have to sell. It's only a matter of time, and you will sell to me, not George."

"Why? Why not to George? And why is it so important to you? No, I know the answer to that. You feel the same way I do. But how can that be?"

"I'm not sure we do want the same thing. I wish I could be as certain as you are, Victoria. But the choices are not as simple as you believe. I shall have to make sure you can't refuse me."

Now it was no longer Jasper the gentleman who was holding me, trying to impose his will on me, but some wild, unbridled force. I was frightened by the strange, new feelings aroused in me.

A Bitter Legacy

"Go. You must go," I choked out. "I need to rest—to think."

"To scheme and plot, if I understand you. You've Lansdowne blood in your veins right enough," he said.

"You could not have insulted me more deeply!" In my anger, I twisted and turned, but he held me.

"You have plenty of determination," he conceded. "But please remember my warning, which I have given you for your own sake, even though you are a Lansdowne," he said before releasing me and finally leaving.

I could still feel the imprint of his fingers on my arms, and the mixed excitement and apprehension he'd induced in me. Outside it was darker, the clouds more lowering, the wind stronger. Jasper was out there—and Jasper spelled danger to me, somehow. I knew it.

Chapter Two

The next day the weather had changed utterly, as it often does by the sea. The sky was a bright November blue, kept clear by a steady onshore wind, and the sun, although weak, was warm. In answer, my spirits lifted and the dark fears of the last few days vanished. I was glad to be away from Seadale, glad at last to be doing rather than waiting. I was used to a busy life, and too much time alone to brood and question did not suit me. Too many unresolved questions hung in the air, too many crosscurrents had been stirred up. Now I was on the move, and I would sweep them all before me, including Jasper Thornley, and let fresh air and fresh ideas and a glorious future replace them.

In view of the weather, we had hired an open

A Bitter Legacy

carriage, and the back was piled with as much of our luggage as possible. Our trunks, in storage in Whitby, would follow soon. At last on our way to Lansdowne Hall, it was impossible to hide my excitement at seeing the place I had dreamed about and had imagined so often, for the first time. My mother had described it in such detail I felt I knew every brick and stone.

We soon left the coast behind and entered into woodland that would form cool glades in the summer, and crossed and recrossed a small river over arched stone bridges. We passed through several small villages, too, of the same dark stone, and low, squat, and four-square houses. They were definite contrasts to the gracious gables and extensive wood-built homes I was used to in Boston, but they were attractive in their own way and suited the landscape.

Our route took us further inland, and up the valley, or dale as I learned to call it. The river was now a lively stream, or beck, and our pace slowed as the road rose steeply. My heart skipped when my mother said, "Now we are entering Holmby Village. My, but it has grown since I was here last."

Grown! It was little more than a street, and a very steep street indeed, each house several feet higher than its neighbor, with an inn at each end and two provisions stores. But what did it matter? Whitby was near enough and a bustling little town, and there was York on the other side of the moors.

Taking a gentle bend in the road, we left the village behind, and then, as we rose still higher, the trees were, too. We were almost at Sleights Moor, at the edge of the vast North York Moors which, far from being wild and desolate, were fresh and inviting and stretched as far as the eye could see. The purple heather was abundant, the bracken dark and wet, and the red berries provided an occasional splash of color, while a hawk hovered high above. Mama and I pointed all these sights out to each other, but I knew we were approaching nearer to our destination when she became increasingly distracted.

"We're nearly there," she said suddenly. "I recognize this little dip in the road, and there's the stream crossing the road. It's quite deep when the snow melts in spring. Just at the top of the rise is the gate."

Stone gryphons crouched on the solid gateposts, and the curving drive was lined by rhododendrons which would be beautiful in May, red and pink my mother had told me. I clenched my hands and my heart raced. Now we rounded the bend and—there it was!

"Oh, no! What's happened to it? What have they done?" my mother cried in horror.

Above a heavily studded door was a two-storied tower complete with crenellations and a flagpole. At the ends of the old manor were turrets, and here and there a stained-glass window. The walls were covered with ivy and the bare trunk and branches of virginia creeper. Behind the main building, I knew, was the original medieval hall around whose shell the rest of the house had been created.

"It isn't exactly how you described. Those towers are new, aren't they?"

"Some is as I remember it. Those decorated windows, the chapel over there. But it used to be so graceful, so stylish—and now this."

"I do hope . . . You don't think the original hall has been knocked down, do you?"

"No, I can just see a portion of the roof. See, there."

She had begun to recover from her shock, as the baggage was unloaded, and we stood uncertainly on the sweep of gravel to the front of the house. Although we'd announced our arrival time at Mr. Pontefract's office, no one, it seemed, was going to greet us.

Then the front door opened a crack, and a small boy ran out, his golden curls bouncing, shouting, "Hello, hello. I'm Tommy." He was obviously Adele's young son, and would be as handsome as she was beautiful when he grew up.

"Hello, Tommy." My mother smiled and leaned down to give him a hug, while I stroked his fine silky hair.

Adele came hurrying out. "My son," she said

proudly. "He's given that dolt of a nurse the slip again. If she doesn't look out, she'll be dismissed." She took Tommy's hand possessively, then said, "You'll have to meet the servants. They've insisted on lining up in the entrance hall. Sophie's idea, I think." She shrugged carelessly. "She gets these strange notions."

I pressed my lips. I wasn't going to fight with Adele—yet. I wanted to absorb every second of my mother's homecoming.

We entered the house, and I looked around at what was now mine.

The hall had dark panelling, with a wide deeply polished staircase leading up to the gallery above. On the wall were two suits of armor on either side of crossed pikes, two gloomy landscape paintings, and even a stag's head, at which I had to hide a smile. Then I was aware that Sophie was speaking to us so quietly I had to strain my ears to catch her words.

"This is Mr. Gandy, the butler, John, the footman, Mrs. Ackroyd, the housekeeper, Mrs. Randell, the cook, and these are . . ." Her voice trailed away in a series of maids, with Ned, head driver and groom, and the gardeners last.

The hall was filled with people, more than I'd expected, though if I had thought about it, a titled household would have double or triple this number of servants. I should have realized it would take all these people to run such a large estate. Numerous mouths to feed, bodies to clothe, persons whose welfare would be my concern. A wave of panic seized me. Where would I find the money? Was I equal to the challenge of managing such a household? Then I caught sight of Adele eyeing me, waiting for me to give way, which immediately steadied me. I began to greet each of them calmly and correctly, as I'd been taught.

Once I had squared my shoulders and lifted my chin, I was able to assess each of the servants in turn. The younger ones were clearly more in awe of me than the more experienced among them. Mr. Gandy stared straight over my head, punctilious in his behavior. Mrs. Ackroyd dropped a quick bob, but her small black eyes were watchful in her pinched face. Ned gave a cheerful grin, but Mrs. Randell, the cook, greeted my mother with genuine warmth and the familiarity of friendship.

"Welcome home, ma'am," she said, her broad face glowing.

I remembered how she had featured often in my mother's stories. I had come to imagine her domain, the kitchen, as a haven of peace in a household often at odds with itself, at least in later years. It had also been the scene of much jollity, as well as good food. I was glad that we had at least one friend, someone we could trust, at Lansdowne Hall.

Now I was able to survey them all with satisfaction. In six month's time this was going to be my little kingdom, not Adele's, or Great-uncle Samuel's—not even George's or Sophie's. I closed my eyes for a moment, the better to savor our triumphal return.

"You can all go back to your work now. Enough time has been lost," Adele said brusquely, and I wondered if hers was a kind hand or a vicious one on the reins of the household.

As the servants began to disperse and Adele moved away with Tommy, my mother said quietly, but firmly, "Our rooms, Adele. Will you or Sophie be showing us up?"

Adele made a noise of irritation. "Rosie will do it," she said, and called to one of the maids. "You can share Rosie as your maid. She usually helps Sophie, but you won't mind, will you, Sophie? I suppose I can spare my own Elise to come to you, not that you bother much with your dress. Now I have some letters to write. I need your help, Sophie."

Sophie had been irresolutely standing by, but, far from being a presence that could be overlooked, there was a tension about her that made one aware of her all the time.

"Thank you for making us welcome," I said to her. "Shall we see you at dinner?"

"Oh, yes," she said. "And I had to do this, don't you see? The house must be properly introduced to its new people, has to get the feel of them."

A Bitter Legacy

I stared after her retreating back as she glided away, having ignored Adele's command and heading off to her own business. I wondered if I'd misheard her, but she'd definitely referred to the Hall as if it were a person.

As we followed Rosie up the stairs, a young woman, dressed in blue and a large white apron, with the copperiest red hair I'd ever seen, appeared on the half landing.

"It's that little rascal Tommy," she said to Rosie. "Hasn't he given me the slip again?"

"Maire, come down here!" Adele commanded. "I want a word with you and it will be my very last warning. You'll be on the next boat back to Ireland if you let my son wander unprotected once more."

"I'm in for a dressing down again," I heard her murmur to Rosie as they passed each other, and she gave us a little curtsy. "Sure an' isn't he just a normal little boy? She'll suffocate him, she will."

I could sympathize with her, having been on the receiving end of Adele's sharp tongue.

Alone at last in my new bedroom, I walked excitedly around, admiring its size, the opulence of the big brass bed and its counterpane of flowered silk; the richly patterned red Turkish carpet; the tasseled ropes that held back the curtains, the walnut escritoire; and the big carved oak press for my clothes.

When my mother joined me, I said, "Well, Mama, how was your room? This is splendid.

I feared they would try to hide us away in an attic, preferably with a ghost for company. Rosie tells me there's even a bathroom with proper plumbing next door."

"I—It's comfortable." She frowned and bit her lip. "Victoria, I want to talk to you."

We sat side by side in the window seat. "Look out there, Mama, there's the beautiful cedar tree you described to me, and the parkland almost as far as the eye can see, with just a hint of the moors beyond. What a splendid homecoming!"

But she was shaking her head, looking very serious. "Vicky, listen to me carefully. You know that I haven't been happy with any of this, and I told you when the letter arrived from Mr. Pontefract informing me of my father's death that we would make this journey because I wanted you to see where you were born. It was also my last chance to see my old home."

"Hardly your last chance. This is our new beginning."

She glanced away. "When we first heard, perhaps I hoped, though my father never said . . . But during the sea crossing, I had plenty of time to think and I know now my conclusions were right. We don't belong here. I feared it all along, but now I know there's nothing here for us. We're Bostonians through and through."

"How can you be so sure when we've only spent one week in England?" I burst out heatedly, deeply disquieted. "You haven't given it any time. We'll soon settle in."

"Don't tell me that you aren't a little disappointed," she said shrewdly. "The house is not quite as you imagined, the weather has been dark and dismal. Can you imagine a winter imprisoned here, cut off by snow?" She shuddered. "We're used to busy city life. I'd forgotten all the inconveniences here in the rosy glow of memory. I really believe that home is where our hearts are and that's America.

"No, Vicky, George has offered us the perfect solution. He will buy the Hall, so that it stays in the family, and we can return to our old life in Boston once we have finished our business here. We can tour England, of course, perhaps the Continent, too, before we go home," she added quickly when she saw the expression on my face.

I'd thought her subdued manner ever since the reading of the will was due to being overcome with emotion. But I'd been wrong. Instead, she'd been reaching conclusions, decisions.

"But living at Lansdowne Hall, your home, is what I've been hoping and dreaming for all my life! I've never felt I belonged in Boston, but here, in this house. I know I'll come to love it just as much as you did. You've described every inch to me."

She shook her head. "That was wrong of me, and I blame myself for making you unhappy with our home in Boston. What is Lansdowne Hall, after all? Just bricks and stones and glass.

I tell you, Vicky, if we don't leave, it'll bring us nothing but sorrow."

I laughed. "Since when have you had the second sight, Mama? Look, if we had been left the money as well as the Hall, you would not be saying these things. You're only worried that we won't be able to keep up the house. I promise you I'll find a way. It'll be all right."

Her eyes filled with sadness. "Darling Vicky, sometimes I think you're doing this for me, rather than for yourself. I wish you'd believe that it's not what I want. If only you weren't so stubborn! It's at times like this that you remind me of your father, and how I wish he'd had a hand in your upbringing. You'd not be so headstrong then. He seems so close to me here, too, after all these years."

I was silent for a moment, out of respect for her memories, then burst out, "Please, Mama, give me some time. I want to get to know the Hall, and perhaps you're right, I'll be homesick for America and want to go back."

My ruse seemed to work. I hoped that, given time, she'd fall in love with her old home again and not want to leave. She said, "Of course you must have time. Enjoy the house and park, meet local acquaintances, get to know your family. You're young, and this is an important experience for you. But I beg you, don't lose sight of George's generous offer before he changes his mind."

A Bitter Legacy

This was the ideal moment to tell her that Jasper, too, had offered to buy the Hall. But the words would not come. Normally, I would have kept nothing as important as that from my mother. Since there had only been the two of us we were more than mother and daughter. We were friends, and I could not understand my reluctance to part with Jasper's secret proposition. It made me uncomfortable. It was as if, though he and I were opposing forces, we were also private allies.

I told myself that the truth of the matter was that I knew his offer was laughable or part of some plot. So instead, I asked, "What on earth made Grandfather Lansdowne make such a crazy will?"

"I just don't know. I managed to have a private word with Mr. Pontefract, and there were no private letters or papers to be found. My father destroyed them all before he died apparently. Nor was there a codicil to the will."

"He must have had some plan in mind?"

She looked out the window. "Who knows? I cannot pretend to understand my father, though I've had twenty years to think about him, any more than to say that the Lansdowne name and heritage were everything to him. He wanted to build an empire to ensure his immortality. Nothing and no one would be allowed to stand in his way. And that included me when I chose my own husband instead of the man he wanted, who is now Sir Gransby and whose estate lies alongside ours." She sighed, still gazing out the window, still remembering the past.

"He was a good father, if remote. Caroline, William, and I had no complaints when we were children, and young George adored him, wanted to be with him rather than with us. But later on my father changed, his ideas grew bigger." She caught my eye. "I shouldn't be telling you this."

"Please go on. I'd like to know everything."

"No. In fact, I'm making a new resolution, to turn my back on the past. I've wasted too much of our lives looking back. This visit will be an exorcism. We must both live in the present from now on."

"But what about my father? Will you forget him, too? You've always hoped that—"

"I'll never stop hoping that somewhere he's still alive, unless we actually discover how and when he died. Now, Vicky, you'll see the wisdom of my words, I know you will. At the moment you're excited by the idea of exploring new horizons, and that's as it should be. I'll leave you to finish settling in, and then we'll dress for dinner."

I had no intention of changing my mind, however, and felt guilty deceiving her. We had never had a major clash of wills, and the last person I wanted or needed to battle with was my mother. But I refused to let go of my dream.

A Bitter Legacy

It was, anyway, as much for her as for me. For the first time, I felt a link with my grandfather. The Lansdowne heritage was everything to him. And so it was to me.

I had dressed in a dark blue silk with embroidered flowers at the hem, and as I entered the dining room, I realized that my gown could at least compete with Adele's splendid silk taffeta. I had hoped that dinner would be a special occasion. However, although everyone had changed to evening wear, they had not changed their behavior. George was out on business, and already I missed his merry presence. Sophie concentrated on her plate, to my relief, but made the oddest remarks. Great-uncle Samuel kept up a conversation with Adele about a family my mother and I did not know, and about whom they chose not to enlighten us. The housekeeper, Mrs. Ackroyd, supervised the serving of Mrs. Randell's tasty dishes. Judging by the exclamations over some of the food, I guessed that the cook, at least, had put on her best show to welcome us.

I disliked the way that Mrs. Ackroyd's beady eyes slid over me. I was under no illusion that she was glad I was here. All in all, dinner was no celebration, but a quiet, awkward affair. I was glad to leave the table and go into the drawing room, while Great-uncle Samuel mercifully took himself off to the library for a cigar and brandy.

I fidgeted for a while, listening to my mother engage Adele in conversation, while Sophie turned the pages of a large old book, her lips moving as she talked to herself about the illustrations. Then I could no longer stomach the prospect of listening to Adele's showing off her prowess at the piano, or singing, or displaying her watercolor portfolio, or her expertise as a mother. I abandoned my patient mother and Sophie to her, took a candle, in case some of the corridors had not yet been provided with gaslights, and set off eagerly to explore.

Downstairs were the dining room, library, and parlors. On the first floor, the west wing contained my and my mother's rooms and bathroom, Sophie's and Adele's rooms, and, up the turret stairs, the nursery. On the way, I stopped to look at the portraits on the wall of previous generations, Albert's brothers, sisters, and parents, all dead now except for Samuel. There was a similarity between them in the severity of their expressions which contrasted with their rather thick, sensuous lips and piercing eyes. Or perhaps it was because they had all been painted by the same artist.

There was no resemblance in any of the paintings to me except for my chestnut hair which was like my mother's. But my thick curls, the

A Bitter Legacy

shape of my face and build were all from my father.

The house seemed enormous to me, as I was used to an apartment of only four rooms. The corridors went on forever, and the servants' quarters below and the attics were like warrens. I admired carved wooden tables, Chinese vases and brass bowls, dried flowers, and china. Then I went upstairs to the nursery, where Tommy was asleep. Maire was mending clothes by the fire, her copper hair gleaming, as she softly sang a magical tune in her native Irish tongue. She shook her head when I tried to speak, held her finger to her lips, then pointed to the sleeping boy, her expression anxious. Doubtless Adele had given her strict instructions concerning the number of hours Tommy must sleep, and that he must not be disturbed. This one time I agreed with Adele and tiptoed quietly away.

I continued my exploration with a growing sense that something was missing. I couldn't fault the upkeep of the house or its comforts, but I didn't feel I belonged to the Hall, or that it belonged to me.

The east wing was similarly laid out and decorated, only here were Samuel's and George's rooms, as well as guest bedrooms. It wasn't until I reached the turret steps that I found a doorway which didn't correspond with the west wing. It was low and arched, its door plain wood, its handle a round iron ring. I had to stoop to go through. And I found something. Only it wasn't what I'd been looking for.

I stood in a sparsely furnished solar in the medieval hall. In the candlelight, the walls seemed to bulge and waver, and were so old that the plaster had altered its shape. I crossed to the tiny round window, virtually a spyhole, which the nobility had used to watch the company in the dining hall below in order to check who was friend and who was foe. It was dark down there, immensely dark, despite the bright silver shafts of moonlight streaking through high, arched windows. At the far end of the solar was a dark shadow which, when I approached it, was the opening to a spiral stone staircase.

Immediately, I knew I had to go down and raised my candle high. I began to descend, bending my head to avoid bumping it on the rough stone ceiling, though I'm not tall.

Then, just before I reached the bottom, I shivered. There must have been a draft, because it was distinctly and suddenly chilly. But as soon as I emerged into the hall, the temperature changed again. If anything, it was warmer. I glimpsed dark hammer beams high up above, a few items of heavy oak furniture, and a long refectory table against one wall. There was a pleasant smell of furniture polish, too. I was about to leave when I heard a scuffling sound. I strained my eyes into the dimness beyond the light of my candle.

A Bitter Legacy

"Is someone there?" I called out, my voice echoing slightly.

There was another scuffle, followed by a slight rustling. I was afraid to go forward and afraid to retreat, too, into the claustrophobic confinement of the spiral staircase.

"Who is it? Is it a mouse?" I called out more loudly, trying to raise my spirits by the sound of my own voice.

"In a manner of speaking, a mouse, cousin. Just a mouse." The voice was startlingly close behind me, and I whirled to see Sophie, pale in the candle's glow.

"It's you! I'm so glad. I was imagining all sorts of horrors!" I said with relief, not thinking to question what she was doing here in the darkness, all alone.

"You've been exploring, I expect," she said, her voice louder and more confident than usual. "I saw through your excuse about having a headache and going to bed early. I've used it myself before."

"Yes, and I should love to see this room in daylight," I answered, taken aback by her unusually revealing remark.

"It's lovely then, too, but different. I like to come here at night best. No one knows I'm here, and I have it completely to myself. It's *my* place, though I don't mind you being here, of course. Come on, I'll show you."

She began to lead me around, explaining the

long and bloody history of the building, of past battles of the folk who'd lived here, of the rich tapestries, and beautiful gold and silver that had graced the table, all long since sold by succeeding, more profligate generations.

She knew every detail of the medieval hall, and managed to bring it alive before my eyes. She seemed to grow in confidence and stature as she talked. That long-ago time was her world, not the present-day reality. Indeed, when her narration wound up the history of fifty years ago, she'd reached her limit of interest and finished abruptly. After I pressed her, she reluctantly went on to explain how Albert Lansdowne had made a fortune out of exploiting the modern world's hunger for minerals. The Hall had been in ruins then, and he had bought and restored it and given it a new name—his own. That was one more thing that I now understood about him. But Sophie had no interest in her own family. She enjoyed the more romantic stories of those titled nobles who had built, lived in, and fought over Lansdowne Hall.

Then she said, "But this is the real reason I come here. Hold up your candle. Higher. Look up there."

On the white wall, between two windows, hung a portrait, the head and shoulders of a beautiful woman. Her blond hair was pulled smoothly into a braided chignon. Her merry smile and laughing eyes were full of life, and

A Bitter Legacy

she wore a striped muslin gown in the Empire fashion from a bygone era rather than the crinoline of her own time, and a sparkling diamond necklace.

"She's lovely but—" I shuddered involuntarily—"she seems almost *alive* up there."

Sophie nodded, pleased. "You feel it, too. She *is* alive—to me. That's Leonie, Adele's mother. I was four when she married Grandfather Albert. No one else loved me, not even my own mother. I was different, not like the other children, but Leonie was so kind, she cared for me. We were friends, that's what she said, and we shared our secrets. She always came to tuck me up and kiss me good night. Then, three years later she died, the year after Adele's birth, but that love had been enough for me. So I come here at night to share my secrets with her still." She suddenly smiled self-consciously and smoothed a wisp of her hair. "I don't really believe she's alive, but it helps me remember."

"No, I understand and thank you for telling me."

"Oh, that's all right. You're a stranger, not one of *them*, not really a Lansdowne. You won't be here long, anyway."

"Why, what do you mean?" I said, startled.

"George says, you'll take his money and leave. There's no other way, he says. You have to do it." She clasped my hand. "Not that I want you to go, of course, and until then perhaps we could be friends, like me and Leonie. Though I don't know how I could bear to live away from this place. I would always long for it."

My anger at George dissipated as quickly as it had come when I realized that he'd only been trying to reassure Sophie about her future.

"We *can* be friends because I shall stick to my word. I want to live in Lansdowne Hall and make it home for me and my mother."

Her mouth drooped. "But the money. George said . . ."

"I'll find a way," I said firmly. "But you have a home here as long as you want, don't forget that. And the portrait shall be yours." How could I turn out such a vulnerable creature?

"Oh, thank you. Then of course George will stay, too. I'd never leave George. There'll be just the four of us and Leonie." She sighed, turned to look back up at the portrait, her lips moving silently as she talked to it, and then she laughed. "Oh, Leonie has just reminded me that Uncle Albert was a very clever man. I don't think you can find the money. You'll have to sell to George!"

"And does Leonie know why Albert Lansdowne made this new will, when he had promised everything to me?" I asked carefully.

She looked at me, her eyes gleaming. "She doesn't really talk to me, you know, only . . ." She cocked her head to one side. "Yes, that's it. He had to have a very good reason. Only you've got to find out what it is!"

She was puzzling. A sort of girl-woman, whose childish voice and ways sat uneasily in her adult body. She seemed deliberate in cultivating a drab and dowdy look, for she could be almost pretty when she was animated, as she was now.

"I think I really do need to go to bed," I confessed as fatigue began creeping up on me. "It's been a long day, with so many new experiences."

"Then I'll come with you to make sure you don't get lost."

I was glad to have Sophie's company on those spiral stairs. Once again that blast of cold air raised the flesh on my arms, and set my scalp tingling. I couldn't help being afraid, even though I felt no threat to my well-being.

Sophie left me when we arrived at George's door, saying she was going to fetch some of his shirts to mend. "He says no one can do it as neatly as me. Good night, Vicky, and I hope you don't have too *many* bad dreams."

Once again, just as I was feeling I had the measure of Sophie, she said something disconcerting. One moment her large, doe-like eyes were affectionate, the next there was something knowing, almost sly in their depths. I wondered if people had been over-protective of the sallow "different" child so that she'd never had to grow up, or if she really was incapable of taking care of herself. I suspected she was more wily than anyone might think. So far, she was disposed to like me. So far.

At the top of the main stairs, as I was on the way to my room, I met Adele. She raised her perfect brows at me. "Surveying your new domain? And why not?" Her laugh tinkled gratingly. "And did you discover any ghosts or rattling skeletons?"

"No. Why, are there ghosts?"

She shrugged. "The medieval banqueting hall is supposed to have a White Lady, but I've never seen her. And of course it's haunted by Sophie and her ridiculous devotion to my dead mother."

"You know about that? She thinks it's a secret."

"Everyone knows, and so does she. It's just a game she plays when she pretends to confide in people. You mustn't think she's simple, though. Oh, no, she has plenty of cunning. Well, what did you think of the Hall?"

"I like it very much and I—"

"Like? *Like?*" Her face darkened with anger. "There are those of us who *love* this house. If you can't offer more than a lukewarm liking of it, then the sooner you accept George's offer and leave, the better for all, especially Lansdowne Hall."

With that, she pushed past me and went to her room, leaving me surprised at her outburst.

A Bitter Legacy

I seemed to have touched at least one deep and real part of her, though the rest of her was as showy as a *papier-mâché* doll.

As I prepared for bed, having said good night to Mama, I thought of the ghostly White Lady and wondered if she was locked forever on those spiral stairs. I had felt abnormally cold there, and was now sure that it had to be her. Perhaps she had decided to greet me. And I instinctively knew her presence wasn't a malign one. She, at least, was on my side. Now that Albert Lansdowne had done his worst, it was the living I had to guard against, not the dead.

Great-uncle Samuel was at breakfast when I went down the next morning on my own as my mother was taking tea and toast in her room. He looked out from behind *The Times*, and with difficulty forced himself to say, "Good morning."

"And isn't it? Bright and sunny," I replied happily. "I shall go out walking."

He snorted at my frivolousness. "I, however, cannot take advantage of the good weather. Have to work. Go over the general accounts. Not the kind of responsibility a young girl would be willing to shoulder even if she knew how."

"On the contrary. I would like to stay and look at them with you. I want to learn as much as I can about my new home and its business."

His frown deepened as he rattled his newspaper, using it as a shield against me. "Hardly a suitable subject for you or any young lady. The business does not concern you at all. That's George's province, though the lad relies on me to assist him. Couldn't do without me."

"I assure you, Great-uncle Samuel, that I've had as good an education as any in England, and figures don't frighten me at all."

His face reappeared from behind the paper, his skin mottled with anger. "Then they should! And what, may I ask, is the point of wasting your time on such inappropriate pursuits when you'll be forced to see sense, settle for George's offer, and return whence you came? I shall decide what you're to be told."

I smiled, refusing to be riled, and sat down, having helped myself to a grilled breakfast from under the warming dishes on the sideboard. "So old-fashioned! You'll have to show me some time, you know. We won't be leaving. I can't think why everyone says I shall sell when I won't."

He grunted and muttered something while retreating behind his paper again. I didn't hear exactly what he said, but I caught the reference to "Albert."

"Great-uncle Samuel, why do you think Grandfather decided to leave Lansdowne Hall to me?"

Irritated, he finally put *The Times* aside. "He had a stroke three years ago. Changed him. Does

A Bitter Legacy

some, y'know. Couldn't move much, couldn't talk much. But would he hand the Hall over to me and George? No! Damned..." With an effort, he controlled his temper. "My opinion, young lady, is he went senile, and Pontefract's as much to blame for letting him make that will. Old-fashioned, stuffed shirt Pontefract."

I laid down my knife and fork thoughtfully. "All these years, as far as I knew, he never gave me a thought. I never received a letter, a present, nothing at all. How did he even know I was still alive?"

"Albert had his methods," Great-uncle Samuel said shortly. Then, aware I would not leave him in peace, he stood up, made a noisy show of folding his paper, and put it under his arm, ready to march out.

I stopped him with another question. "What I can't understand—and it seems no one can, as it surprised us all—is why he changed his mind at the last minute and gave the mines and their income to George? I thought perhaps he might have explained himself to you, his brother."

He marched as far as the door, had one arthritic hand on the handle, then swung round. "Explain himself? Albert? Master of all? Maybe Pontefract knows but he ain't telling."

Alone, I stared at my plate of cold sausages, then thrust it aside angrily, and rang the bell to ask for more hot tea. For a moment I'd almost found myself feeling sorry for my grandfather, a vigorous man reduced by physical disability, but resolutely I stamped on that spark of compassion. He did not deserve it, and it had been a just end for him because of all the misery he'd caused. My mother had thankfully escaped, but all the others, even George, had had to jump to his commands all their lives. Maybe that explained Aunt Caroline's nervous illness.

My hatred flooded back in full force as I thought of his compiling secret information about me, and then deciding to use me as a pawn in his game, the one he still intended to play even though he was dead. Because there was no doubt in my mind that that was how he had seen me, as a minor pawn. He hadn't chosen this course of action because he might have cared for me, but to use me for his devious plot.

But I would find out what it was, and I would defeat him! This pawn would become a queen!

My breakfast finished, I informed Mrs. Ackroyd that I was going for a walk. She pursed her lips in disapproval, but her training made her keep silent. However, I was determined to treat the Hall as home, not behave as if I were a guest or a transient visitor. I wrapped a warm shawl around my shoulders and put on my bonnet, against the morning chill, and went out into the wonderful day.

The dew on the grass spread silvery-gray across the park, and dissolved under my boots.

A Bitter Legacy

The sun was melting away the haze of mist in the air, and a light breeze lifted the hair at my neck, tickling me. In a nearby copse, a wood pigeon cooed softly. I breathed deeply and walked steadily on, away from the gray-stoned house, the smoke rising from its tall, sentinel chimneys.

My goal was the woodland ahead, on the other side of which lay a river, which formed one of the Hall's natural boundaries. I hoped to get some ideas for raising the money I desperately needed during my walk. Certainly, I could not complain about the maintenance of the grounds, which had been properly landscaped so that there was always some new, beautiful vista to admire. As with the interior of the house, I couldn't fault Albert Lansdowne on his care of my inheritance.

It was worth fighting for after all. I had much to think about, much to learn. But for now, what did it matter? I was free to walk, to run, to do whatever I pleased.

It took longer than I expected, to reach the edge of the wood, over half an hour's brisk walk. During that time I had seen no one and no other dwellings, except for a glimpse of the gamekeeper's cottage in the distance. Many of the trees, though virtually leafless, looked familiar, similar to trees in Boston, and they were well spaced. I loved shuffling my feet through the orange and yellow leaves, pale reflections of fall's colors on the other side of the Atlantic, but no less pretty for that.

After a while the trees became denser, and there was more undergrowth, but I could hear the sound of running water and pushed on until I reached the river at last. It was swollen by the recent rain, the fast-running water a peaty brown from the moors. I peered into it, wondering how many fish it contained and whether there were enough to make me a fortune. As the river was only some four feet across and not a rushing torrent, I doubted it. This was not the river of gold I had hoped for.

There was a narrow margin of grass between the rushing water and the woods. I followed it, enjoying both my freedom and the knowledge that I was walking on *my* land and becoming familiar with my very own kingdom. Even when the path narrowed and became slipperier with mud, as no grass grew on this part, I went on. I hardly noticed that it had become more of a struggle to get past the trees and bushes, so lost was I in my own scheming thoughts. Then I noticed up ahead that the river widened into a pool with a weir at the far end. On the other side were the roofless walls of a ruined building. Perhaps an old millhouse, I thought, looking for the paddle wheel.

I clung to the supple trunk of a young alder sapling, trying to round this last obstacle to reach the pool. With one foot poised over thin air, I heard a noise in the undergrowth. I

A Bitter Legacy

stopped, looked around, but could see nothing beyond more bare trunks, holly bushes covered in glossy green leaves and scarlet berries, and other fir trees. I shrugged. It must have been a squirrel. All the same, I felt very alone, and the reassuring presence of the Hall seemed very far away. The only sounds were the gurgling of water over the weir, and that noise, like scratching.

I swung my foot to the ground on the far side as it began again. I stopped, quickly glancing over my shoulder. Nothing. A little prickle of fear trickled along my spine. It was ridiculous! To be afraid on such a sunny morning in a pretty wood when . . .

Something suddenly burst up from under my feet with a terrible screech. I pulled back, startled, desperately flinging one arm out to keep balance, but my other hand lost its hold on the sapling, and I was clutching at nothing. My booted feet made their last fatal slide on the slippery mud and then I fell.

The icy-cold water took my breath away. It closed over my head and, as if in a dream, I was looking up at the pale surface. I struggled, but my clothes were soaked, so heavy and clinging that I could hardly move. I broke the surface, gulped in precious air, and tried to call out. But my mouth was full of cold river water, and I sank again.

Somehow, I managed to rise above the water

once more and then came the terrifying realization. Although the surface of the pool had looked quite calm, beneath it was a powerful current which was now sweeping me relentlessly toward the weir. I redoubled my efforts, my hands already numb with cold, trying not to hear the dull, deep boom of the barrier getting closer and closer and silencing the sounds of my own struggle.

And then suddenly my head was above the surface and I was drawing ragged, gasping breaths into my water-filled lungs. In my terror I lashed out, but inexorable arms gripped me fast, and I was dragged onto the bank where I lay, coughing, my head pounding. Hands pumped my back, and I could feel water trickling from the corner of my mouth.

At last I was able to turn over and sit up. Jasper Thornley crouched at my side, his face like thunder.

"Damn you! How could you be so careless of your safety—and to go out alone, too!" He almost shook my shoulder.

"Why not?" I demanded weakly. "These are my grounds." A coughing fit seized me. I began to shake uncontrollably and then inexplicably to laugh.

The blow of his hand on my cheek snapped my head to one side, but my body at last relaxed.

"Come on," he said. "You must get out of those wet clothes before pneumonia sets in. My horse is not far, just on the other side of the woods here."

"But I've been walking for hours. We must be miles deep into the woods," I pointed out shakily.

"Right here the trees are only about fifty yards deep. You've been following the perimeter, and circling round behind the Hall."

He helped me up and picked up his coat from the ground where he must have flung it before jumping in to rescue me. He put it around me and supported me with an arm around my waist. My legs shuddered and trembled, but somehow we managed to force our way between the trees.

"How—how did you know where I was?" I asked. "Did you hear me scream?"

"Scream? It was more like a pitiful gasp. Fortunately, I heard it. I came to see you and your mother, and Mrs. Ackroyd told me you were out walking. Your footsteps in the dew told me which direction you'd gone, and I rode along beside the woods, hoping to meet up with you. Vicky, how did this happen?"

"How? I didn't fall in from choice, if that's what you're thinking."

"Neither can I believe you'd be so clumsy as to fall in accidentally, either." His tone was grim.

Why was he angry with me? Now was the time when I needed sympathy. However, my own answering anger warmed me, though I managed to keep my voice level. "Did you hear or see anything unusual in the woods? I heard a strange noise and then something—I think it was a giant bird—attacked me."

He laughed harshly. "There are no such things as giant birds here in England, or wolves, or bears. You probably startled an ordinary blackbird. The largest around here would be a pheasant. Nowhere near the size of an eagle." He paused. "Though, of course . . . Describe it to me."

"Nor do we have bears or wolves in Boston," I told him. "This creature was large, dark. It was beating its wings against my face. I thought it was going to peck out my eyes. What do you think it was?"

Instead of answering me directly, he said, "Here's my horse. Up you go," and swung me up easily, then mounted, cradling me in his arms. I could feel the thudding of his heart through his wet clothes, strong and steady, reassuring and exciting to me.

Drowsiness was now threatening, and to keep myself awake, I asked, "Why did you want to see me?"

"I wanted to know if you'd come to your senses yet after your first night at the Hall."

"No, I won't sell—to you or anyone."

He took a deep breath. "Victoria, surely you understand that someone in that house doesn't want you here, any more than they do me."

A Bitter Legacy

"Of course I do. They already know that I want them to leave, to find homes elsewhere, though I did tell Sophie she could stay. But they've had plenty of time since Grandfather Albert died to get used to the idea."

I looked up and from his grim expression saw that he disagreed with me. "This is not the time to talk, when you're already shocked. Let me at least warn you. What the Lansdownes want they have ways of getting, whatever the cost. And they want the Hall."

"Why is that worse than *you* wanting it? At least each of them has a strong legitimate claim. You were only the nephew of the second wife. And I, too, want it, but I'm the lucky one, because I'm the legal heir."

I heard an odd sound and looked up. He was looking ahead, not at me, but I could have sworn I saw a slight gleam of laughter in his eyes.

"Jasper," I said, reclaiming his attention. "Why did Grandfather Albert forbid you from coming here anymore? Why did you quarrel with cousin George?"

His face darkened. "I'm surprised you don't know yet. I thought George wouldn't waste any opportunity to blacken my name."

In answer, I sneezed and began to shiver uncontrollably, the wet clothes clinging to my body feeling colder and colder. Jasper muttered under his breath and kicked his horse into a canter.

Then, abruptly, following his own train of thought, he asked, "Why don't you want to return to Boston? All your friends are there, it's where you grew up. You can't have any memories of England, because you were a baby when you left. Were you so unhappy there that you prefer to live amid the rigors of Yorkshire and among strangers who are your enemies, too?"

"No, I was never unhappy in Boston." His words brought a sudden rush of memories: clear blue winter skies; graceful white steeples, broad streets, and clapboard houses; neighborly warmth; childhood excursions and games; and my many good friends. I closed my mind to them with an iron will. I had a new purpose now.

"It's because this is where my destiny lies. I've always known it."

"Destiny! That's a mighty word." His tone was mocking now. "What does Alexandra—your mother—think of this mad venture? She was always a gentle dreamer, but you're made of harsher stuff. Perhaps she's changed."

"No!" As always I rushed to my mother's defence, though as yet he hadn't criticized her. "It's true she told me all about her home and childhood, but only because she was so happy here. It helped her through the difficult times, particularly when I was a young girl and we were very poor. Then I felt as if I knew the Hall myself."

A Bitter Legacy

"I've been told that your father's Boston family rejected you."

"Yes," I spoke slowly, remembering. "But my mother never spoke ill of anyone. She never changed from the woman you remember, never became bitter.

"All during my childhood we had to endure the taunts and snubs of rich Boston society, belonging neither to the poor nor to the rich. With hardly a complaint, my mother worked long, hard hours, teaching music, taking in sewing, stitching exquisite embroidery for pitiful sums, to bring me up, and buy me an education and good clothes. Can you wonder that now I intend to make up to her for all that?"

We were close to the Hall now, and he reined his horse to a halt and spoke quietly and urgently, "So you're doing this for her. Do you think she wants revenge, too?"

Outraged, I pulled myself from him, even though it felt painfully colder away from the protection and warmth of his body. "Never! In fact, she—" But I wouldn't give him ammunition by telling him that even my mother was against me in this.

He sat quite still, making no effort to reclaim me, while I heard nearing footsteps crunching over the gravel.

"Which is it, Vicky? Face the truth. It's not for her, it's for you, so that you can play at being a princess. But this castle is no fairy tale, believe me. I—"

I couldn't stop myself, but I was angry beyond words now. I delivered a blow to his cheek that stung my palm, but did not even make him wince. I could not bear the way he had deliberately twisted my words. I had opened up my feelings to him, and he had painted them black and thrown them back in my face.

He took my wrists and held my hands easily to one side, his face so close to mine that I could see the bottomless dark pupils reflecting my own pale face.

"Listen to me, before it's too late. One day soon you'll be begging me to help you, to save you from the Lansdownes."

"Never!" I cried again, as Rosie's and Ned's hands reached for me, and lifted me down. "I'd never come to you!" Despite my brave denial, Jasper's words were burned deeply into my mind.

The word that I was drenched and feverish spread as I was borne upstairs, and hearing my mother's voice in the distance, I had only one thought. They all knew I'd gone out. Mrs. Ackroyd could have informed anyone, or they could have seen me from the windows of the Hall, as they obviously had when I returned with Jasper. He had found it easy to track me. So, too, could have anyone else.

Had it really been a wild bird that fright-

A Bitter Legacy

ened me so much that I'd fallen into the water? Or had someone sinisterly, deliberately stalked me, like some quarry, until they had spotted their opportunity, making a vicious attack look like an accident? These were wild thoughts, but although I wanted to deny he was right, everything Jasper had said fitted. And now, to my increasing discomfort, I thought I could feel disappointed eyes watching me secretly, malevolently. . . .

Chapter Three

I lay in bed and shivered in uncontrollable bursts, despite the hot bricks at my feet and the many blankets. Although I protested, I was secretly glad that my mother insisted on sending for the doctor, and was relieved when I heard the hooves of the messenger's horse speeding down the drive. I wanted to sleep, but I was too frightened. Every time I closed my eyes, I was underwater again and felt myself choking, unable to breathe, while everything went black. . . .

My mother was careful not to be angry with me, yet I could see she was worried as I shuddered again. I felt as if I was frozen to the core and would never be able to get warm again. I tried to laugh. Had I been saved from drowning

A Bitter Legacy

only to die of pneumonia?

But when Dr. Cooper arrived, he was brisk and reassuring in his diagnosis.

"Aye, she's young and fit," he said in his dry, quick manner. "A good sleep is all she needs. Give her all these powders mixed with water, and I'll leave some for tomorrow for good measure."

"Is that all?" my mother asked anxiously as he handed her the prescribed powders, and she emptied the first sachet into the glass that stood ready at the bedside.

"That's all, but if she begins to run a high fever, let me know. I doubt she will though."

I drank the potion obediently, then lay back. With a light touch to my forehead, my mother followed Dr. Cooper to the door, where she detained him with a hand on his arm. I was already beginning to drift into sleep as the drug took effect, but I could hear their hollow, whispering voices quite clearly.

"Dr. Cooper, you've been the family doctor here for some years, so you must know our history. Did my father speak to you of us—of me?"

"I'm sorry, he did not mention you, but your daughter, yes. He told me he planned to will the house and grounds to her."

"But just the Hall. What of the income? What can he have been thinking of?"

I managed to force my heavy lids open and

saw that Dr. Cooper's eyes were both shrewd and sympathetic behind his thick-lensed spectacles. "When I asked him, he said, 'You'll see, you'll see. A sprat to catch the mackerel, that's what she'll be.' And he laughed, yet I knew he wasn't senile. That's all he ever said about it."

They went out, and their voices faded. I fell asleep, filled with renewed loathing for the man who was using me as his puppet for his own purposes. *We will see*, I thought, *who comes out on top. It will be me. It will be me....*

I slept through the rest of that day and night, awaking late the next morning. I felt well enough to get up, but my mother would not let me. When she left the room for a few minutes, I tried to stand, but was so weak I was glad to climb back into bed again before she returned. My struggle to survive, to live, had nearly used up all my strength.

When she entered, I asked, "Mama, what happened to Jasper?"

"Adele insisted that Dr. Cooper attend him, too. She said she would not allow 'that man' to have any excuse to blame her for negligence. The doctor ordered that he should rest, and so Adele had a room prepared for him over the coach house."

"I'm surprised he agreed to stay," I said. "He doesn't like any of us except you, of course."

"Hush now, don't fret. You should drink this soup and then sleep some more."

A Bitter Legacy

For once, I did as I was told.

The next day, when I asked about Jasper, she reported that he was well but staying for one more night.

"But what has he been doing all this time?" I asked.

She smiled. "I've been to visit him. He's resting, as ordered, as you should be."

Still, I frowned. "That doesn't sound right. Surely he'd be up and about by now. He only got slightly wet."

"Vicky, if I didn't know you better, I'd say you were ungrateful. He saved your life, and I shall never forget that." She took my hand and squeezed it. "I nearly lost you, and you are the dearest thing in the world to me. You still haven't explained why you took off all alone the other morning. I was always very careful about your safety in Boston, but here you seem to think the same rules don't apply. I want you to promise me"—and her voice was as firm as I'd ever heard it—"that it'll never happen again."

I stared at the half-finished bowl of soup on my lunch tray, suddenly no longer hungry. For the first time my mother's fussing over me was irksome. I was an heiress, nearly a woman! But now was not the time to fight her on this issue.

I gave a genuine shudder, and said, "I promise I shall make every effort never to fall in a river again. Oh, Mama . . ." I trembled again, remembering vividly the water closing over my head, the icy wetness choking my lungs, the certain knowledge that I was going to die. . . .

"It's all right." She smoothed my forehead. "The promise you've made is good enough for me. We all learn by our mistakes. Don't think about it if it upsets you or it'll impede your recovery."

"I don't mind talking about it. That way it's less like a nightmare. I've never been so frightened as when that bird flew out."

"But to allow a harmless creature like that to startle you . . . you're not usually so easily shaken."

"I'd heard strange sounds in the bushes, and I know everyone will say I disturbed a pheasant or a grouse, but they would be wrong. I know what happened, Mama. It was large and black and it attacked me!"

She looked troubled, but unconvinced. "It happened so fast I expect in your imagination it has become a much more terrifying creature than it actually was," she suggested. "And of course the bank was slippery after all the recent rain. George went to look, and he didn't find anything out of the ordinary. Try not to think about it anymore."

I sighed and moved restlessly in the bed. "You're right. I just feel so confined here, yet I don't feel strong enough to get up. I've finished the last novel the maid fetched from the

A Bitter Legacy

circulating library. If only Great-uncle Samuel would show me the accounts, that would give me something to do. Perhaps you could persuade him to change his mind?"

She shook her head. "Uncle Samuel was always the most stubborn of Lansdownes, and he's old now, and difficult to persuade to change his ways. But if he and Mr. Pontefract reassure us that all is well, that's enough for me. Why go over old news and figures?"

"You ensured that I attended one of the best academies in Boston, so now you mustn't complain that I know too much," I said playfully. "You don't want me to forget my mathematics, do you?"

She laughed. "Uncle Samuel has already accused me of raising a little monster." She assumed his stern expression. " 'A little singing and embroidery are quite sufficient,' he told me yesterday, 'for any girl's education if she wants to find a good husband.' " She became serious again. "Perhaps he's right. I had such high hopes of Henry, yet he didn't offer for you, and the girl he did marry had none of your spirit and beauty."

Mention of my former beau was still capable of hurting me. "Henry never gave me to believe I was anything more to him than a sister." I'd persuaded myself of this to salvage my pride.

I could still remember the pleasant thrill of his kiss beneath the mistletoe, of dancing close to him. Then he'd become engaged to Kitty Masters and I knew why! I was good enough for a flirtation, but I was not good enough to marry, even with my small dowry. My parentage was in question: even my mother's marriage to my father was still not accepted by his Boston family. But things were different now. I had a name, I had a family. Possession of the Hall was balm to my aching heart. Henry must already be regretting his choice! But Mama knew none of this.

"Have you been scheming behind my back?" I teased, looking slyly at her.

She smiled. "One day we'll have to discuss matrimony, but not now. I want you to rest."

She kissed my cheek, and then, before she left the room, she turned the gas lamps off, and my ears hummed in the sudden silence as their hissing ceased. There was an occasional crackle from the fire as a fresh piece of coal caught and flared into life. Shadows leapt along the walls. The curtains were partly drawn against the dark dank November afternoon, and I drifted into a doze, my head dull and dazed despite my brave words earlier.

I didn't know if I was awake or dreaming. But my mind was filled with fearful fancies, at first unreal, but then taking the shape and solidity of the Lansdowne family, mocking me in a frieze along the wall. Adele's light taunting laughter never reached her eyes, Great-uncle

A Bitter Legacy

Samuel frowned in shaggy-browed disapproval, warning me off. Sophie's pale, ethereal face turned away from me, and George's merry laugh hid something I was sure, but what I didn't know. All of them hated me, wanting me gone from their lives!

They seemed to writhe in the air around my bed, coming closer, crushing me with their combined presence, so that I could hardly breathe, then suddenly they parted and were swept away by a newcomer. It was Jasper I could see in the background, an enigmatic shadow in profile. But was he with them, or was he apart from them? I couldn't make sense of it. Then they closed ranks again, were reaching for me, determined to be rid of me. . . .

Crack! I shot upright, my heart hammering, stared round at the unfamiliar surroundings, then sank back onto my pillow. I knew I had just had a nightmare. It was a relief to see my ordinary everyday surroundings lit by soft firelight.

I drank some water to ease my dry throat and brushed back my hair from my damp forehead. I was still troubled by my terrifying dream. Worse, I knew it wasn't a fantasy. My mind hadn't just created murderous phantasms out of nothing. I recalled Jasper's words: "They don't want you here. Soon you'll be begging me to save you."

It was true, I thought, that I couldn't trust

anyone in this house except my mother. What secrets did Sophie have to whisper to dead Leonie? What lengths might Adele go to to keep the Hall and a home for her son? Why did Great-uncle Samuel fear to share the records of the house accounts with me? And George, easygoing George, might he too be unwilling to give up his power, unwilling enough to take some action?

I couldn't forget that anyone could have tracked me, and that, unlike me, they all, including Jasper from his childhood days, knew the woods and river well. Someone had wanted to frighten me away or worse. Sophie would say it was the White Lady, but the creature that had attacked me had been no ghost, but a trained animal. I knew my memory was not in doubt and that I could tell the difference between the plumage of a game bird and the black feathers and large, horny beak of the bird that had flown directly at me from the side.

Nor could I forget Jasper's rapid appearance at the river. Could it have been coincidence, good luck on my part? But something whispered in the back of my mind, reminding me that he had threatened that he would make sure I could not refuse his offer. He could have staged the accident just to frighten me. In which case, he'd succeeded very well.

Once again, that chilly feeling of being one against many overcame me.

A Bitter Legacy

* * *

The next day I woke without remembering any dreams. Late the night before my mother had noticed my flushed cheeks and gave me more of Dr. Cooper's sleeping powders, and for once I was glad to slide into blackness without any troubling thoughts. But now I felt heavy-eyed yet stronger. I got up and remained in my room, dressed in my warmest clothes and a shawl around my shoulders.

Left alone for a while, I grew gloomier, and when I went to the window, the bleak scene outside complemented my mood. It was sleeting heavily, the bare tree branches were shiny wet, and slushy puddles dotted the gravel drive. A heavy weight settled on my heart. Could I ever come to love it here, or was my mother right and I didn't belong? It was similar and yet totally different from the land I was used to, and Jasper, too, was right. I did miss being in a busy city calling on my friends. Here there was nothing but trees, grass, gray skies, and rain, and the people were as dour and difficult to know as the landscape. I felt I hadn't a friend in the world.

Maybe the rest of my family was right, too. It would be impossible for me to run this great house, to find some way to pay for it all. The burden of it pressed down on my shoulders, felt too much for me to bear. I was suffocating and helpless to save myself, just as I had been in the pool.

I had just reached the depths of self-pity when my mother came in with a tray of refreshments, smiling brightly. "Here's George, come to cheer you up, and he's got a present for you, too."

"Cousin Vicky," George strode over and kissed my hand with a flourish. "This is such a miserable day, but I've found something which will cheer us both up. I found this last rose in the kitchen garden behind the house."

He presented his trophy, a lovely white rosebud, beginning to unfurl, with a hint of pink at the edges of its petals. "It reminded me of you, opening on the threshold of your new life, and it matches your complexion perfectly."

"Careful"—I had to smile, rallying as he promised from my low spirits—"or I might believe you or start blushing, in which case you'd need a red rose. But it is beautiful and it smells of fresh, clean air. Thank you."

He grinned delightedly and sat on a low stool at my feet, stretching out his long legs. Today he was dressed in the height of fashion, and the bright plaids added to the effect of dispelling my gloom.

"Now we can have a good long talk. I know I've neglected you since your terrible ordeal, but you know that only important business could have kept me from your bedside."

"I'll find a vase," my mother said, and exited the room, leaving the door ajar for propriety's sake.

A Bitter Legacy

"How are you?" he inquired more seriously. "You gave me quite a fright the other day, and I blame myself entirely for what happened."

"But why?" I asked, taken aback by his forthright approach.

"Because I should have been there to show you around instead of leaving you to wander alone. At the least, I should've warned you about that weir. I've come to ask your forgiveness and to make you a promise."

"But it wasn't your fault. I was happy to explore on my own," I said to reassure him.

"Great-uncle Samuel had a few choice words to say about that, of course." He assumed our elderly relative's forbidding expression, and said, " 'The girl has no sense of propriety. She's been allowed too free a hand.' "

I had to laugh at his accurate imitation, but said, "I hope he didn't say that to Mama's face. He's being very unkind to her."

"Don't take any notice of the old codger. I don't. He thinks he's head of the family now that Albert is dead, but, of course, he isn't. For one thing, I've always looked after Sophie and me. As for Adele, she leads her own life. She's the widow of a substantial businessman, and has her own position in society."

"You and Sophie are very close," I observed.

"I suppose she does look on me as her protector, and I should be very honored, Vicky, to be yours, too. In fact, having you here is a good thing all round for me, livens the place up a bit. For a start, I want to hear all about America, and then when you're well again, we'll ride out together. There are some breathtaking views, and perhaps we'll have time to see them before winter and the snow come. Then—"

"Oh, George," I interrupted him, laughing again, "I can't keep up with you. But it does sound fun. And will you show me the Lansdowne Mines, too?"

He stared at me in amazement. "The mine workings! Ugh! They're not worth visiting. Nothing to see. Don't worry, I won't take you anywhere near them."

"You misunderstand me. I really would like to see them. Isn't it because of them that Grandfather Lansdowne became so wealthy? They're part of our family's history."

His expression changed in a moment from warmth to coldness, and I held my breath, not knowing what was to come. After all, I hardly knew him. But then he nodded, and said, "Of course, why not? But in the spring, when the weather's drier. They're depressing places at the best of times, and it annoys the men, too, to have strangers about. They think women bring bad luck. I'd have to prepare them for your visit. Besides"—George leaned forward conspiratorially— "Uncle Samuel and I rarely go ourselves. We have first-class managers to run them. And, of course, I wouldn't want to expose you to the slightest danger. The miners are a special breed, you know, and they resent outside interference. I spend my time selling our minerals, and renting out use of our freight line and shipping berth. Now, how about a game of cards?"

"Of course, I'd love to, but, George, what was the promise you were going to make?"

He laid his fingers against my cheek. "Only that I promise not to let my lovely cousin out of my sight, and that I'll protect her from all harm," he said softly.

My heart melted. It seemed I had a friend here after all. My desire for revenge, I realized, was taking secondary place, and was mainly now directed at Great-uncle Samuel. George and Sophie could not be blamed for what had happened to my mother and me, but Adele was another matter. She had made her enmity toward me clear from the start.

When George left, my sullen mood had entirely vanished, and I felt much better. Now, I saw that the Hall was just a house, and my family like any other, with their normal squabbles. I had let my imagination be fueled by Jasper's words until it blazed into phantasmagoric life. Now it was quite clear that he had been lying to me because he wanted the Hall. I would never trust him again.

I looked forward, therefore, to joining everyone for dinner the next night when I was fully recovered. This, I determined, would be a fresh start, especially as George promised to be there.

I chose to dress in a dark blue satin, which would complement my dark blue eyes and chestnut hair. Rosie, who had now been assigned as a personal maid to me and my mother, worked on my hair. Her deft and expert fingers styled it into a highly elaborate fashion, talking all the while of household events, punctuated by exclamations about my hair's thickness and intractability under the curling tongs. She herself had smooth, perfectly behaved brown hair, and when she smiled or laughed, which she did frequently, her broad almost plain face was transformed into being very attractive. I could see why Adele did not use her. Adele would think her far too talkative and overfamiliar, but I was glad of her cheerful company.

"Thank you," I said when it seemed she was almost finished. "I never knew it was possible to make my hair look so pretty. Is it your own design?"

"Aye, it is, Miss Vicky. You see, Elise, Mrs. Roberts' maid, she's been copying hair styles from these French magazines, and I've no intention of letting her outdo me."

"Adele's and my heads are being used in a contest then?" I teased.

"Oh, no, Miss Vicky." She was horrified. "I was trained in the Countess of Wear's household. I was hired when Miss Adele—Mrs. Roberts—married." She tutted. "Then she took on Elise because she's half French, and I thought I'd have to go, but Miss Sophie took me over. Only *she* won't let me touch her hair. Insists on doing it herself." She tried to catch my eye in the mirror, but diplomatically, I avoided making any remark about Sophie.

"Those must have been happy days, when Mr. Roberts was alive?"

At first I thought Rosie hadn't heard my question as she attended fussily to an obstinate curl, then she said carelessly, "Happy enough, until he died. It was a terrible tragedy. He was crushed when one of the mine trucks skipped a rail and fell on him. To this day no one knows what he was doing there."

I gasped and trembled. Now I understood George's reluctance to take me to the mines, though of course I would surely be safe in his company.

"I knew I shouldn't've told you. It just slipped out, like. They told me not to. I'm that sorry, Miss Vicky," she said, her cheeks flaming.

"I'm perfectly all right," I reassured her quickly. "Who told you not to tell me and why?"

"I don't know as I should—"

"Rosie, contrary to what you may have been told, I am not a child, nor am I liable to faint at the mere breath of trouble. Was it my mother who spoke to you?"

I could see her struggling with the truth, and then it came out in her usual honest way. "Mrs. Roberts instructed me t'other day. 'See you watch your words round Miss Hunter,' she said. 'She's come to throw us all out of our home, and I don't want it made any easier for her. I don't want you talking about our private business, especially mine.' But I don't suppose it can do any harm, you knowing how Mr. Roberts died, can it? Besides, it doesn't seem right to keep secrets from you."

"None at all," I assured her, inwardly raging against Adele. Even though she had only spoken the truth, she had tried to set Rosie against me from the start. It was my good fortune that Rosie made up her own mind on such matters.

At last I was ready. As I descended the oak staircase, I became more and more nervous. For some reason I couldn't forget that the last time I'd seen Jasper I'd been in his arms, and I knew he might be there. As I reached the great stone-flagged hallway, I heard the murmur of voices in the drawing room, and for a moment, hesitated, before taking a deep breath and marching in.

Adele and my mother were seated at either side of the fire, Sophie nearby on the chaise longue. Great-uncle Samuel stood broodingly behind Adele. In the center of the room, George and Jasper stood facing each other, George heavy-set and his hair almost burnished in the

A Bitter Legacy

lamplight, Jasper rangy and saturnine, quite unlike his Aunt Leonie.

"Good evening, everyone," I said cheerfully, and all faces turned toward me.

"Victoria, I hope you're completely better. You understand, I cannot allow any risk of Tommy becoming infected in any way. Therefore I could not visit you in your sick room." Adele's tone was false and brittle, unsuccessfully trying to draw my attention away from the two men, who had clearly been quarreling.

"Only a head cold, hardly the plague," I told her lightly. I was reminded yet again that if George and Sophie were fast on their way to becoming my friends, Adele was entrenching herself more and more as my enemy. I was therefore gratified to see a sour twist to her mouth as she took in my toilette, and I thanked Rosie silently.

"If it hadn't been for Jasper, she might not be alive," my mother said, continuing the conversation I'd interrupted.

"That still doesn't explain why he was trespassing. I've kept quiet before for Vicky's sake." George looked at me and gave me a warm smile which I returned. "But I will be answered now." He glared at Jasper.

"Hear, hear," rumbled Great-uncle Samuel.

Now Jasper turned to acknowledge my presence, and looking into his cold gray eyes was like a sudden dousing of ice-cold water, like falling into the river all over again, but this time without anyone to save me.

"Are you—are you all right?" I inquired, finding it difficult to meet his gaze. "I wanted to thank you again for saving my life."

"Be sure, cousin Vicky, that Jasper Thornley did not save you for your own sweet sake but for some master plan of his own," George said belligerently. "He doesn't always save lives, only when it pleases him."

A muscle twitched in Jasper's cheek, but he spoke coolly, "And since when has saving lives mattered to you?"

My cheeks flamed, but I spoke up, "This—this is my house now, and I want you both to stop. If I have no objection to Jasper visiting us, then he can stay as long as he wants."

"Have you forgotten two trustees are here, and we say Thornley goes." Great-uncle Samuel's tone was caustic. "Furthermore, I have nothing to be grateful to him for. My opinion, he's long outstayed his welcome."

"It's not up to you whether Jasper goes or stays," Adele added. "You're not twenty-one until next spring and this house isn't yours until then—and until then I'm mistress in this household."

I clenched my fists, then remembered in time that I was too old now to stamp my foot. I looked in appeal to my mother, but she was staring down at her hands, twisting them tightly in her

A Bitter Legacy

lap. I was on my own, defending Jasper against the Lansdownes.

I opened my mouth, but Jasper spoke first, demanding of Adele, "You're saying that Victoria has to ask your permission first before receiving visitors?"

She looked away uncomfortably and did not answer, to my surprise, leaving it to George to do so.

"I deem it an honor to serve and protect her, and she has agreed to let me. No gentleman would stand by and let her be bothered by such as you."

"I beg you!" I pleaded, and even Sophie seemed to echo my words. "Please, George, listen to what Jasper has to say."

"There's no need, Victoria. I'm leaving anyway, now that I know you're completely better. Remember, though, that there are two sides to every story, won't you?"

With those quiet words, Jasper was gone, leaving me staring at each of the others in turn.

"What is it?" I asked. "Mama, can't you tell me?"

She stood up. "I think we should go upstairs," she said calmly and, as she passed Adele, she added, "ask Mrs. Randell to send a tray up, will you?"

Adele, stiffening in annoyance, complied, reaching out to ring the bell.

George caught my hand before I left. "Vicky,

believe me, I would have spared you this, but Thornley has forced the issue into the open himself. I'll speak with you tomorrow."

We went into my room. I now felt quite exhausted and wanted nothing more than to brush out the hair I'd felt so pleased about an hour earlier and to go to bed. But instead I said, "Mama, tell me, what has Jasper done?" I knew she wouldn't lie or prevaricate.

"I never heard it before, as the friends who wrote me wouldn't repeat such vile gossip, but George told me everything just before you came down tonight. Remember the day of the reading of the will when he said, 'I have not forgotten. None of us have.'? Some time after my brother's death, Father and Uncle Samuel began to receive anonymous letters accusing Jasper of... Well, saying that William's death could have been prevented. A servant, who was later dismissed, was discovered reading the letters, and he spread the rumor to Holmby Village and beyond. Some did not believe the gossip but some did."

I held my hands to my side, afraid of what she was going to reveal, yet I had to know. "In what way, prevented?"

Before she replied, she sat down, or rather sank down, in the chair before the fire, still glowing brightly, and patted the ottoman. I sat at her feet and gazed up into her face, like I had so many times before, and waited.

A Bitter Legacy

"Jasper denies it, of course," she said, "but the stories linger on, as they always do in this part of the world—bitter feuds in a bitter land. Jasper, it is said, could have saved William, but he rode away and let him bleed to death when he fell from his horse."

I wanted to deny it, but hadn't I heard those whispers in my own mind, that Jasper was following some devious course all his own? "And Grandfather knew this?"

"Yes, he must have. I do know he ordered that the Thornleys should never be allowed on our land again."

"I wish there was some way we could discover the truth," I said vehemently. "Was there an actual witness to this deed?"

She smiled and laid a hand on my hair. "Still righting wrongs? I remember when you first went to the academy, you came home crying at the injustices of the world. My dear, brave daughter, you must learn to be prudent, or trouble will find you."

"I see now what he meant when he was leaving, that there are two sides to every story. He has his own version of what happened, of course. Mama, what do you think?"

"Like you, I think we should give him a chance to clear his name because surely that's why he's returned here. And I, too, want to know the truth about my brother's death. As you say, without a witness we only have hearsay. I know too well how gossip causes grief."

I was silent a moment as her words sank in. "But how can we when he's not allowed to come to the Hall?"

She took my hand. "There's time enough for that. You must get some rest. Get into bed and I'll give you a little supper when it arrives."

She tried to stand up, but I held her back. "How can I rest when I know there's something else on your mind, too?"

"But you've only just recovered."

"I'm as strong as a horse. Tell me."

She looked away, but I saw that the muscles in her jaw were tightly clenched.

"I intend to visit my sister, your Aunt Caroline, as soon as possible."

"Mama, not alone, surely. It will be too distressing. Wait until I can come with you."

"I've already spoken to Jasper about it, and he has promised to arrange everything, as well as come with me."

"But why Jasper?"

"No one else would go. Uncle Samuel went recently to inform her of our father's death, Adele claims that she cannot leave Tommy, while George understandably has pressing business. As for Sophie . . ." She did not need to complete her sentence. I had never yet seen Sophie leave, or speak of going outside her beloved Hall and its grounds.

"I want to go as soon as I can. It's been too

A Bitter Legacy

long, too many years, and so I turned to Jasper for help. I've been out of England for so long that I don't even know how to get there. But I must see for myself if what they say is true and there's no hope for her. Perhaps when she sees me..."

"Mama, what is wrong with her? Is she quite mad? Does she recognize anyone?" I asked softly.

She winced at my questions. "I discussed her condition with Dr. Cooper, who has examined her on a few occasions, though she rarely falls ill. He says that she is very gentle, usually quite calm, but she seems to have no memory of the past. As if her mind is blocked, and so she lives continually in the present. Sometimes, though, pieces of memory surface, and then she becomes very fearful. She always was a very anxious person, inclined to worry about the tiniest thing. She lived in a world of her own much of the time, painting and drawing. She was so talented."

"Sophie lives in a world of her own, too," I observed.

"Vicky! There's nothing wrong with Sophie. She's just a little eccentric, that's all. She should get out and about more. I expect Adele leaves her too much by herself. We can change that. But first I must see my sister."

"Of course we must go, but do you think we can trust Jasper?"

"I think we should give him the benefit of the doubt for now, don't you? But what's this 'we must go'?"

"I'm coming with you," I said firmly. "And to prove I mean what I say, I shall get into bed right away."

She hesitated, then smiled, nodded, and kissed my cheek.

Two days passed quietly, in which we familiarized ourselves with the Hall, slipping into its routine of mealtimes and formal observance. If I missed our more casual life at home with only one servant to help us, I told myself that I had to get used to my new life. This was the station to which I had always aspired, therefore, it must be better than the old one.

Although George promised to spend some time with us, again he was called away on business, this time to visit his solicitor in York, and during his absence, I missed him. Most of the time Great-uncle Samuel ensconced himself in the library, smoking his cigars and dealing with his "papers," though I suspected he paid more attention to his port wine decanter and to dozing in front of the fire.

Adele fussed over Tommy, who had a slight stomach upset, and so we ate alone with Sophie. It did seem, as we told her more about our life in America, that she was taking an interest in life beyond the boundaries of the Hall's parkland.

A Bitter Legacy

Then, on the morning of the third day, we prepared for our trip to visit Rosebank, the asylum where my Aunt Caroline was. My mother had told Sophie that we would be out for the day and where we were going, but prudently omitted to mention Jasper. I noted and resented that for the first time in our lives we were resorting to subterfuge, in however mild a form. But not for long, I told myself. Soon I would be mistress of all.

I arrived on the doorstep before my mother, and was surprised to see Rosie deep in conversation with Ned, who had agreed to drive us. They stood close together, not actually touching, and yet there was a sense of intimacy between them. I coughed lightly, and Rosie jumped and looked around.

"You're ready, miss," she said, hurrying toward me. "I was asking our Ned to take a message to my mam in Whitby while he waits for your return. You won't tell Mrs. Roberts, will you?"

"No, I won't tell her I saw you talking to Ned," I promised, "Though you must be more discreet in the future."

She flashed me a grateful smile as she hurried into the house. She may have been asking him to carry a message, but I felt that more had passed between them. I knew that some employers disapproved of such liaisons, and some openly forbade them, but not me. Rosie had a right to her own feelings, in my opinion. I certainly would tell Adele nothing.

My mother soon joined me, and we climbed into the small carriage. Ned was a man of few words. He was young and strong with thick blond hair tinged with red, perhaps a lingering trace of Viking ancestry. From the way that he went about his work, always politely and never surly, he managed to convey his own aura of disapproval, though whether of us in particular or of the Lansdownes in general, I didn't yet know.

We bumped over roads made worse by wintry weather till we joined the main thoroughfare into the fishing town. We left Ned at the West Cliff, where brash new houses and hotels spoke of better times to come, arranged a time to meet later, then made our way to the railway station. We followed the estuary, which was crowded with fishing boats, or cobles, and noisy with the hammers of craftsmen building boats in the now reduced yards. Across the water, the narrow old houses of the fisher folk huddled together against a brisk wind, tall chimneys breathing smoke which was snatched away and dispersed in the clear pale sky.

I was uneasy about seeing Jasper again. Why had he looked at me so coldly the other evening, despite my defence of him? We had been physically close, I had told him my secret dreams, he had saved my life, and now it was as if he was

A Bitter Legacy

deliberately holding me at a distance. But why? I was frustrated by the way he avoided revealing himself to me. He fascinated me, undeniably, but was it the way a snake fascinates a rabbit before going in for the kill? He provided a kaleidoscope of various impressions, and I was responding in an equally kaleidoscopic manner.

When we did meet and settled into the train, the accusation that Jasper had left his friend William to die weighed heavily on my mind. Why, I'd thought a thousand times, would he have done such a thing? Though also weighing on my heart was the private knowledge that he wanted Lansdowne Hall. Had he always wanted it, and why was it so important to him?

I raised none of these questions. Instead, we talked about the weather, and Aunt Caroline, and then he and mother recalled the long-ago past, before William died, when it seemed everyone was happy—a golden age. I learned that Jasper's mother was dead and that his father was a semi-invalid, living in the south of France for his health. Jasper managed a vineyard there, working for a French count. When he described Provence and his life, I could almost forget the present and pretend we were sitting under blue skies with the Mediterranean just beyond silver-leafed olive trees.

My mother and I occupied the window seats, and Jasper sat beside my mother, to allow room for his long legs. As he talked, I studied him. His face was tanned from the sun, as I supposed he spent most of his time outdoors, tending the grapes. I tried to picture him there, but I could not. For me, he was inextricably linked with Yorkshire, its moors, its bleak stone houses—and the Hall.

At least he no longer looked at me coldly. Nor was there any sign of that complicity between us. He was remote, giving all his attention to my mother. I wondered angrily if, having failed to persuade me to sell him the Hall, he was now playing up to my mother, hoping that she would convince me.

He suddenly looked up, caught my naked gaze, and at last emotion entered his eyes. A blazing look that saw inside me, through me. I felt as if all the air had left my lungs, and, shaken, I quickly glanced away and out of the window, though I was oblivious to some of the prettiest scenery in Yorkshire. I was afraid, afraid of what Jasper could do to me, make me do. When I dared look back, he was quite self-contained again, so that I thought I had imagined his penetrating gaze.

As we drew closer to our destination, we fell silent, each of us dwelling on what we were about to encounter. I was dreading what we might discover.

Our first stop was the ancient moorland town of Pickering, with its steeply angled streets and louring castle. At the railway station we hired

A Bitter Legacy

a carriage that took us beyond the outskirts yet not quite into the country proper. When we turned up the drive of Rosebank Gentlewomen's Asylum, some of my distress was eased when I saw it was a pretty, whitewashed house set back from the highway along an avenue of poplar trees and amid pleasantly landscaped gardens. It stood four square, tall chimney stacks and three storeys of sash windows staring blankly at us.

"I wrote to inform of our arrival," Jasper told us. "I didn't want the superintendent to have any excuse to turn us away. Some doctors claim that seeing relatives upsets a patient, but I do not agree."

By now we had alighted, and Jasper had rung the bell.

"It looks well run as far as I can tell," my mother said nervously.

"There are more modern, humane treatments these days, on the Continent at least," Jasper said as we waited for the door to be opened. "Let's hope those methods have reached this part of Yorkshire as well."

The superintendent of Rosebank, an imposing woman both in height and breadth and with a stern but composed expression, led us to Caroline's room. The house was oddly quiet. No laughter, no crying, no conversation.

Before I could comment on this, the superintendent told us, "The doctor insists on plenty of rest as part of our regime. It soothes and refreshes. The patients sleep mid-morning and mid-afternoon, but Caroline will be awake, pending your arrival. However, you mustn't expect too much of her. Her lucid periods come and go. She may not recognize you."

"Is she worse now than when she first arrived?" my mother asked.

"I wasn't here then, but I looked at her records before your arrival, and talked to the doctor in charge. She is no worse but no better, either. We found that the cold bath cure was not successful." I noticed Jasper frown. "And instead, she spends much of her time painting, which absorbs and pleases her. She was very talented once, I believe?"

"Yes, she was," my mother confirmed.

"At least, she is not one of our guests who requires the special treatments."

"What do you mean by that?" Jasper asked.

"Why, when a patient behaves uncontrollably, we must find ways of restraining them. There are certain measures that have proved successful. Not only for our safety, but that of the inmate's, too, you understand. Some of these people can be quite self-destructive." She sighed heavily. "We do what we can, and that's little enough. But the cold water jets and the long immersions . . . Ah, here we are."

I was glad we had reached Aunt Caroline's room. I did not want to hear any more details of the regime. At least it sounded as if my aunt had not had to undergo any of those rigorous methods.

A red-faced woman, introduced as Caroline's attendant, let us into her room, and I saw my aunt for the first time. She was sitting by the window, staring out. Her hair may have been a fine brown once, but now it was thin and graying. She looked much older than my mother, even though she was four years younger. Her forehead was creased in an anxious frown which had scored deep lines in her skin, and her lips moved silently. Her attitude was one of apprehension. She wore a simple pale blue gown, like a uniform.

The room was plain and sparse, containing a narrow metal bed with gray blankets, two wooden chairs, but no rug or carpet. However, it was scrupulously clean and warm, being heated by hot-air ducts. But what struck me most forcibly was the series of paintings on the walls. Terrifying mixes of orange, red, and black in vivid splashes that never quite added up to anything recognizable. They spoke of an inner torment that I found deeply disquieting.

"Here are your visitors," the attendant said in a loud voice, as if Caroline were deaf.

She stood up obediently and, avoiding looking at us, said softly, "Good afternoon, do sit down. The weather is so . . . oh, no, I mean, tea will be here directly once Mary . . ." She frowned, looked at her attendant, who was shaking her head. "Oh, I'm not—"

"Caroline, it's me, your sister, Alexandra. I've come all the way from America to visit you and to bring my daughter, Victoria, to meet you."

Aunt Caroline started at the sound of my mother's voice. She darted a quick glance at her and in her eyes was a question. But it was quickly replaced by fear, and she looked off down to the side again.

"Yes, you do know me. I haven't changed all that much. Let me give you a kiss in greeting." My mother went toward her, her arms outstretched, but Caroline started back nervously, hiding her hands behind her.

"I can't . . . allow it . . . to be touched," she said, her voice more high-pitched than before.

"She has her funny little habits," the attendant said flatly.

"Would you mind leaving us?" my mother flashed at her in a rare moment of anger.

The woman raised her eyebrows, but said, "I'll be right outside, and I won't be locking the door."

Then mother said coaxingly, "It's Alex, Caroline. Remember how we used to play together? How you used to show me your drawings?"

Aunt Caroline had been looking lingeringly at the closed door, having watched her attendant

A Bitter Legacy

leave. But now she again looked at my mother and this time did not look away. "Yes, Alex, I think I . . ." A brief expression of comprehension passed over Caroline's face, like sunshine across a cornfield, then was gone. Bewildered eyes looked at my mother, then reluctantly at me, then back again. That flicker of recognition came again, as Caroline strove to understand while Mother talked patiently to her, constantly referring to events that had happened in their childhood.

"And look, here's Jasper, too." My mother stood aside. "You must surely remember him."

Both Jasper and I had been concentrating on my aunt's responses, and now he moved into her line of vision. I expected her to duck her head once more, but this time, inexplicably, her face convulsed.

"You! I know you. You're the one! William! That's it!" Caroline held up her hands to ward him off.

"No, Caroline, this isn't William, but Will's friend, Jasper Thornley. They used to ride together—" my mother began.

"William! That's it. He was there . . . I saw blood . . ."

Now Jasper stepped forward, brushing me aside, and gripped her arms, while my mother and I stared, aghast.

"Yes? What did you see? Think! Think hard!" Jasper commanded harshly, unrelentingly.

"Yes, there's something. I saw . . . No, no, it's all wrong. It's upside down." Her voice rose to a scream. "He's the one! He killed William! He killed my brother!"

Chapter Four

Confusion reigned. Caroline's attendant hurried in, her anger mixed with concern for her patient.

"There, there now, it's all right," she soothed, her words at odds with her rough tone, yet she seemed to care for Caroline in her own way. She put her hand on my aunt's shoulder, turned her away from us, and propelled her to her bed where she persuaded my aunt to sit down. Then she turned on us. "You'll have her waking everybody up, and then we'll never get them settled for the night. You must leave—leave now."

Caroline was tearful, like a child, making a loud noise of protest and screwing her face up. In between the strange noises, it was clear that she was very frightened. Only her attendant's calming hand kept her from curling up and hiding her face.

My mother started toward her imploringly, wanting to hold her, but Jasper held her back. "There's no more we can do for her," he said.

I recovered from the shock of Caroline's accusation, put my arm around my mother, and supported her from the room. Caroline's wailing and the attendant's shushings followed us down the corridor. Already there were murmurings behind the closed and locked doors, ominous rattlings and creakings, and the occasional attendant looked out to watch us pass.

"I must—I must see the superintendent," my mother insisted.

"What good will it do?" I asked. "She's already told us Aunt Caroline's condition doesn't change, and hasn't changed in all the years she's been here."

"At least we've checked that she's well treated and comfortable, so you can put your mind at rest on that score," Jasper added his weight to my argument. "Whoever chose Rosebank, chose wisely."

"Of course they did!" I snapped at him. "Even Grandfather Albert would make sure of that."

"Ah, yes," Jasper shot back, "your beloved grandfather. So you approve of what he did now."

I pressed my lips together in annoyance. "You're a Lansdowne through and through," he'd said, and I'd hated him for it. He was mocking me for changing my mind.

"He was right to ban you from his land, judging from what Aunt Caroline says."

I forced myself to look at him, dreading that I might see guilt on his face. Instead, there was a challenging, sceptical look in his clear gray eyes.

"But there must be hope," my mother was saying. "I cannot bear to leave her here like this, my dear sister Caroline . . ."

Jasper and I continued to argue around her.

"I told you there were two sides to the story."

"Perhaps there were two sides to Grandfather Albert, too," I retorted. "And perhaps you have two sides—a good and a bad. How can I judge when you haven't told us your version?"

"At least wait until you're outside before settling your differences," my mother remonstrated, and so we fell silent, on either side of her, each holding onto our claim, until we left the building.

Once outside I took a deep breath of clear cold air, and only then realized how tense I'd been the whole time we'd been inside. My mother was probably even more so, and in answer to my thought, I felt her tremble, and her face was paler than I'd ever seen it.

We persuaded her to get into the waiting chaise, and I was doubly glad now that I had kept my resolve and accompanied her. Glad that I could help her in her distress. Glad that I'd been witness to Caroline's accusation.

Now I turned to Jasper, and said angrily, "Is it true, then, what she said? Did you leave your friend to die in that cowardly way? Or do you claim she's too mad to know the truth?"

"If I was guilty, would I deliberately confront someone who could accuse me? Who was a witness?" Jasper asked curtly, his mouth a thin line.

"Perhaps you were trying to find out how much she remembers," I flung back at him.

I was satisfied to see him flinch slightly. I knew I was punishing him, though as yet I didn't know why.

"That's enough, Vicky," my mother admonished sharply, leaning out from the chaise. "I'm sure that if there was any doubt about the way my brother died, Father would have investigated it. She must be misremembering or misunderstanding the story that the others have been repeating, that Jasper abandoned William when he was injured. But, Jasper, you say that William was quite well when you left him that day?"

"But, Mama, why should Aunt Caroline immediately think of William's death when she saw Jasper?" I protested.

"She associates the two for some reason of her own. Now let Jasper answer."

Jasper and I stood facing one another, my

A Bitter Legacy

mother looking on as referee. At a word from Jasper, the driver walked a little way off, out of earshot.

"Are you willing to listen to me?" Jasper demanded. "Or is your mind already made up?"

"I'm listening," I said, biting my lip to stop myself from adding, "and please make your side of it believable."

Jasper began to speak, his eyes looking beyond us, reflecting on the past as he recalled that day. "Will had a new horse for his fifteenth birthday, and he and I were racing each other. I knew a short cut, and arrived back at the Hall and waited for him. After an hour I became worried and went to look for him. I found his body and brought it back. It's no wonder Caroline associates me with his death. But I did not kill him, nor did I leave him to bleed to death."

He was struggling with powerful emotion, his voice husky as he remembered his friend's death. Mama stretched out her hand to him, and I knew she believed his story. I wanted to as well, but something stopped me from trusting him.

"And I believe," my mother said softly, "that that was the start of her . . . her illness."

"I don't remember clearly. I was filled with grief for Will. We all were. Everyone loved him, and he deserved that love. But, yes, I think it was not long after that Caroline became ill.

I didn't see her, and she'd always been very private anyway. For a long time I thought she had broken down from grief."

"But you don't think that now?" I said.

He met my eyes steadily. "There were no rumors about my supposed part in Will's death until sometime afterwards, then there were evil letters, and the poison began to spread. The whispers started, and there were quite a few bloodied noses while I tried to get to the bottom of it, but always the source of the malicious lies eluded me. Then my father was advised to leave England, and both of us were glad to make a fresh start in a new country, and put sorrow behind us. Though we could never forget, we put the past out of our minds and we were happy. Until this past year."

He looked away, and I wondered what it was he didn't want me to read in his eyes. "Then I suddenly concluded that I had to clear my name. I had to find out the truth of what happened. The news I received made it imperative."

When he looked at me, his expression was veiled again. He stepped back. "Now you've heard my side. I won't accompany you now that you know the way, and you'll be safe enough. Then you can make up your own minds about what I've told you."

As we drove away, I forced myself not to look back. Why did I care about him so much?

Our return journey was bleak. The sky had

A Bitter Legacy

clouded over, a keen wind blew, and the countryside looked dark and uninviting, paralleling our mood. My mother sat for a long time with her eyes closed, tiredness etched into her face, and every now and then her lips would move, as if she held some imaginary conversation.

Meanwhile, I went over and over the scene in my mind. On the one hand, I knew that Jasper wanted the Hall, which he'd offered to buy from me, offered secretly, for some reason. What if he had *always* wanted it so badly that he was prepared, if not to kill for it, then at least not to do the right thing?

On the other hand, the truth as he told it still left questions. Why had Grandfather Albert banned him from the house before the rumors started? If there were no truth to them, why had so many people repeated them?

If only there had been a witness, I thought again, someone out on the moors that day. A sudden thought struck me, and a cold chill ran down my spine. Suppose Caroline *had* been there, *had* seen what happened. It was said that she'd "forgotten" much of her life. Had she seen something so terrible that she'd deliberately forgotten everything? If so, and if Jasper were guilty, why would he be trying to jog her memory? None of it made sense, including the fact that he'd chosen this particular moment to make his move. Why was that?

Was it because he sensed the Hall's new owner was vulnerable, an easy target? He certainly made me feel vulnerable. I had to find out what my mother thought.

"Mama," I said, and she opened her eyes. "I'm sorry about—"

"Vicky, I know you want to protect me, but sometimes you forget that I am the adult and you the child. And despite what you see as my weakness in my soft judgment of others, I haven't yet brought us any harm, have I?"

Now I was truly contrite. I hadn't realized that she had read my mind. "Not weakness. You are too kind sometimes, I feel."

"Better that than to judge too harshly. Isn't that exactly what you find at fault with your grandfather?" She smiled. "I accept your apology."

I was confused. I did not like the implications of what she had just said. But I went on, "If William was such a good rider how—"

"Accidents can happen even to the best of riders," she interrupted.

"Grandfather must have been heartbroken."

"Especially as he'd bought the new horse for William. He shot it himself, I was told. At first he blamed himself, and then George's father wrote me that Father blamed me, too. He lost two of his children right after each other. I was told to forget ever coming home again."

She didn't sound bitter, but I felt the bitterness

A Bitter Legacy

for her. "But it was Grandfather who drove you away, refusing to accept my father just because he was an American and he didn't choose him for you."

She wouldn't meet my eyes and hesitated before replying. "It wasn't quite as simple as that. There's something I've been putting off telling you, though I don't know why."

Alarmed, I leaned forward. "What is it? You mean Grandfather didn't forbid you to marry father after all?"

"Yes, he did and we ran away to get wed by special license. When we returned, we stayed at the inn in Holmby Village and sent messages daily for two weeks to the Hall. Then to my delight, Father gave in and accepted what we had done. It was after that that the trouble started."

I frowned in bewilderment, dreading what she was about to tell me. Had my father abandoned or mistreated us after all? Whatever it was, it must be bad, because she had avoided telling me all this time. She would only do that to protect me. "Quickly, Mama, tell me, please," I begged.

She tried to compose herself and then, as the train rattled and swayed through the countryside, I learned at last what had happened to my father, whom I'd never known, a loss I still mourned.

"I've told you often enough how your father

was a great explorer and geologist, and how he used some of his family's vast fortune to map new lands, rediscover ancient treasures. On his travels he was accompanied by another man, Richard Eyne, and they sank equal amounts of money into this joint venture. Spenser was on the verge of a brilliant career, you know. He kept a rough journal of his adventures, filled with drawings and wonderful descriptions, which he intended to write up properly and have published. He showed it to me, but I don't know where it is now.

"When I met Spenser, he'd been invited to give a series of lectures, and I attended. He told me that Richard Eyne had died when gangrene infected his wounds while they were in a swamp. Spenser tried to amputate, but it was too late . . . He lost the heart for a while to carry on alone.

"While Spenser and I were staying in Holmby Village, waiting and hoping for Father to come round, the landlord of the inn told us in confidence that he'd overheard some strangers in the snug talking about Spenser. It was hearing the name that made the landlord listen, and it was wicked words he heard and they were now being openly repeated. That Spenser was a cheat, a rogue and a ne'er-do-well. That he had no money, it was all Richard's. That he'd killed Richard and stolen all his money, and could never go back to America, where he was

A Bitter Legacy

a hunted criminal. That his rich Boston family was all a lie."

I listened, mesmerized by the sound of her voice, revealing her most painful memories of the past. Finally she had unburdened herself of the horrible stigma attached to my father, the shame and ostracism they'd had to endure till he could not tolerate being treated as an outcast any longer, and had disappeared one night.

"These rumors reached Father's ears just after he'd recognized our marriage. He was enraged, but he always stuck by his decisions, and therefore only said to me in private, very coldly, that I'd been a fool and would have to live by the consequences. He never referred to the matter in public. But everyone else did.

"Spenser didn't leave a letter, and no one saw him go. It was my belief, and still is, that he did it to stop me from following him. Of course, those who believed ill of him said it was proof of his guilt. But I knew he'd gone to Boston to fetch real proof of his identity."

"Only he never came back," I whispered.

"No, he never did. I waited. There were no letters. You were born. Still, I waited. Then I could no longer stand the pitying stares. I was branded a dupe and, worse, my marriage was called a sham, so I determined to follow Spenser to Boston. Father said he would never speak to me again if I went—and in a sense he didn't."

Jean Davidson

When she'd reached Boston, my father's family decided she was a fortune hunter and would not accept us or the marriage certificate. And, of course, Grandfather refused to answer any of her letters asking for help in proving who she was. I knew that part. But I was stunned by the revelation that my father had been accused of cheating and lying.

"Ironic, really. In England Spenser was dubbed a liar, in America I was. So you see, I can sympathize very much with Jasper's attempt to clear his own name," my mother continued. "And you can perhaps find some understanding for your grandfather's last, lonely years. All his surviving children were gone, one way or another."

"He had Adele, though," I reminded her, but I could not imagine her being a comfort to anyone, least of all her father. Certainly she never mentioned him, affectionately or otherwise. "Not everyone is lucky enough to have a second family. And he only had himself to blame for not writing to you."

"Yes, if only he had been able to unbend a little toward the end, perhaps . . . Ah, well, I like to think that leaving the Hall to you was his gesture of reconciliation."

I could not answer that. To me, his will dividing the land and income was simply another pull on the strings with which he still controlled us.

A Bitter Legacy

"But never," my mother concluded, "in all the correspondence I received from my friends—for of course those few communications I had from Lansdowne Hall were strictly business—was there any mention of Jasper being involved in causing William's death in any way. Letters from disinterested parties. So you see, Caroline, shut away for all those years, must be deluded."

I nodded. "Perhaps."

My mother took a deep breath. "We're nearly in Whitby now. Vicky, I know this must be difficult, unpleasant for you, and I wish I had chosen a better time to tell you, but it was unavoidable. I knew it had to be soon, for at any moment I expected someone to refer to those dark days. Now, too, you'll understand why I'm so reluctant to stay here. Many of those same people who were prepared to believe the worst are still here and I fear it's only a matter of time . . . If you have any questions, you must ask me immediately."

Shock had blanked my mind. I could think of nothing to ask her, except why she had shut me out all these years, and I already knew the answer to that—for my own peace of mind.

"Do you see the connection?" I asked. "Both my father and Jasper were driven away by rumors. Although they occurred some years apart, the same person could have been spreading them. There are certain types of people who delight in spreading such stories. Jasper must be looking for that person now."

My mother's face brightened. "Yes, and perhaps we can, too. I had thought it was all too late, but perhaps after all we might still find out what happened to Spenser."

I had little time to myself over the next few days, and perhaps it was just as well that I couldn't brood about my father and the injustice done to him, and his disappearance. My mother had stood by him and always denied that he was guilty of the charges laid against him so long ago. I was angry that a malicious tongue had robbed me of my father. At the same time I had to let go one reason for hating Grandfather Albert. It hadn't been because of him my father had left, and that made me unhappy, too. I didn't want it to be possible for my grandfather to have any redeeming qualities.

As for Jasper's guilt, I simply postponed coming to a final conclusion. Indeed, so powerful were my conflicting emotions that I felt as if they might overwhelm me, and after a while I deliberately put them aside, glad of the distractions that followed.

We did not mention our visit to Aunt Caroline, and no one thought to question us about it, beyond a casual inquiry about her health. George had returned again, and we played cards and talked and sang together. Sophie, too, came out of her shell and took

A Bitter Legacy

me around the Hall, regaling me with its past history, holding my hand and complimenting me and saying we were friends. Great-uncle Samuel continued to avoid me, but I was grateful for that. My questions about the Hall's finances could wait a little longer, while gradually I absorbed my new surroundings, and recovered my strength.

I also played with Tommy, slipping up the spiral stairs and passing time with his red-haired nurse, Maire; Adele kept her distance and did not forbid it. She regularly went visiting, though she never invited me along. It was a constant surprise to me that Adele could have produced such a delightful, loving little boy. It seemed that only Tommy had managed to melt Albert Lansdowne's heart, for he often referred to his grandpappy, and asked when he'd be back "from heaven."

Meanwhile, my mother spent more and more time working alone in the attic, saying she wanted to look through the chests and trunks, seeking anything of her own, mainly books and clothes. It seemed to me, though, that she was searching for something specific, too, but whether it was a revival of old memories, or something physical, I didn't know. After her revelation about my father, she had retreated emotionally, and I couldn't reach her and she refused my help.

In the light of my new knowledge about the

past, I looked around me with fresh eyes. I did try to bring up the subject of my father with George and with Adele, but they brushed my questions aside, saying they had been too young to know much of what took place. Only the rumors about William's death had come to them. I didn't ask Sophie, however, as she seemed always to have inhabited a world of her own.

There were moments when my mind was not distracted as I tried to plan for our future. But invariably I always wound up thinking about Jasper. I couldn't keep him from my thoughts. I went over and over the few facts I had, and could not decide whether Jasper was guilty even if only by neglect of William's death, or whether he was innocent. I only knew that the idea that he could be guilty disturbed me deeply, and I longed for it not to be true. I knew that that was why I'd lashed out at him.

Then, one evening George came in to dinner in an even more ebullient manner than usual. "What a gathering of beauty!" he said, looking around the table. "What a lucky man I am. How can I bear to be parted from you ladies when I have to go away on business."

Adele pursed her lips, but even she was flattered. George was right about her, of course. Her hair that evening was dressed in softer, looser clusters of curls and ringlets, and for once she brought to mind the portrait of her

A Bitter Legacy

mother, except her face was harder and lacked Leonie's warm radiance. Sophie, too, had taken more care than usual with her dress. But I felt that George's compliments were especially aimed at me. His gaze was brighter and more lingering when it met mine.

"Tomorrow," he said, "I want to take you out on that promised trip. The weather should hold. Will that suit?"

"I'll look forward to it," I replied, beaming back, then was slightly concerned when I caught an odd look in Sophie's eye. Hardly malevolent, she wasn't capable of that, but something dark and unpleasant. "Unless anyone else would care to join us?" I ended awkwardly. "Sophie?"

Everyone else declined, but Sophie looked eagerly at George who immediately declined for her. "She has to take care of her health," he explained to me. "The cold is bad for her. Isn't that right?"

Sophie nodded meekly, and I felt sad at the restricted life she led, but I also understood that this was really the life she wanted. She would be frightened to go out.

"I can't wait to see the full extent of the Hall's grounds and any other Lansdowne holdings you care to show me," I said.

George grinned delightedly. "Impetuous as always, Vicky. You shall see all, I promise."

"You shouldn't encourage her, George," Adele protested. "Isn't it enough of an insult that Victoria is to inherit this house without involving her further in our affairs? We all know that if she refuses to sell, it will disintegrate around our ears, destroyed by her childish whims."

"On the contrary, when I take over, the Hall will shine again," I declared proudly.

"Ha! And what makes you think that a—a colonial like you could play a part in English society?"

"Boston is not a colony, and society there is a good deal politer than here, if you're anything to go by," I retorted.

"But you have no money," Sophie said softly, and I looked at her sharply, but she quickly looked away, and I could not tell if her remark was deliberately vicious.

"I have plans," I said defiantly.

"Impossible," Great-Uncle Samuel snorted. "It's time you owned up, my girl. You just want to make trouble for us. Admit it now. You've no intention of running this place. You only want to turn us out of our home."

The latter was painfully close to the truth, but I opened my mouth to retort to the former, when Mama spoke up. "Let this be enough for now. No more quarreling about events we cannot foresee."

Her words were followed by an eerie silence that made the back of my neck prickle. The unspoken accusations were deafening, and they were all aimed at her. If it weren't for her,

A Bitter Legacy

I wouldn't exist, and none of this would be happening.

At last George broke the silence. "Quite right, quite right. And I admire your spirit, Vicky, I really do."

I was thankful to George for helping avert a further outburst, and I wasn't entirely unhappy about the confrontation. At least now I knew who comprised the implacable forces ranged against me: Adele and Great-uncle Samuel, while Sophie vacillated on the sidelines, depending on her jealousy of her beloved George. While in George I had found, though an amused one, an ally at last.

The next day was chilly but bright for the end of November. George was solicitous, tucking a tartan rug around my knees before taking the reins himself. It was wonderful to be out with no other purpose than our own pleasure, and my heart was light as we bowled down the drive in an open gig to the gateway.

We followed the rutted lane that took us around the outside of the parklands of Lansdowne Hall, heading in the opposite direction from Holmby Village and Whitby. It was strange to view our land from the outside. I remembered the woods as empty and chilling, the river cold. But with George beside me, laughing and joking, I admired the clever landscaping of the grounds, and the magnificent panorama stretching to the horizon, a sea of brown and duns and greens, rather than of gray and blue water.

"You can almost glimpse the sea from certain spots up here, even Whitby itself. There's no mistaking the ruins of the Abbey, which has many stories attached to it, and was one of the earliest and most important Christian churches in England. Yet there were pagans worshipping here long before that. See that standing stone there?" He pointed with his whip, "There are quite a few scattered across the North York Moors, but no one knows their significance. Our ancestors were always busy hereabouts, making something of this remote wilderness. There's been mining here since the Romans."

I pictured the moors, alive with men digging, burrowing, altering, and stealing the earth's riches for their own purposes. As yet, the land wasn't radically changed, but I wondered if at some future time all that would remain would be the scars of our leavings, and where would this wildness be then? For a moment I experienced Jasper's and Adele's love for this landscape, and although I missed the social and cultural climate of a big city like Boston, here one could be set free, could become even more than oneself.

"What are you dreaming of?" George asked, breaking into my reverie.

A Bitter Legacy

"Tell me, do you love all this?" I spread my arms wide.

"Ha! I see bigger horizons than this. By a trick of birth I'm an industrialist, but I want more than this. My heritage may be work, not leisure, but I intend to change that and create my own heritage. Do you know how we acquired the Hall?"

"Sophie told me the history of its titled family, but she wasn't much interested in her own, and Mama told me only about her childhood."

"Then I shall tell you now. The Lansdownes have been living here since about eighteen hundred and twenty. At that time the Hall belonged to the nobility, but the eldest son was a wild, dissolute character who gambled away his entire fortune and then bet the house and grounds on one throw of the dice. It fell into disrepair for a while, until Uncle Albert made his fortune speculating on the stock exchange and bought it, and later the mines and so on. Of course Lansdowne wasn't his real name. He changed it so that it sounded more like the gentry."

"I didn't know that. Then what is our real name?"

George grinned. "Plain Smith. Uncle Albert did not like anyone to remind him of it. He thought Lansdowne had a better ring to it. What d'you think? Like the sound of Smith Hall, or Smith's Mining and Industrial Railway?"

I laughed. "And is that where we are going

today, to Smith's Mines?"

George grimaced. "You have an unhealthy interest in those unwholesome places. No, I'm taking you to lunch with friends in a nearby village."

I was unreasonably disappointed. "But as they are the basis of our wealth, and now yours—"

"Still the mines! What a strange girl you are. But then that's your fascination. So different, so refreshing. In the spring, I promise, but you wouldn't want me to work when I'm having a day of rest, would you?"

I shook my head, contrite. I'd been thinking only of myself again.

"For now I'm looking forward to showing off my lovely cousin, as Adele has so far neglected to do," George added.

"She and I are not set to become friends."

George smiled again. "Adele has only one person close to her heart—herself."

"She loves her son, though. Strange that Grandfather did not leave anything in trust for Tommy, when he loved him so much."

George was quiet for a moment, then sighed. "The sad truth is that his mind was wandering a great deal. He hadn't been well for some time and he left most things to me and Uncle Samuel to deal with. It was something that we . . . well, none of us liked to accept. That the old man had changed so much."

"Then I'm surprised that Adele didn't try to

persuade him that Tommy deserved part of the Lansdowne inheritance."

"Roberts left her a well-off widow, and she intends to marry someone even richer, perhaps with a title. No doubt she's happy with that as a provision for Tommy."

"She must look like a good catch," I agreed generously. "All the same, when she loves the Hall so much, I'd expect her to want something of it for the future, even if Tommy doesn't bear the Lansdowne name."

"This is a strange line of questioning, cousin," George said thoughtfully. "What are you trying to find out?"

"Nothing. Just trying to understand Adele. Oh, look, what are those men doing over there? Playing football?"

The roofs of village homes and a church spire were visible over the brow of the hill, but on the open grassy ground to our left was a gathering of fifty or so men in rough working clothes and cloth caps.

"This is no holiday. Those men should be at work!" George said, whipping up the horses and heading for the group of men who, I now saw, were being addressed by a speaker.

One of the men saw us, pointed, and shouted. In the next instant, they had become a yelling mob, racing toward us, shaking their fists. Then the two leading figures stooped, pulled up clods of earth, and hurled them at us. I heard pebbles rattle against the side of our gig, but none came inside.

"What's happening? Why are they angry with us?" I demanded, my voice shrill.

George stood up, raising the whip, and lashed out with it at the men, who stopped and gathered in an angry knot just out of range.

"Keep your distance," George commanded loudly. "You're breaking the law. Disperse now, or I'll take action."

"Nay, the law's on our side now," a voice came from the crowd, and the others muttered in agreement. "You're no longer above it, Lansdowne."

"Then I'll remember the ring leaders, and they'll be punished. Depend on it." Abruptly, he sat down, whipped up the horses, and we were away.

I glanced back and saw that, rather than follow us as I had feared, the men were walking in the direction of open country. In only a few minutes we'd crested the rise and the first houses of the village were within hailing distance. George hauled on the reins until we were at a trot.

"Are you hurt?" he asked, and I could see he was shaking with suppressed rage.

"Only shaken. Why do they hate us so? What did that man mean when he said you were not above the law?"

George waited until we reached the main square, then halted the gig, "We'll be safe here.

A Bitter Legacy

Perhaps it's best you should know how things stand round these parts, then you'll see why you can never go to the mines, where those men should have been working today. It's not me or you they hate, so much as our wealth. Jealous of something they cannot have, they resort to violence. This isn't the first time. But such meetings have been banned by law for many years, and some say still should be. No matter, the important thing is they are under contract to work for me, us, and that's where they should be now. I shall make sure the militia are called out."

"Is that really necessary? Those men looked desperate. Surely it wouldn't hurt to listen to their grievances and explain to them why they're wrong."

George gave a short bark of laughter. "Explain to that mob! The voice of reason counts for nothing with them. They're a pack of dangerous animals and should be treated as such. Now you see why the mines were left to me. Too much for you, a young woman, to handle," he said grimly. "And now, too, you see what awaits you should you take up your inheritance."

"But I thought you said there were first-class managers?" I objected.

"And do you think they'd obey a slip of a girl?" he asked patiently. "No, just consider yourself lucky that you only have the Hall and park to worry about. I have tried to hide these harsh realities from you, but perhaps this is a lesson well learned."

"George, I can't help thinking there's more to it than that. They may have simple demands that—"

"Simple! I'll tell you what they want. They want my power and money. They want your Hall. Are you willing to pack your bags and leave it to them? I thought not. Then let's hear no more about it. There's nothing to be done, and it'll all blow over very soon. I'll see to that."

Despite the pleasant visit and peaceful journey home, I could not shake off the memory of that frightening moment when those men, hurling abuse, had charged at us. George's explanation did not allow for any argument, and I knew he had to be right. Violence was not the answer to any problem. Those men should not have threatened us. Yet, although I'd been afraid, I found I did not hate them. They'd departed peacefully enough. I was curious to know more, not fully satisfied by George's explanation, which he obviously believed.

Moreover, the events of my day out with George and our conversation injected me with fresh purpose, too. I decided to put the echoes of the past behind me and concentrate on my plans for the future. I had to find a way to take up my inheritance, and so a couple of days later I decided to go and see Mr. Pontefract

A Bitter Legacy

at his office in Whitby. My mother declined to come with me, when I asked her the evening before my projected trip, as she didn't feel too well, and, indeed, I thought she looked waxy and pale.

"A rest in bed and some of Mrs. Randell's beef tea and I'll be fully recovered by tomorrow." She smiled as I prepared to go down to dinner. "It's only a cold."

"Promise me you won't go up to the drafty attic, nor out in any of this foggy weather, while I'm gone tomorrow. And you'll rest here by your bedroom fire tonight. I'll come in and read to you later, if you like."

"Very well, but I do have something to finish up there, and then I will have a nice surprise for you when you get home."

"Then you've found what you were looking for?" I asked delightedly.

"Not exactly," she replied mysteriously. "But I do have this for you. It's not much, just a christening gift from my mother, which I wanted to pass on to you." She handed me a small brooch of silver and pearls, with her name scrolled in a delicate filigree.

My throat constricted, and I grasped her hands in mine. "Mama, promise me you'll take good care of yourself."

"Foolish girl, of course I will. And you, too, tomorrow. I know Mr. Pontefract will speak sense to you, and I can put you in his good hands. Anyway, what harm could come to me in my own home?"

I should have been glad to hear her refer to the Hall as her home again, but her words made me shiver with foreboding. It was a bad start to the evening, which, without my mother's calming presence, became yet another scene of Lansdowne pigheadedness and conflict.

Dinner, as always, was strained. Great-uncle Samuel engaged George in conversation about hunting and shooting, Adele discussed the finer points of her outfit for a forthcoming engagement to which, naturally, I had not been invited, while Sophie nodded, tried to hide the fact that she ate very little, and looked off to the side, really in a dream world of her own. Afterwards everyone went to the drawing room, including the men, while I wondered how soon I could leave and go upstairs without attracting unwelcome attention. However, Great-uncle Samuel spoiled my plans.

"For heaven's sake, stop your fidgeting, Victoria. A man can't enjoy his cigar with you twitching continually."

"In fact, I'm rather tired." I tried to yawn. "I've got an early start tomorrow, too, so perhaps you'll excuse me if—"

"An early start? Why's that?" George inquired pleasantly.

"I'm going into Whitby," I said, then decided to throw caution to the winds, "to consult Mr.

Pontefract about my future."

"Do better to discuss it with your trustees—your elders and betters in every way. We can give you all the advice you need. Already have, in fact." Great-uncle Samuel frowned in his disapproving way. "Still, I suppose this is one of Alexandra's fool-brained ideas."

"No, it's all my own fool-brained idea," I retorted. "My mother's not coming with me. She hasn't finished sorting through her boxes in the attic."

"A rather pointless exercise, I would have thought," George said. "Surely her old clothes are all out of date or don't fit. Why doesn't she give them to the servants?"

"Oh, there's much more than her old clothes which have been kept. I haven't seen for myself, but she's already given me this lovely brooch, and there are other things, too, she has to give me. But I can manage perfectly well on my own."

"But so lacking in style," Adele declared. "People are already gossiping about your peculiar American habits, without your adding to the talk by galloping about the countryside alone. You do realize no one will marry you if you carry on this way."

"Then that will suit me just fine, because I don't intend to marry, but will remain mistress of the Hall."

This earned me a half-admiring glance from Sophie, surprised silence from Adele, and an amused look from George.

"Bravo," he said. "The best way to catch a husband is not to look. However, I do think I should come with you. Can't you wait a day or two? I have one or two things to attend to here tomorrow."

"I'll have company enough with Ned, and I don't want to delay, but thanks. Or are you worried about the mine workers? Did you call out the militia?"

"No need. That problem has been dealt with. One disgruntled troublemaker stirring up discontent. One rotten apple to be thrown out. Now they're back in line again. So I know you won't come to any harm, as long as you promise me that you'll hurry home afterwards so that I may see you tomorrow evening."

"I promise, and I'm glad the trouble is over now."

I presumed George had told the others about what had happened, and I looked for signs of interest at the end of the story. But Sophie was busy rolling and unrolling her napkin in different ways, Great-uncle Samuel merely nodded in agreement at whatever George said, while Adele had other thoughts in mind.

"You're spending more time at home than usual, George," Adele said sourly. "Are you sure your precious mines and petty business deals can spare you? I wonder if you're planning something."

A Bitter Legacy

"Dearest Adele, you would be the first to know my plans, if I had any. But I was going to ask you about the company you keep and whether *you* have plans for the future?"

I took the start of another bickering row between George and Adele as my opportunity to leave the room without interference, though Great-uncle Samuel glowered at me. How I longed for my birthday in the spring, when at last I would be free of these irksome relatives!

The next day I set off cheerfully for Whitby. A thick fog had blown inland from the North Sea during the night, and Ned and I made slow, but steady, progress, and I was not too late for my appointment.

Mr. Pontefract was dressed, as before, in a black tail coat and top hat, dark clothes of an old-fashioned cut, and his fleshy nose and cheeks were reddened by too much fresh northern air. His bluff and bracing welcome was most warming.

"Come and sit by the fire, Miss Hunter, and tell me what I can do for you on such a raw day."

"Miss Victoria, please. You are our family solicitor."

"Not entirely correct, any longer, I'm afraid, but Miss Victoria it is."

"But surely, it was you who drew up the will, wasn't it?"

"Albert Lansdowne continued using me, true enough, but Master George has been looking after the Lansdowne business interests ever since Albert had that minor stroke two years ago. He couldn't speak very well, though his mind was still clear, and he handed the reins of business to George and Samuel at last, who'd been waiting long enough in the wings. George transferred to a sharp new law practice in York, though I told him they'd charge twice as much for no better service."

I was pleased. Already this forthright North countryman had dropped the affectations of correct address, and spoke his mind about the family he knew well. He would only tell me the truth, rather than diplomatic lies.

"So you're not sure how much money George has now?"

"Enough to be able to borrow more money to buy the Hall from you, if that's what you're thinking. But you want my advice on how to keep it, don't you? You were very definite about that at the reading of the will. Do you still feel the same way?"

"I do. My grandfather, whatever I may think of him, left the care of the Hall to me, something I'd only dreamed of. I need information on how to keep it. But Great-uncle Samuel refuses to tell me anything, George thinks I need protection, while Adele and Sophie . . . Well, you know them as well, probably better, than I do."

A Bitter Legacy

"Maybe you do need protection. I heard you had an accident. That's not changed your mind, either?"

"No. I'm determined not to let the Hall go. There has to be a way. Perhaps leasing some of the parkland or the stables, or selling a little bit of the land."

"It'd bring in buttons, lass, but I'll do as you ask, and see what prices you can get. You could always go to George, of course. I can't tell you what income he has now, but it must be enough. Perhaps a loan?"

"Not without offering something in return, and the only thing from me he wants is the Hall, and I want the house and grounds to be totally mine."

He quirked his eyebrows in what I took to be approval. "Aye. Your grandfather thought you wouldn't easily be beaten."

I frowned. "But how could he know what I'd be like?"

"He said to me, 'John, if I know anything about character, adversity will have molded that young lass, and polished her till she shines, and all the best of the Lansdownes will be polished in her, too. I'll leave the house to her, and that'll put the cat among the pigeons.' I told him he should leave you be, but he'd have none of it."

I felt cold. I didn't want to think that Albert Lansdowne's blood might be flowing in my veins. "My grandfather was a vindictive old man, and though I speak ill of the dead, I for one am not sorry. He died without one word of forgiveness for my mother, and all because she disobeyed him once by following her husband to his native land when she refused to believe he'd abandoned her."

"Albert expected the world to do his bidding," Mr. Pontefract said candidly. "He was a law unto himself, and none dared gainsay him."

"He was cruel, and I'm glad he's dead!" I couldn't stop the words tumbling out.

Mr. Pontefract only shook his head sadly, not at all shocked. "He was tough and cantankerous, that's true enough, but his worst sin was stubbornness. Once he'd made up his mind, you couldn't shift him because he thought it looked weak to change his mind, even though he wanted to."

"You're thinking about the way he treated my mother. Did he regret it then?"

"Possibly. Maybe if he hadn't had that stroke, he'd've written to her, but he wouldn't want her pity, couldn't bear pity, not Albert. No, I was thinking of the way he treated the Thornleys."

My heart quickened. "You mean Jasper's family?"

"Aye, that's right. Jasper takes after his mother with that black hair, but his father, Leo, and his Aunt Leonie were both silver-blond. Viking throwbacks, maybe. Anyway, Leo Thornley's business went through a rough patch. He was

A Bitter Legacy

always too optimistic and borrowed too much. Leonie persuaded Albert, after she married him, to help her brother out. Except Albert insisted on very severe terms. In the end Thornley's business failed, and he lost everything—house, horses, possessions, the lot—to Albert."

My mind whirled. Why hadn't Jasper told me this? "If Grandfather had been kinder, then Jasper would have had his own family business now?"

"Perhaps. Certainly it affected Leo Thornley's health, and so did Leonie's death not long after. So he took his family and went to live in France."

"Jasper has good reason to hate my family," I said. "I wonder why no one has told me this. Not even Jasper has mentioned it."

Mr. Pontefract leaned forward and poked the fire into more life. "Ah," he said at last. "Maybe I've said too much, then. Doubtless Thornley has his reasons for keeping quiet. I don't know who else might know the full details. But you should know."

"Did you hear the other rumors, too? About William and Jasper?"

Mr. Pontefract shook his head. "Only that the two lads were the best of friends until Will's tragic death. That and your mother running off made Albert even harder than he had been before."

I felt myself go red. "She didn't run off! She went to find her husband."

"Everyone said he was a ne'er-do-well and only after a slice of the Lansdowne inheritance. Sorry, Miss Victoria, but I'm only repeating what everyone believed. Albert thought he was only trying to make his daughter see sense."

"Or he spread the stories about my father himself out of sheer spite because his daughter wouldn't let him choose her husband for her!"

"Never. He may've been hard, but he was honest. Albert would never have pulled a trick like that."

"I know he was your friend and you have to defend him, but I'm sorry, I stand by everything I said about him."

Again he shook his head sadly. "I hope there's not a day when you regret those words, Victoria lass. Remember, you've got your own life to live. Don't let the past ruin your future."

Mr. Pontefract's words of warning pounded in my mind as I clattered down the stairs to the fog-bound world outside, along with the information he had just given me. I had been searching for Jasper's motive in wanting to buy the Hall from me and now I had it. He wanted revenge against the family who'd ruined his. And if I had at last discovered the truth, how could I hold it against him? Wasn't I bent on the same course? Perhaps that was the bond between us, hatred for Albert Lansdowne.

Hearing Mr. Pontefract tell of the old man speaking of me had chilled me. It made him

A Bitter Legacy

real in a way he hadn't been before, both less and more threatening. I half expected him to loom behind me suddenly, place his grasping hand on my shoulder, begin to bend my will to his—and then I collided with a man turning from the street into the stone passageway.

It was Jasper Thornley.

Chapter Five

His long, lean body filled the entranceway, blocking my path. So dark had been my thoughts, that for a moment, he took on the aspect of the devil himself, unsmiling, fixing me with his piercing gaze. Remembering the circumstances under which we'd parted only days before, any normal words of greeting seemed inappropriate.

"You've been to visit Mr. Pontefract," he stated rather than asked. "You've been discussing Lansdowne Hall. Can I hope that you've come to your senses and that you realize that it's impossible for you to live there?"

"My affairs are private, Mr. Thornley. Would you tell me what *your* business is here with Mr. Pontefract?" I said. He was close to me, too close, so that he must surely have heard the rapid beating of my heart.

"Your affairs are not fit for the ears of a would-be murderer, that is," he said, and smiled, which was more a grimace, and I caught a glimpse of his even, white teeth.

"I—I do not know what to believe."

"Then accept the truth. I tell you again, I had nothing to do with Will's death. I had hoped that Caroline would be able to tell us what she knew, but I fear her memories are almost entirely lost to us."

"She did remember you. She accused you!"

"She became ill just after William died. Her memories of the time, such as they are, are confused. If I'd known, perhaps I could have helped her, but I could only think of William."

"Your explanation sounds reasonable," I said in a low voice. "Mama thinks you are innocent."

"Some comfort then, though you take the part of the other Lansdownes." His voice was grim. "You've judged me and decided against me. I was right when I said that pure Lansdowne blood flows in your veins."

He didn't want my sympathy. It was something else he wanted, needed, which made me feel trapped, overpowered. I tried to move away from him, but there was nowhere I could go. Passers-by were like ghosts looming out of the thick sea fog.

"Can you blame me? From the moment we met, you've made it plain that getting your hands on the Hall is the only thing that matters to you. And now I learn that Grandfather Albert is to blame for bleeding your father dry, which you neglected to tell me. How much more have you kept from me? What else can I think except that you want vengeance, after suffering so long in exile."

He looked at me pensively, some of his anger seeming to drain away, then he said at last, "Yes, I can see the way it must look to you. And it's true. I did miss my boyhood home. But it's really you who think you've suffered in exile, isn't it? The Princess Pretender."

"Haven't I every right to be? Haven't I suffered enough? And now you want me to suffer some more, but I won't. You'll see." Then, as he continued to look down at me, my next words came out in a rush, "Please, forget the Hall. You ought to leave the country. Whatever happened in the past, if rumors start to spread again, you could be in danger. I beg you, is it worth it? Is it really what you're looking for?"

He put his hand under my chin and held it firmly, examining my face in minute detail, as if trying to sear it into his memory for all time, and his eyes were haunted. "I don't know yet what it is I'm looking for. But I will bear your warning in mind, if you heed mine. You may

A Bitter Legacy

think that you are beginning to be accepted, but don't believe it for a moment. Schemes are being laid, as cleverly as always. You wouldn't be able to understand just how devious at least one person is."

His intensity frightened me. I tried to lighten it with flippancy. "Are you talking about my family? No, they haven't accepted me, and never will. Sophie is a bit odd, Adele is haughty and cold, Great-uncle Samuel wishes me at the North Pole. Only George is kind to me."

He released me. "There's something you should know about Samuel and George and those mines they profess to manage. The men work there in the most primitive conditions."

Immediately, I could hear those yells, see the missiles being thrown at us. "George—George is kindness itself, but Great-uncle Samuel, yes, I could believe him guilty of neglect. There's been some trouble recently, but it's all been cleared up now. What have you heard?"

"That the Lansdowne mines are abysmally run-down. Safety measures have been cut to the bone, and men and women hurt . . . Yes, women still work there."

"Then I should tell George. I'm sure he doesn't know. It's Great-uncle Samuel who—"

Jasper laid a heavy hand on my arm. "No, don't say anything to George yet. Let me bring you the evidence, then will you listen?" His mouth twisted.

My heart began to race again. "Perhaps," I said.

And then he was going, on his way to see Mr. Pontefract. He brushed up against me in the narrow confines of the passage, leaving me to collect myself before I could continue on my way.

Outside I had to look right and left to get my bearings. I felt dizzy from my sudden encounter with Jasper. I hadn't realized how much he'd been in my thoughts until I actually saw him in the flesh. I had also learned many things, and felt I needed time to understand them fully.

I still had time to complete my own purchases in town before I met Ned, so I headed for the shops. I bought some toiletries for myself and my mother, a toy that took my fancy for Tommy, and I lingered for a while in front of a display of jet jewelery, for which Whitby was justly famous. I thought of the brooch my mother gave me last night and which I'd worn to dinner, now safely tucked away in a drawer. I eyed a pair of earrings which I thought would suit my mother. But, mindful of our slender budget, I decided against buying them, knowing Mama would approve of my decision.

We had been forwarded money by Mr. Pontefract to pay for our passage from America. Though we had always rented, we had man-

A Bitter Legacy

aged to put by some savings, which my mother and I thought we would only need to last us until we reached England. Since the bitter blow of the changed will, we now had to eke out our slender resources, which was an added pressure on me to sell the Hall, of course. Now we were financially dependent on the family, which I disliked intensely.

My thoughts drifted to the conversation my mother and I had had with Adele about the matter. After I had fully recovered from my fall into the icy river, and before we had visited Aunt Caroline, Adele had called us into her private sitting room on the ground floor, with Mrs. Ackroyd a brooding presence in black standing behind her, the old witch guarding her beautiful young mistress.

"Quite frankly," she'd said, "I have no wish to help you, but George insists we must be generous. You are to stay here and to avail yourself of everything we have. Do you hear that, Mrs. Ackroyd? They're to be treated as part of the family."

"We are part of the family," my mother pointed out equably.

"Oh, you know what I mean. I hope, however, that you won't take advantage of us in this respect."

"You're so gracious," I said, "And in return I graciously allow you the use of *my* cutlery, *my* china—"

"Victoria, Adele didn't mean to sound unkind I'm sure," my mother interjected while Adele sprang to her feet in rage and Mrs. Ackroyd clasped her chair to stop it from falling over.

"None of it's yours until your birthday, and it's a very long time until *then*. We'll see if you're so eager to stay next March!"

Her words rang ominously in my mind again as I recalled them, which I did from time to time. But I resolved not to think about Adele any longer as I made my way up Flowergate to my rendezvous with Ned. He was still stowing the provisions he'd been asked to buy. We obtained eggs, milk, meat, and grain locally, but from the town we bought tea, sugar, coffee, and at wholesale prices. I watched as Ned tucked two final wooden boxes on top.

"What's in those?" I asked, curious about the foreign markings stamped on them.

"Master Samuel's port wine. Comes special all the way from Portugal. He don't hold with these new French wines, or with cognac, but sticks to the old ways."

And the more expensive ways. I judged there to be six bottles at least. Great-uncle Samuel was a man who liked his comforts, the more costly the better. He would not like to feel the winds of change to come. Another ominous thought.

Once we were on our way, I no longer had the distraction of the busy streets and shops, the bustle of the crowds. I dreamed of the future

A Bitter Legacy

and made it as rosy as I could, with myself and my mother at the center of a great social whirl, while my impoverished relatives watched enviously from the sidelines. And Jasper, yes, even Jasper, would be forced to acknowledge me.

When I arrived, the Hall—I still found it difficult to call it home—was quiet. No one came to greet me, and all the doors leading from the hallway were firmly closed. I took off my outer coat, damp from the heavy mist, and shivered involuntarily, though I wasn't cold. Suddenly weary, worn out by the struggle to fight and keep on fighting, I began to climb the stairs, intending to find Tommy and my mother. I wanted to give Tommy his gift and my mother her purchases and report on my conversation with Mr. Pontefract. After I would change into dry clothes for dinner. It was dark on the landing, and standing in the gloom, I wondered why no one had lit the gas lamps.

The door to my mother's room opened, and I heard quick footsteps. It was Rosie, her face white and strained in the light of the candle she carried. "Miss, oh, miss, your mama's been taken right poorly while you were out."

My heart thumped with alarm. I threw off my weariness and hurried along the landing to her. "Where is she?"

"In bed in her room. Dr. Cooper's with her now."

"Doctor! Rosie, what happened? Was it an accident?"

"I don't know!" She tried to reassure me, her natural honesty warring with kindliness. "Just a chill, I'm sure. Aye, that's all it can be. It couldn't be anything worse, could it? You see, she didn't come down to luncheon, and as no one had seen her since breakfast, we went up to the attic, Mrs. Ackroyd and me. We found her lying there in a dead faint, and she's not woken since."

"Thank heaven you went to look for her. What does Dr. Cooper say?"

"He's only been with her a couple of minutes. Mrs. Roberts sent for him straight away, but he was not at home, and we had to wait over an hour for him."

We were standing outside the closed door to my mother's room now, talking in urgent whispers. I both longed and dreaded to go in.

"Adele must have been very worried then, to act so quickly."

Rosie made a wry face before saying, "More like she wanted to make sure it was nothing that would harm Tommy, even though the dear lad's not had a day's serious illness in his life. She'll be weakening him, I reckon."

"Perhaps, but she's right, we must stop any infection from spreading. What does George say? Does he know?"

"Caught the news just as he was going out.

A Bitter Legacy

He said she probably needed a lie down. But everyone's frightened till we hear the doctor's verdict."

"I'm sure George is right. I'll go in now. You'd better light the lamps up here."

The strange hush in the Hall had now been explained. Everyone had withdrawn into their rooms, anticipating with fear the doctor's diagnosis. In Mama's room the now familiar sight of Dr. Cooper's short, round body was bent over my mother's body. He turned around to me, his small, steel-rimmed spectacles catching the light, and frowned.

"I've just come back from Whitby," I explained unnecessarily. "How—"

"Wait," he commanded peremptorily and turned to his patient.

Obediently, I moved back again, then was startled to see, on the other side of the bed and initially obscured by Dr. Cooper, Mrs. Ackroyd. Those black-button eyes, the unnatural stillness of her wiry form, the pursing of her thin, gray lips, all shouted disapproval of me. I had never seen so clearly before her dislike of me. Natural anxiety brought a flood of guilt. She seemed to be silently accusing me of being an ungrateful daughter and that if I'd been the usual, dutiful sort, taking care of my mother instead of gallivanting off on my own, this wouldn't have happened.

Not true, I cried inwardly. My mother had

seen me off with her blessing. Only this morning I had begged her to rest. What more could I have done? I clasped my hands in silent prayer, my eyes fixed on the bed. I could hear my mother's ragged breathing, and occasionally a slight moan, which jabbed at my nerves. I could not believe that this was happening. It was all a bad dream from which I'd awaken soon.

At last Dr. Cooper was finished, and Mrs. Ackroyd assisted him with swift, silent movements to pack away his things. Then he washed his hands in the bowl of water she provided before speaking to me. He could not hide his puzzled frown.

"What is it? Is it more than a chill?" I asked. Dread names floated through my mind: rheumatic fever, pneumonia, pleurisy.

He shook his head. "I'll be honest with you, Miss Lansdowne—"

"Miss Hunter."

"Yes, of course. As I was saying, to be honest, I don't know what's wrong with her. There's no fever, no sweats, no chills. Her lungs seem sound. However, though regular, her heartbeat is weak and slow, very slow."

"Then she's had a heart attack? Or a stroke, like Grandfather Albert?" I suggested.

He paused in drying his hands, then shook his head. "No, there are none of those signs. To be truthful, I've never come across anything like it before. Nor would it have made any difference if I'd been here earlier, from what I've heard, as there's been no deterioration."

"She's always had excellent health," I protested.

"All the same, she's sunk into a coma." He paused, his eyes meeting mine in a level gaze. "I know her sister is in an asylum, has been for years."

"My mother is not insane, or catatonic," I declared loudly, while Mrs. Ackroyd watched and listened. "As for my Aunt Caroline, it's only her nerves."

"I think I will be the judge of that," the doctor said acidly. "Though I think you're right. I'll consult a colleague of mine at York Infirmary. Meanwhile, I've prescribed some powders. For now, keep her warm, give her liquids from a spoon. She should swallow those quite easily. And keep her company. Talk to her. Try to bring her back from wherever it is she's gone."

Mrs. Ackroyd escorted Dr. Cooper to the door, then she stopped to look back at me. When he was out of earshot, she said, "More than you bargained for, miss, eh? Such a shame." Then she was gone. The words were an expression of sympathy, yet it was clear she meant the opposite. How I hated the sound of her voice, thin yet grating, with its false accent mimicking Adele's. They'd been innocent words, yet I'd heard the gloating behind them.

Left alone with Mama, I sat by the bed and took her nearly lifeless hand in mine. It was cool, her skin papery. As I smoothed her hair from her forehead, just as she had done when she nursed me through childhood illnesses, I pushed the black thought that she could die from my mind. I was going to nurse her back to health again, and failing that, I would *will* her to recover.

At the same time, both Jasper's and Mr. Pontefract's warnings chased themselves around in my mind. In a way they were both being proved right, that Lansdowne Hall would bring me nothing but trouble and grief. And yet, it only made me more determined to prove them both wrong.

I sat by my mother's side all night, my mind numb with shock. Rosie brought me food and drink, and offered to sit with me, but I refused, telling her to get some sleep. The next morning I was hollow-eyed and exhausted when she came in with a tea tray at half past six and made up the fire.

"You must rest, Miss Vicky. You won't do your mother any good by getting ill yourself. I'll wake you if there's any change."

Blearily, I stumbled to my room, fell on my bed without washing or undressing, and was asleep instantly. I was awakened much later by a gentle tapping on my shoulder. Mrs. Randell was leaning over me, her broad face filled with concern.

"Mrs. Ackroyd will be after my blood if she finds me above stairs, but I had to hear the story from your own lips about Mistress Alexandra. Here, I've brought you some strengthening soup."

Between mouthfuls of the hot, restoring liquid, I told her every detail. When I'd finished, she was frowning. "I can't understand it," she said. "She was always the sturdiest of them all. She ate the same as me yesterday, and I'm not ill, so it can't be the food. I wonder if it's some sort of shock she's had?"

"You've given me cause to hope," I said. "I'll try to find out if anything unusual happened yesterday. Perhaps something she discovered in the attic? Meanwhile, she's able to swallow, so we must feed her the best we can."

"You just rely on me, lass. I know what's best for an invalid."

And, even though I wasn't an invalid, I believed her, because my strength returned after eating her soup. I emerged to discover that Mrs. Ackroyd, much to my surprise, had offered to share nursing duties with Rosie and me. I could only assume that Adele had actually ordered this, giving the housekeeper more reason to resent me.

Gradually, the shock wore off and I became more accustomed to Mama's appearance, and was not every second expecting her to die. I could tell at a glance how she fared. Now it grieved me that none of the family came to ask about her. They pursued their own lives, either oblivious or glad of my distress.

My mother's condition remained unchanged. The powders were fetched, and in consultation with Mrs. Randell, I concocted various mixtures, with honey, lemon, and herbs, as well as giving my mother beef tea and other clear soups. She swallowed all these, but her eyes remained closed, her breathing and pulse slow.

I met Sophie on the stairs on the third day when I was returning from a brief walk outside in the blustery wind to clear my mind. I was pleased to see someone new and was eager to talk, but Sophie kept her distance and stared at me from opaque eyes.

"They say no one knows what's wrong with your mama," she said. "Adele is frightened that we all might die. But I know we won't."

"How do you know that?" Hope rose inside me. Had Sophie come across this strange illness before?

"She's having a long rest, that's all."

"But how do you know?" I persisted.

She looked at me slyly. "The ghosts told me," she said, then smiled when she saw how taken aback I was. "No, I puzzled it out for myself."

A Bitter Legacy

I couldn't tell what she believed. The little flicker of hope she'd raised died instantly, cruelly.

"Adele says you're not to go near Tommy, either. She—"

"As if I would be so thoughtless as to endanger Tommy when I love him as much as anyone," I interrupted. "Rosie's told me that she's isolated him in his room for now, even though Dr. Cooper says there's no risk."

"I know. I told her you'd never hurt Tommy." She moved closer. "Is it true that Dr. Cooper has sent for the surgeons and they're going to operate?"

"That must be wrong. He's never said any such thing to me," I protested. "She's not in pain, just sleeping, like in a faint."

"Someone told me the doctors would have to cut her open, to investigate what's going on inside her."

I seized her shoulders. "Who? Who told you these lies?" I almost shook her in my horror. "It can't be true. I won't let those butchers near her with their knives."

"I think it was Mrs. Ackroyd who told me." Sophie's dark eyes were luminously large. "You'll have to face it, Vicky, if it's the only way to cure her. There's nothing you can do to stop them."

"Stop being ghoulish, Sophie. There's no question of Victoria's mother being operated on. Mrs. Ackroyd has got it wrong, as usual. You can let her go now, Victoria."

George, who had joined us unseen, pried my fingers from Sophie's shoulders, his face sterner than I'd ever seen it. "Will you leave us?" he said to his sister. "I want to talk to Victoria alone."

She looked from one to the other of us then, realizing he would not relent, touched his sleeve in a helpless gesture, and walked away.

As soon as she was gone, George subjected me to a fierce scrutiny, then said, "Cousin Victoria, I've been informed that you were seen hiding in a doorway with Thornley having a secret meeting when you went to Whitby. Learning of the tragedy that he has brought on this family, the very fact that he's been forbidden to enter this house, must mean something to you. I can hardly credit your disloyalty."

"He denies everything."

"What do you expect? It's not him I'm concerned about, it's your underhanded behavior."

Aghast, I said, "I didn't arrange any secret meetings. I went to see Mr. Pontefract, as I told you. And what if I did speak to Mr. Thornley? I've done nothing to be ashamed of," I told him hotly. "It's your informant who should be ashamed of spying and spreading gossip!"

George raised an eyebrow. "No spy, merely a chance remark by an acquaintance in Holmby, friendly neighbor to neighbor. Victoria, please understand that I'm worried for your safety. He's already caused the death of one family member. I don't want it to happen again, for you to be next."

"But, George, if you believe him guilty, why hasn't he been brought to trial?"

"Don't think I don't feel bitter about that. But there was not enough evidence. Somehow he managed to wriggle out of it, perhaps by intimidation on his part."

Boldly, I suggested, "Perhaps there are no witnesses because the rumor is—was—false."

"Or is it that you would have it so?" he asked quietly.

I looked away. "I'm just trying to be fair. Remember, my father was made to leave because of false rumors, too. I believe that someone here is trying to destroy our family. Therefore, despite what you say"—I could not bring myself to mention Aunt Caroline—"I'm trying to give Mr. Thornley the benefit of the doubt."

"Of course, Vicky." George's tone was conciliatory now. "I'm only thinking of you. I know you'd be too proud to speak out if Thornley was forcing himself on you, but I can help. You've not had a father or brother to look out for your interests, but now you have a whole family. There's no need to feel vulnerable any longer."

I was now thoroughly confused. I had begun to consider George my friend, and I gladly accepted this further demonstration that he cared for me. I, too, had perceived Jasper as in some way dangerous to me, and I, too, had been prepared to believe Aunt Caroline's accusations. Yet, perversely, I rebelled at the thought that George was telling me who I could or could not speak to.

I lifted my chin, and said levelly, "He has not been forcing his attentions on me. On the contrary, like you, he wants the Hall. He's even offered to buy it. The truth is, we met by accident outside Mr. Pontefract's office when he asked me again to name my price."

To my surprise, George laughed uproariously. "Why, Thornley could never afford it. He's virtually penniless and has to grow grapes to earn a living. He's an adventurer, preying on an innocent and generous-hearted young woman. Don't deny it, I've seen him playing on your sympathy. He's a cheating con-man, and, besides, I only offered to buy this pile of stone to help you out. I promise you that in future I won't fail you. Thornley won't be allowed near you again. Because I—"

"You're a fool, George!"

We both spun around and saw that our voices had roused Adele from her siesta. She stood in the doorway of her room, wearing a long silk robe, her hair cascading over her shoulders, her face white with anger. Ostentatiously, she kept her distance, hissing down the hallway, "Can't you see she's playing us against each other? I'd rather *she* kept it, vile creature that she is, than she sell to anyone else, even Thornley. I won't let it happen."

"You don't have any say in the matter, Adele," I said coldly. "You, too, have judged and condemned Jasper Thornley, I see."

"Everything that George has told you about that—that heartless creature is true." Her eyes flashed icy fire, like diamonds. "As for having no say, don't forget I'm a trustee. If there's some way to get rid of you, I'll find it!"

Fuming, I hurried away. Adele had stated her position even more clearly. She was my implacable enemy. With her and Great-uncle Samuel so firmly against me, and with my mother ill, I had only George to support me, and now I had just alienated him. In the back of my mind, I suppose I had nursed a foolish fantasy that, despite everything, we would turn out to be one happy family. How wrong I'd been.

Then I heard footsteps behind me. It was George.

"Vicky, I'm sorry I was cross with you, and don't let Adele upset you. She has a quick temper, and she doesn't always mean what she says. You know she's afraid, we all are, of the changes you bring, and she has Tommy to think of, too."

"I understand that she's just threatened me,

but I suppose you're right," I conceded, hot tears stinging my eyes. "You could at least have asked about my mother."

"Of course. How unfeeling of me. It's just that you come first with me." Gently, he took hold of my hands. "If you must blame anyone, blame me for caring too much about you. But since you arrived, my life has taken on new meaning." He raised my fingertips to his lips. "Give us—me—time."

I smiled at him gratefully. George's hands were warm on mine, and strength flowed from them. "I know I can count on you."

"At the least as your friend," he murmured, and stroked back a curl of my hair. "Whatever the circumstances."

I desperately wanted the comfort he offered. If only Jasper hadn't cast doubt about him in my mind, I could become very fond of George. And what of George's words about Jasper? Which one of them should I believe?

Later, keeping my lonely vigil at my mother's side, I remembered the tenderness in George's eyes and voice, and wanted to believe that he was sincere, and found more there than comfort. I could become very fond of George indeed.

That night the first snows came, which were early for this time of year. There were just a few weeks to go before Christmas, and what a bleak prospect that was for me, with my mother

A Bitter Legacy

still in her coma. Not only would it be my first Christmas away from home—in Boston, that is—but it would be the first I had spent without my mother. My Lansdowne relatives were no substitute.

Dr. Cooper returned several times. He reported that his learned colleagues were fascinated by the case, and once one of them accompanied him, in top hat and fancy waistcoat and carrying a gold-knobbed cane. But none could throw light on the mysterious illness. My only comfort was that my mother's condition did not deteriorate, as daily Rosie and I turned her, rubbed her arms and legs to stimulate the circulation, washed her, talked to her, and fed her liquids teaspoon by teaspoon.

The snow gradually accumulated till the Hall stood marooned in a sea of white. Deliveries were erratic, but Mrs. Randell had ensured the larders were well stocked. She was glad to add to her supply the odd brace of game birds or bag of fish that were brought from time to time.

But George complained that the early weather had brought vermin scavenging too close to the grounds, and Great-uncle Samuel said something ought to be done about them, though as usual he did nothing. Bitter winds howled around the Hall at night, keeping me awake with their gusting shrieks in the chimneys, and I imagined the wild animals prowling restlessly outside.

Cooped up in the house, we all grew restless, except for George. He came and went on horseback to Newcastle and York, mentioning names, but bringing no one back to the Hall with him, and I wondered if he was ashamed of us all in some way. Yet he seemed cheerful.

Great-uncle Samuel complained endlessly of rheumatism and other minor ailments. He cast me baleful looks as if his afflictions were my fault, and sat all day alone by the library fire, guarding the records of Lansdowne Hall. I'd looked in once or twice and seen him nodding in the great leather armchair, his foot propped up, glass and decanter by his side, but alert enough to look up if I ventured too far into the room.

Adele at last relented, after first requesting me to keep to my own room, and allowed Tommy out to play in the snow with Maire. Her red hair was the only color in the monochrome of black and white stretching as far as the eye could see. Black branches and twigs, black underbellies of the heavy clouds contrasted with dazzling white snow. I should be used to snow, but in Boston it was quickly cleared away, and there were skating and slides and children pulling each other on toboggans. This was dreary, empty, imprisoning snow, the only laughter coming from Tommy and Maire as they threw snowballs at each other.

I tried not to dwell too often on my old life, but I found myself questioning more and more

A Bitter Legacy

whether my dream of inheriting Lansdowne Hall, of establishing my mother and myself at the center of a glittering social life, had any real substance. But I had been determined to be avenged all my life, and since our summons to England, it had blossomed to the exclusion of all else like a great ugly poisonous mushroom. I could see nothing else except my resolve. What else was there?

As yet, none of the others had made any arrangements to move, although my twenty-first birthday was only three months away. Still, they expected my defeat, and I expected to triumph over them. So we watched one another, waiting for the first crack to show, the first sign of defeat.

George kept to his word and sought my company when we were both free. Those were few but pleasurable times, helping me forget my anxiety for my mother briefly. We would sit in the small parlor, George clearly indicating that Sophie wasn't welcome to join us, which made me uncomfortable. We played cards and parlor games, and he would talk and make me laugh, though afterwards I couldn't remember what about.

When he was away, I would find myself in Sophie's company. She would slip silently in to my mother's room while I read aloud to Mama, hoping that her favorite poetry or novel would make her stir. I would suddenly become aware of another presence and, the skin on my neck crawling, would glance around. There Sophie'd be, watching me fixedly, sometimes with her head cocked to one side, in that calculating way of hers. Then she'd nod, and say, "Dearest Vicky, go on. I won't disturb you. I do love to listen to you."

Other times she'd bring me her drawings to admire. She would happily explain what they meant, because each of them told a story rather than represented a landscape, and were distinctly odd.

At least Adele kept well out of my way. Occasionally, I would hear her voice raised in imperious command, or I would see her leaving the house in yet another resplendent new gown, looking utterly ravishing yet haughty. I couldn't understand why we couldn't be friends, why she was the way she was, cruel and cutting. Such beauty wasted.

All the same, there were moments when I was alone and unoccupied, and chafed at my confinement. I longed to know what Mr. Pontefract had discovered, but no letters arrived for me. And on those quiet days of toil and care and worry when I wished to be doing something for my future but could not, I would think of Jasper. I thought of his gray eyes, of his spare, rangy body, of his square shoulders. He reminded me of one of those "vermin" George had mentioned. I imagined him circling the Hall like a great wild fox, or the shadow of a thin gray wolf, choosing his moment to pounce. I would remember the closeness of his body, the sensation that he'd been about to touch me when we stood close together in the passageway below Mr. Pontefract's office. Could it be, as George hinted, that I had an unhealthy fascination with evil?

I also made my way up the narrow, wooden stairs to the attic, to make sure my mother hadn't left anything up there. In fact, I was curious about the mysterious something that she'd promised to show me, and hoped that I might find what, I didn't know, but I guessed it must be connected with my father.

As I walked past heaped boxes, broken furniture, odd shapes under dust sheets, I fingered the small brooch she'd given me and which I always wore, as if it was a talisman that would help me locate her secret.

I soon saw where she'd been working. These trunks were dusted off and still stood open. I searched quickly, but the trunks largely contained clothes and books, some bric-a-brac, and just one packet of letters. Though I scanned these intently, they were all from her closest friend, now living in the far southwest of England. I didn't linger, for all these items filled me with sadness as I imagined my mother as a young girl, before life had dealt her such harsh blows. I carefully closed the lids and went downstairs again.

I headed to my own room to rest, after glancing in at my mother and glad to see Elise with her instead of Mrs. Ackroyd who always made me feel so awkward. I stopped, however, when I heard a hammering at the front door, and then shouts from below. I quickly ran along the landing and leaned over the bannister.

The great hallway seemed to be filled with men, George striding among them, putting on his hat and coat, his voice loudest of all. In fact, there were only five other men, four standing together, their caps respectfully removed, while the fifth talked energetically with George. He was of medium height, heavily muscled, and carried a stout stick. I guessed this must be Mr. Brown, the mines manager, whom George had mentioned a few days ago. As I hesitated, wondering whether to go down, Mrs. Ackroyd brushed past me, and said, "I should stay here, miss. They'll not be wanting women down there." But she went on down herself.

Great-uncle Samuel emerged into the hallway, blinking and swaying slightly. There was a sudden lull as the other men exited the house.

"Get ready," George said to him. "We have to go out."

"What? Can't Brown see to it?"

A Bitter Legacy

"Dammit, this time we have to see what we can salvage." He glanced over his shoulder. "Brown says they won't start work until we're there and they can see the color of our money. You'll have to open the safe."

The old man departed, grumbling, and Mrs. Ackroyd suddenly glided out of the shadows, carrying an extra woolen cape for George.

"We shan't be back tonight," George said, beginning to pace restlessly. "Inform the household, will you? Dammit, these lazy good-for-nothings have a lot to answer for." Then he headed out the door, and Mrs. Ackroyd climbed silently up the stairs.

"What is it?" I asked. "What's happened?"

"Subsidence and flooding at Stickle Mine," she told me.

"An accident you mean? How bad is it?"

"There'll be plenty injured," she said with cold relish. "Perhaps some dead, too."

I shuddered with horror, remembering how Adele's husband died, glad that she'd sent Tommy away for a few days. I could almost hear the cries of the trapped men, the screams of pain . . .

Mrs. Ackroyd passed me, and I seized the opportunity to run down the stairs, eager to offer my help. Perhaps I could make up bandages or organize hot food. Obviously, help was needed, because whoever Mr. Brown had marshaled needed bribing, which disgusted me.

George had already gone, but I met Great-uncle Samuel shrugging into an old-fashioned wool cape. He lowered his bushy eyebrows at me, but I was not intimidated.

"The accident. I want to do something," I said.

"You, miss, can go back to your room and stay there," he growled. "No female fussing required." He brushed me aside, stomping out the door in George's wake.

I frowned with frustration at being continually shut out. Surely George would listen to me. I hurried outside into the few swirling flakes of snow, but the men were already well under way down the drive. I watched until the last lantern and last torch had disappeared, then suddenly realized how cold I was. I could do nothing to help after all, except pray, and was just turning to go indoors when I saw two dark shapes on horseback emerging from the gloom across the park. I waved, then waited for the men to reach me, thinking they had come about the accident, too, intending to direct them to the mine.

They were nearly upon me when I recognized, with a jolt of shock, Jasper Thornley. In the porchlight I thought the man with him looked familiar, but wasn't sure.

"Have you heard about the terrible accident?" I asked urgently. "George and Great-uncle Samuel have already gone to help."

A Bitter Legacy

"Aye. More like to see what they can salvage from the wreckage," Jasper's companion muttered, then began to cough.

I peered up at him. His voice was familiar, too, but I could not place him.

Jasper jumped down. His face was set like granite, though he looked tired. "You promised to listen to the evidence if I brought it," he said. "This was the only time Jem could come, and we learned on the way about the accident, so it's just as well they're all away. Jem can talk to you in peace. Is there somewhere we can talk safely and privately together?"

I didn't hesitate. "Come around to the kitchen. I'll find Mrs. Randell and ask her to find us somewhere, and we can trust Ned to keep quiet about the horses. He's sweet on Rosie, my maid, so he will do anything I ask so that I'll allow her time to see him!"

"I know Ned," Jasper said. "He's a good lad and to be trusted."

I looked at him in surprise, then remembered. Of course, Jasper knew far more about my home than I did.

We skirted the outside of the house, where all was thankfully in darkness. I slipped in through the pantry and the passageway, and caught Mrs. Randell alone in the kitchen. She simply nodded when I posed my request. After greeting Jasper quietly, but with affectionate warmth, she led the way to her own little parlor beyond the kitchen via its own passage, and no one saw us. She brought us some hot drinks, and then she left us alone. In the light I saw that Jem had only one arm, the other just a stump. He also coughed frequently, a chesty cough that wheezed in his lungs and sounded painful.

"I'm sorry about your fellow miners," I said. "As many will be saved as possible, be sure of that."

"We're sorrowing for them and waiting our turn."

"Don't give up heart," Jasper urged.

"No one can guarantee accidents won't happen," I began. But Jem, jaw set and fist clenched, interrupted, "Mebbe not. But you can try damned hard to avoid one, by not letting the support timbers rot, by not using outdated, rusty equipment, and by making sure the water don't get in. Flooding, that's what we expect daily, that or a landslip. Those mines are a deathtrap for all who work in them."

"I know mining is a dangerous job," I said slowly, while my mind's eye insisted on replaying the scene when George and I had been mobbed by men hurling insults and stones, about which I hadn't told Jasper. "Surely if they're in such a poor state, you should speak to the manager. I know George has every confidence in him."

A Bitter Legacy

"Brown?" He laughed bitterly, and then began to cough in painful spasms. When he spoke again, it was between gasps. "He knows already, but why should he care? His orders come from above, and anyone who complains gets turned off, like my brother. I daren't complain because I've got a family. I get paid pitifully little because I can't do much like this, though it's better than nothing."

"Couldn't you find other employment?" I asked, my cheeks burning at his contemptuous statement about "orders come from above."

He looked away. "Not when we signed the contract. There was no work, and we were desperate. Contract says if we go, the militia come after us."

"But surely that's illegal," I cried, and looked to Jasper for confirmation.

"Now you know my business in Whitby," he said quietly.

"I thought," I said, "that laws were being passed."

"Aye, laws in London, but here it's Lansdowne law, and we've no rights to force changes—yet," Jem added ominously. "My brother tried, and he's hunted now, living rough, in fear of his life. They're afraid he'll talk, see. But he won't, because of me and my younguns."

"How many children do you have, Jem?"

His face softened momentarily. "Four, and

the bairn, not yet christened, though we hope before Christmas. And that's another thing. This winter our wages are being cut because we can't get much out, with the mud and water after all the rains we've been having."

"But surely repairs can be carried out?"

"They can but that costs money. Same as the maintenance of the houses that go with the job. Our upstairs is so damp we all sleep down in the kitchen. If only I could do something . . ." Jem's excitement caused him to cough again, an ugly, wet whistling in his lungs. "Not that I have any say in the matter now. This happened when some dynamite blew." He nodded to his stump. "I was going to be thrown out of our house till Mr. Thornley helped us."

As Jem and Jasper talked, I listened with growing horror to the tale of neglect at the mines, and the way all petitions went unanswered. We talked quietly, stopping at the least sound from outside, but the maids were elsewhere and so far we were safe. Once or twice Jasper got up to check the door, but no one was there. However, Jem began to get restless, wanting to leave before he was discovered at the Hall by a returning Lansdowne, and I saw genuine fear in his eyes.

"You can believe me or not as you like, Miss Hunter," he said. "I'm known as a troublemaker by your family."

A Bitter Legacy

"It could be that my relatives are too proud to listen to you, but I'm sure they'll listen to me. I'll do what I can for you and your family. I'll speak to George as soon as I can."

When we were outside, I drew in breaths of the pure, clear air, and held Jasper out of earshot while Jem fetched the horses. "What's wrong with him?" I asked. "Is it influenza?"

"No, it's the dust that gets into miners' lungs. These minerals are dangerous, I'm convinced of it, and get into every crevice. An occupational hazard." He paused. "Vicky, be careful how you tackle George. For one thing, how will you explain your new knowledge?"

"I'll say I've been overhearing gossip, and, Jasper, I'm still sure that it must be the manager's fault. Those mines represent George's future fortune, so why would he allow them to deteriorate? That way the return on his capital will simply dwindle away. It's a question of good housekeeping."

"A shrewd point. I think you'll find that, when the legalities are over, he'll sell as fast as he can. George is more interested in his social life than business."

Jasper took my hand in his and lifted it to his lips. His touch sent a tremor running through my body, and for a moment I longed for him to hold me and kiss me properly. It seemed he felt something of that, too, because when he spoke again his voice was husky. "Is it possible you're revising your opinion of me, Vicky? We must meet again."

I shook my head vehemently, suddenly afraid for both of us, though I didn't know why. His face hardened.

"Then you still think my honor is in question."

"No! We were seen together in Whitby, and George was very angry with me. He does care for me, you know. Besides, my mother is very ill—"

"Vicky, I didn't know. What's wrong?"

Briefly, I gave him the details, his frown deepening all the while. Finally I said, "Besides, now I've told them you want to buy the Hall, too, and they hate you twice as much."

"What? You little idiot! What possessed you to give away our private business?"

I looked up into his shadowed face, its planes and angles hard and uncompromising. "Why keep it secret?"

"Surely it must be obvious to you!"

He grasped me fiercely by my arms, as I tried to explain. Then he said, "Quiet, I must think. I have the answer. Marry me, now, straight away. It can be done."

I stared at him, aghast, then struggled to be free of his imprisoning hands. "Marry—you! You must be mad. Make an alliance so you can get your hands on the Hall, *my* Hall!"

A Bitter Legacy

"Of course. I should have known that that pile of stone always comes first with you, now and always. You should rename it Vengeance Hall. Listen to me, Vicky—"

"No! It's you who wants revenge. You're just using me in all this," I said with a sudden flash of insight.

He groaned, gripping me tighter, pressing me against him. "If only you knew—" he said, then broke off. His lips came down on mine, once, and then he turned and strode to his horse and rode away with Jem without looking back.

Chapter Six

I spent the remainder of the evening as if I was in a fevered dream. Images surfaced and resurfaced in my mind: of the cruel life led by the miners who worked for the Lansdownes; of Jem; of the press of Jasper's body; and of the force of his lips against mine.

I hid all my thoughts from the other members of the household. Only when sitting alone with my mother could I murmur to her everything that had happened.

"He asked me to marry him," I whispered in the dead of night, my throat choked with anger. "He would go to any lengths to get his hands on this house and to get his revenge against the Lansdownes. Why, he didn't even pretend he cared for me, so arrogant is he and so little

A Bitter Legacy

does he think of me. Does he think I'm so weak I'd take any opportunity for marriage? Or did he think that I'd be so overcome by Jem's story that I'd say yes? But never fear, Mama, I left him in no doubt as to my answer. Only why does it hurt so much?"

I laid my cheek against her cool hand, hoping for a response, but there was none. No flicker of consciousness, just the occasional sigh or light groan. She still clung to life, and no one knew how thin the thread was, or how or when it might snap.

Then as I undressed for bed, I remembered that unfortunately, Sophie had noticed my absence from my room earlier that evening when I'd talked with Jem and Jasper. When I'd entered the house, I'd been so preoccupied I'd not noticed her at first, sitting in the shadows beyond the reach of the firelight. I had jumped when she spoke.

"I knew you'd be back," she had said. "I knew you hadn't run away, so I've been waiting for you."

"Of course," I said as calmly as I could. "I can't think of any reason why I should run away from what is to be my home, can you?"

She fingered the dull, dark brown woolen skirt she wore. "I wanted to run away when Leonie died. And when William died. This has been an unhappy house. So I thought that with your mother so ill . . ."

"My mother is going to recover, I'm sure of that," I said firmly, keeping my own doubts and fears to myself. "I shall have to find the courage you did when Leonie died. After all, you're still here."

"I wasn't brave at all. No one had any time for me. George was away at school, Uncle Albert was always angry when he saw me. Then I met the White Lady for the first time, and she helped me to speak to Leonie."

The hairs on the back of my neck prickled. "To—to speak to her?"

Sophie smiled in her sly way. "I don't hear her voice exactly. But they're both in the spirit world now, aren't they? So when I talk to Leonie's portrait, it's as if my words are sent on by the ghostly power of the White Lady, and I imagine that Leonie can hear me and that she is looking after me still."

The lonely, overlooked child then, as now, starved of affection, had found the love she craved where she could. That I understood.

"I think the White Lady is our friend, don't you? Some people say that she drives you mad if you stay awake the whole night in the old hall, but I've done that, and I'm not mad, am I?" she asked, tilting her head.

"I agree she's not to be feared," I said, remembering the sensation I'd felt when I'd gone down those spiral stairs. "Not as long as we love her."

I don't know why I added those last words,

but, as I said them, my neck prickled again, and Sophie stared at me with very big round eyes. Then she suddenly got to her feet and came closer, and for one moment I wondered if she was crazed after all, and stepped back.

"Where have you been anyway? I wanted to play cards and now it's too late."

"I—It's Mama, and—and the accident. I needed fresh air, to think, to be alone." We both looked down at my damp boots.

Sophie nodded understandingly. "I'll help you take those off. George would never forgive me if I allowed you to catch pneumonia, would he? But you shouldn't go walking in the snow at this time of year. You could get lost and die."

"In that case, we'd better not tell George, had we? We don't want to give him something else to worry about."

She flashed me a rare smile. "How thoughtful you are! It shall be our secret. George means more to me than anything else in the world, and I don't want him hurt." She patted my hand. "I'm sure I'll come to love you just as much, though, in time."

Although I wanted her as a friend, I rather hoped she wouldn't become as devoted to me as she was to George. That would indeed be a heavy responsibility to bear.

The next day Rosie told me when she brought my breakfast tray up—I rarely ate downstairs any longer—that someone had been sent with the message that both George and Great-uncle Samuel would not be returning. As soon as we had finished caring for my mother, and I had eaten my own breakfast, I left Rosie in charge and went to look for Adele.

Outside the sky was a dark gray above a dull earth covered by a sprinkling of snow. Inside the light barely penetrated far enough for me to see my way. It was very quiet, too. Usually, I could hear the sound of a distant voice, a light laugh from one of the servants, a snatch of whistling from outside, or perhaps Great-uncle Samuel booming some order, or Tommy's cries of excitement from the nursery. But today the house was shrouded in silence, as if in mourning for those men who had died or been injured.

Adele was in her private sitting room, giving Elise instructions as to what clothes to pack and how to care for them. She made me wait until she had finished her detailed instructions.

"Oui, madame," Elise said, then sailed by me, her nose in the air, as if I did not exist.

"Where are you going?" I asked when the door closed behind Elise.

"I'm collecting Tommy from the Gransbys' and taking him with me to the Grange to stay with Miss Redvers and her brother, and I'm extremely busy. I hope you'll be quick. What do you want?"

"A messenger came. I wanted to know what happened at Stickle Mine. Are the men safe?

A Bitter Legacy

I heard George and Great-uncle Samuel were staying there."

"Hah!" I'd amused her. "They're not staying there. They've gone on to York, something to do with the bank, I believe."

"Then it wasn't that serious?" I asked happily.

"It was very serious. There'll be no more production till it's all cleared up. Several died and scores were injured."

I gasped in shock. "How terrible! Those men will have wives and children..."

I'd amused her again. "The women work there, too, alongside the men. Some of them are tougher."

"All the same, their families will need care. Is there a fund we can contribute to?"

"Why should you care? Father didn't leave the mines to you, did he?"

"Nor to you," I retorted. "Which I'm sure bothers you just as much as not having the Hall. Yet you don't hate George."

"You're wrong. I couldn't care less about the mines. I've never been near them. I don't know the first thing about them, nor do I want to. You're just like Roberts, my first husband, always poking your nose in—and look what happened to him for his pains. I told him to leave them to those who know what they're doing. George and Uncle Samuel have been running them for as long as I can remember for my father, and we've always had enough to live on, so why should I complain?" Adele finished her tirade breathlessly, tapping her fingers impatiently, longing for me to go.

"Then you can't confirm what Jasper says, that the miners are mistreated, the mines themselves in disrepair, so that someone can line their own pockets and falsify the accounts?"

"*Jasper* says!" Her voice was filled with venom, her look was pure hatred. "When were you talking to Thornley?"

"A chance remark at one time." But she didn't want to hear me.

"Because if I find you've been meeting with him, be sure I'll make trouble for you."

"Telling tales to George? Getting him to fight your battles, like Sophie does?" Even as I goaded her, I knew I was wrong.

She was trembling with some emotion I couldn't place, yet for once she controlled herself. "I've never gone running to George. I've always taken care of myself. George learned long ago to leave me alone."

For a moment I saw her as she saw herself, the Frost Queen ruling over her own court, pushing aside the occasional nuisances like myself. Yet she was deeply discontented.

"Meanwhile," she pursued relentlessly, "I have instructed a lawyer to investigate you. Be sure that if there's any loophole, any dirt to stir up, I'll find it, and you will be on your way back to America!"

I could think of no answer to that, and hated the weakness of my position. But subdued, as I returned to my mother's side, I knew that, of course, my position as the legitimate heiress to the house and land was the strongest position. I didn't need to attack, only to defend—for now.

I reported the news about the accident to Rosie, but none of the rest of the conversation.

"My family are all fisher folk from Whitby way," she told me. "And I know how the whole town mourns when someone goes overboard. When a boat goes down . . . Well, it's a disaster, like this." She was silent a moment, her face registering deep concern, then she went on, "You say Mrs. Roberts is leaving today?"

"Yes, she's taking Tommy to the Grange. Some people called Redvers?"

"Redvers still, is it? He's been courting Mrs. Roberts for some time now. Well, quite a few have, though when they heard she wasn't inheriting much, some dropped out, of course, even though she's well off and beautiful, too."

"Well, I haven't met him or his sister. It seems I've met nobody as yet. Nobody even comes to call! It's weird around here, I tell you."

Rosie's reply was, for her, evasive. "It's not your fault, Miss Vicky, but folks is wary. The old master didn't expect company once he fell ill, and the others all look for it abroad, away from the house. It's a poor quiet place now. Neglected, like, wouldn't you say? And now your mama's ill."

I sighed. "I suppose so, Rosie. But it would have been nice to be made more welcome." But even as I spoke, I knew that the past hung over me and my mother like a tainted shadow, and until it was removed, we could not expect to be accepted.

I found myself very much alone with my mother over the next few days once Adele had gone. Even Sophie deserted me, claiming she had a cold and remained hidden in her room, making it clear she didn't want anyone to disturb her. I often wondered what she did in there for long hours alone, but she never invited me in, nor referred to any pastimes except drawing.

Caring for Mama was becoming more and more demanding. She was still able to swallow, and I continued to feed her clear soups and honey-enriched drinks. Rosie's help was invaluable, but I avoided Mrs. Ackroyd's cold disapproving presence as much as I could. But I couldn't fault her nursing of Mama, doubly needed now that Elise had gone with her mistress.

For much of the time then there was nothing to interrupt my thoughts, and I was able to puzzle over all the strange things that had

A Bitter Legacy

happened since we'd returned to England to take up my legacy. And a bitter legacy indeed it was turning out to be. All the same, I'd learned more about my grandfather and didn't hate him so much. But I still blamed him for abandoning us in Boston when my father's family refused to believe that my mother had really married my father. Would it have cost him so much to unbend just once and send one letter, or a little money to help us out of our poverty? My mother had only asked him for money twice, and after that, did not write again. How could I forgive the cold heart that put his own pride before his daughter's well-being?

And so I had never blamed my father for our predicament. As a child I'd dreamed about him, longed for him to return to us. When everyone believed he was dead, my mother clung to the hope that he was alive somewhere. She had not remarried because she was still loyal to my father's memory. Sometimes I had been annoyed with her for her stubborn insistence, believing that she was making herself needlessly unhappy. At the same time, I admired her for the depth of her feelings.

I admired her even more for her quiet determination to make a new life for herself. We could not ignore the wealthy Hunter family, whose name was well-known for their charitable works. But none of it had ever been extended to us, and my mother never asked for a penny.

She would not beg. Nor would she allow me to hate my father's family. She explained that the wealthy were prey to confidence tricksters, and, preoccupied with finding my father, she had not thought to bring any proof of their relationship. Except me.

So I did not hate them, nor did I love them.

Then, one day, when I was ten years old, we came face-to-face with Spenser Hunter's sister in the street outside the library. She stared at me long and hard, then took my mother's arm. "Oh, my dear," she'd murmured. "So it is true. She is Spenser's daughter. It's as if he's come back from the grave."

No public acknowledgement followed as my aunt clearly believed I was the result of an illicit union. But there were gifts for me of clothing and books, and the path seemed smoother for my mother to receive more and more lucrative offers of employment, particularly for her beautiful embroidery.

The Hunter family had genuinely mourned the loss of their second eldest son, certain that he had drowned, and certain that it was his own fault. In their opinion, he should have stayed in Boston, married the respectable girl they had cultivated for him, and become a lawyer—the destiny they had chosen for him. So both of my parents had been rebels, breaking with tradition. Both strong-minded people. It was a revelation to me to see that my mother was strong, after all, but in a quiet way. Could I be as tough-minded? Had I inherited those strengths, or was it true that I was a selfish, bigoted Lansdowne? I felt the two halves of myself pulling in opposite directions, and my palms went cold. Was I determined or pigheaded? Was I right or Jasper?

To distract myself from these unpleasant thoughts, I thought carefully over everything I'd learned. But instead of arriving at answers, I came up with more questions. Who spread the lies and gossip about my father and Jasper, someone in the household or someone further afield? Did Jasper only want to clear his name or was that the first part of a longer reaching vendetta? And why should he ask me to marry him? I could think of no reason except to possess the Hall. But why take revenge on me? I had never tried to harm him.

Only one thing slotted into place. I thought I had recognized Jem, and so I had. He was the one who had shouted at me and George from the crowd, and his brother had been the one who'd thrown the mud at our gig. George had called them ring leaders, rotten apples. Deliberately stirring up discontent against our family. Yet Jasper had spoken of him with affection and trust. Which one of them was right?

Furthermore, at the back of my mind remained the shadow of William's death. How I longed to discuss these questions with my mother. I needed her more now than at any other time in my life. But, I had only myself to rely on, and I was tied to her side, unable to investigate and banish the shadows surrounding me.

In my spare moments, restless and unable to walk outside because of the snow, I would wander through the quiet house, as if touching and examining everything in it would make them truly mine. The crystal, the silver, the paintings, the furniture, many of these were heirlooms my mother had told me about. They were part of the magic palace I'd conjured in my mind, where my mother and I would entertain and be treated like royalty.

But the reality was somewhat different, and as I explored the Hall a feeling of sadness developed and accompanied me like an unwanted wraith. It was a feeling that these objects of wealth and power, collected and imported from all over the globe, used as ballast or trade by the Lansdownes, would never and could never be mine, that I would never find the answers to my questions here.

The carved sandalwood from India, chased silver from London, steel from Sheffield, delicate colored glass from Italy, silk paintings, lacquerwood, and plates from China, rattan cane from Malay, ivory and ebony figurines from Africa, all were solid and unyielding of their secrets. Their strange scents and shapes spoke of alien worlds, casting no light on mine.

A Bitter Legacy

Late one evening I took my finished supper tray down to the kitchen, ignoring the astonished looks of the maids. I wanted to talk to Mrs. Randell. She was sitting beside the fire in her private sitting room, dozing. Her knitting had slipped down into her lap, helped on its way by the claws of a tiny kitten playing at her feet. I touched her shoulder, and she jerked awake, sending the kitten scurrying for safety behind the coal bucket. She laid her knitting aside and stood up, a solid, square figure, her fair hair turning white, a few wisps escaping from her bun.

"Miss Vicky! It's not bad news that brings you down here?"

"There's no change," I told her. "But I wanted to thank you for everything you're doing for Mama."

"Now then, I wouldn't've done less. You look fair done in, too. Sit down and I'll make up one of my special hot drinks. I used to have them ready for the girls when they came in in the small hours from the balls and outings."

"You mean my mother and Aunt Caroline? I thought Aunt Caroline was very quiet."

"Sometimes she liked to shut herself away to do her painting, but she loved to dance and laugh, too. Your ma wouldn't go anywhere without her."

"Do you remember my father? Did he change things?"

She paused, glass in hand, a fond smile on her lips. "Aye, I do. Full of life, he was, and he loved your mother, there was no mistake. You've his eyes and his spirit. And then . . . Such a tragedy, him disappearing like that. He was a proud man, you see, and he'd want to set your mother up proper, not let those lies follow him. I never took any notice of them, but plenty did. What a loss." She shook her head and handed me the drink. It was delicious, the steam aromatic of cinnamon and cloves.

"You don't believe he abandoned us then?"

"No, even though it was strange him going off in the night like that and never even leaving a letter or note."

"Then no one saw or heard anything?"

"That was the oddest part. And it was the beginning of all the tragedies—your mother leaving, which hurt her father deeply because she took you with her, then William dying, and Caroline's nerves shattering . . ." She shook her head again. "Like someone laid a curse on the Lansdownes." She looked me directly in the eye. "Now it's your mother. You'd best take care of yourself, too."

I shivered, though it was warm by the fire in the snug room. "What about Jasper Thornley? What do you think of him?"

"A lively lad he was." She chuckled. "I remember the day he and Master George had their fight out there in the stable yard."

A Bitter Legacy

I sat up straight. "A fight? I never heard of that."

"You wouldn't. Only us servants witnessed it. George, well, he had a hasty temper on him, and Ned was just a little lad, not much more than seven or eight, but helping out already with the horses. Always loved them, did Ned. I don't know what Jasper was doing here. He'd been forbidden the house, and Master William had died. If only I could remember exactly when it was, but it was a long time ago."

"Tell me what you do remember," I urged. "How old were they?"

"Regular young men they were, and not long after the fight Jasper left for France. This is what happened. Ned picked up a bucket of water that was too heavy for him, and he dropped it. The water splashed all over Master George's new leather boots. Soaked he was, and he gave Ned a clip round the ear. I didn't see it myself, but I heard Ned roar, and we all went running to the back door. Jasper strode past, pulled Ned away, and spoke sharply to Master George, though I didn't hear what he said.

"Next thing, Master George had his jacket off and was squaring up to Jasper. There wasn't much between them then. Jasper was taller, but thin, whereas Master George had more weight on him. Such a fight it was, up and down the yard, in and out of the stables. The old coach driver poured another bucket of water over 'em, but they took no notice, carried on till they were bloody and their clothes all torn.

"Now Ned swore that Master George cheated and threw bran dust in Jasper's eyes, but the boy worshipped Jasper, and no one else saw it. Anyway, Jasper was down, and George picked up his riding crop and hit him once, not to hurt him, but the end caught him on the face."

"The scar!" I breathed. "It's very faint but you can still see it."

She nodded in confirmation. "So I yelled out, 'The Master's coming,' and George ran one way, Ned and Jasper the other. Master wasn't coming, but it was time to put a stop to it. Eh, that was a fight, those of us who remember still talk about it."

"Then Jasper would have no love for the Lansdownes, and he and George have never resolved their differences. Did Jasper say that George cheated?" I asked.

"Never said a word. They always hated each other. Two young men like that both want to be cock o' the walk. Another thing, your grandfather drove a hard bargain when he took over the Thornley business. He was possessive of his new bride, Leonie, and wanted to keep her from her family. That was one of the conditions. When she died so young, he blamed himself, but he was too proud to admit it. After that, the Hall became gloomy at the best of times."

She suddenly roused herself, as if to shake off

A Bitter Legacy

those memories, and began to tidy the kitchen. "There now, we'll pull your mother through. She's a strong constitution. I know, I fed her well when she was a wee tyke! And there's Christmas to look forward to. She'll be up and about for the festivities. They'll be a bit different to what you're used to, though."

I closed my eyes. The vivid vision of clean crisp snows, of Boston's streets and steeples, of the faces of friends around the table, gripped me so hard I could even smell the keen north wind from Canada. I tried to tell Mrs. Randell a little of this, and I think she understood. Then I thanked her again and went to bed, though it took me a long time to fall asleep that night. Somehow I had to make the Hall give up the secrets it harbored. What's more, if my mother and I were to survive, and I was now convinced that someone intended that we should not, I would have to redouble my vigilance.

By the second week in December the snow had melted, only to be replaced by more snow, which in turn was frozen hard by early deep frosts. But at least the season of storms was over, and my window no longer rattled at night as the wind howled around the house. Then at last over the next few days everyone began to return, and Sophie emerged from her room. And as the Hall was cleaned and a magnificent homecoming supper was planned, I began to feel the return of optimism, too. I would have my talk with George and find out the truth. Dr. Cooper would surely have results soon of the observations and tests on my mother and a cure would be in sight. And I would make up my mind about both the future of Lansdowne Hall and myself.

On the day of the homecoming dinner, I left Mrs. Ackroyd with my mother in the early afternoon and went to my room to look at my dresses and to make a selection for the evening. I didn't want Adele to outshine me too much. I was looking forward to learning all the news from the outside world, and perhaps there would even be gossip about Jasper. My high spirits had returned full force, and I felt as if a window had been flung open, letting the sunshine and fresh breezes stream in.

I sang happily as I lifted out first one outfit, then another, remembering the circumstances under which I'd bought them, when and where I'd worn them. I was even reminded of Henry, with whom I'd fancied myself in love, and laughed out loud at the idea. I could hardly remember what we found to talk about, and it was even harder to remember his face. He was welcome to his Kitty. I had had a lucky escape after all.

At last I made my choice, and went to the door to see if Rosie was with Mama. It was then that I found a note pushed under my door. In an

A Bitter Legacy

illiterate, almost childish scrawl, it read: "If you want the Truth about your Father, come to the old Hall at Four—alone."

I looked at my watch. It was ten to four already. How long had the note been there? I had not heard anyone deliver it, but then I had been making a lot of noise. I stood in indecision for a moment. Maybe this was some joke of Sophie's, when all she wanted was to lure me into Leonie's presence again.

I looked more carefully at the handwriting, but could detect no resemblance to anyone's. The more I looked at the grubby, stained piece of paper, with its ill-formed letters, the more I was sure it was genuine. Perhaps it was one of the older servants, afraid to be seen talking to me, or someone from Holmby Village who likewise wanted to keep their visit a secret. Yes, that had to be it. The secrecy was to protect whoever it was from later recriminations. There was now no doubt in my mind. I had to find out what this person knew about my father.

My hands shaking with excitement, I hurried along the corridors, hearing the grandfather clock chime four. I hoped that the mysterious letter-writer would wait for me, that I would be in time.

The medieval hall was even more striking in daylight, albeit the pale, filtered light of a gray December afternoon. The stark white of the walls contrasted with the black beams and the black-painted iron chandelier; the high, arched windows were diamond-paned; the floor boards creaked and squeaked as I walked around. Leonie's sweet gaze followed me.

To my disappointment, it was empty. Could whoever it was have already given up and gone? No, I was only a few minutes late. Maybe the person was still on his or her way. I looked up toward the solar window, but could detect no movement. Then I walked around the hall, my shoes echoing on the wooden floor, and finally checked the small door that led outside. But it was firmly locked, and looked as if it hadn't been opened in years. So the stranger must be coming from the main body of the house, and was late, for I hadn't passed anyone.

I walked slowly back to the center of the room and looked up at Leonie. Her skin seemed to glow like a sun-ripened apricot and, such was the skill of the artist, her wise bright eyes seemed almost to be speaking to me.

"Well, Leonie, here I am. It wouldn't be you who sent for me, would it? No, you would have beautiful handwriting," I spoke softly. Even though I was alone, I felt embarrassed to be talking to a portrait, yet she seemed to be waiting, eager to hear what I had to say. "If only you were alive, I'm sure you would have the answer to my questions. Is my father alive somewhere? Why did Grandfather Albert leave me the Hall but no money? What is it that your

A Bitter Legacy

beloved nephew, Jasper, really wants?"

Foolishly, I waited for her reply, and then, because of course there was none, I began to smile. Then I heard a noise, just the faintest sound. I stared at the portrait. Was this a trick? Was someone trying to ridicule me? Make me think I was hearing voices?

A sudden cracking sound made me jump. I spun on my heel and looked around. Nothing. Then there was a rasping noise and creaking. I stood stock-still, trying to locate the source. At last I looked up—and froze in terror.

That vast iron ring, some two feet across, that had once been a chandelier bearing enough candles to light the medieval banquets of old, was swaying. No, it was falling, straight at me. In the instant that it took for me to draw breath, to try to propel my legs to reach safety, I knew it was too late. I could not escape. I had ignored all the warnings, and now I was going to pay for it.

In the next instant a gust of intensely cold air swept over me, buffeting me, and I fell. The iron chandelier reached its destination. I felt intense pain, then blackness claimed me.

I rose, struggling and coughing, then sank again. I was fighting the water, the blackness, my muscles straining with the effort, but I could not lift my head out of the water. I was choking. Darkness came and went, and still I struggled, gasping in choked breaths of precious air. Then at last I saw light and I could breathe. I opened my eyes, murmuring, "I'm free, I'm free."

Four faces were looking down at me. The lamp on the bedside table cast strange shadows, distorting their features, so that momentarily they looked like the stony faces of gargoyles leering down. I gasped in horror. Then one of them moved, and the trick of the light was broken. I could see it was George, with Adele and Sophie beside him, and Mrs. Ackroyd on the other side of the bed.

"Dear Vicky, thank goodness you're all right," George was saying. "When I think how close to death you came, and you lying there so still and quiet, we were sure you must be—". He broke off, shaking his head.

"Sadly not," Adele said in clipped tones. "Whatever possessed you to go poking around in those old ruins? Sophie is the only one who knows her way around that place."

"The ring," I said. "The iron ring . . . It fell."

"The thunder it made startled me," Adele grudgingly admitted. "But Sophie knew immediately where the noise had come from, didn't you?"

Sophie flushed at this unwelcome attention from Adele. "Yes, I knew where it came from. You've upset the White Lady, Vicky. She made it happen."

"What nonsense, Sophie," George said lightly.

A Bitter Legacy

"Let's not frighten Victoria. I'm so glad to see the color back in your cheeks. When we ran in and saw you all crumpled up, white as a sheet, and with that iron monstrosity lying on top of you, well . . ." He was unable to finish, and I was touched by his concern.

"Such a fuss about nothing," Adele said impatiently. "The thing caught you on the ankle and you fainted. Dr. Cooper has strapped it up and he says it'll soon mend."

"The doctor's left a sleeping draught to kill the pain and help you sleep, miss," Mrs. Ackroyd said with a look that said I didn't deserve all this kindness and attention. "You're to drink it now, mixed with water. The doctor said that although it was a terrible accident—"

"No! It was not an accident. It was the White Lady, I'm sure of it. I felt her presence nearby when we went in. She tried to tell me something," Sophie spoke jerkily, and George and Adele exchanged glances.

"Really, Sophie, that's enough. I'll have none of this talk reaching Tommy's ears. I've warned you before about filling his head full of frightening stories about ghosts. This is my final warning. If it happens again, I will not allow you to see him."

Sophie turned a dull red at the threat, but her jaw set in a stubborn line.

"It couldn't be a ghost, beloved Sophie," George said more gently to soften Adele's words. "The fastenings on the old chandelier were rusted through and it fell. It was bad luck that Victoria was there when it did. It could have happened any time—even to you. I'm going to have it removed entirely."

"But, George, the White Lady knows everything that happens," Sophie spoke excitedly, her cheeks still red, drowning out her normal sallow complexion. "I think she only wanted to frighten Vicky away, not to harm her. You mustn't think she's a bad—"

"Enough," George commanded, and Sophie at last subsided, but with a rebellious expression.

"Once and for all, it was an accident," Adele stated.

Mrs. Ackroyd ignored the talk going on around her and had prepared my medicine, but I wasn't ready yet to drink it.

"Someone sent me a note, asking me to meet them there at four o'clock, but I didn't pass anyone on the way, and the outer door was locked," I said firmly, watching their faces.

My words silenced them, then they all spoke at once. I saw that even Great-uncle Samuel was in the room, keeping his distance over by the window.

"What note? Preposterous," he blustered, catching my eye. "No note, nothing. Made it up, I expect."

A Bitter Legacy

"It was in my hand," I told him. "Surely someone found it."

George looked at Mrs. Ackroyd, who shook her head. "I undressed her, with Rosie's help, for Dr. Cooper. There was no note."

"And none of us noticed one in the old hall, though we will search again," George said. "We must try. Perhaps we may recognize the handwriting."

"Are you sure there was a note?" Adele asked sourly. She thought I was making it up.

"I'm certain. It was no dream. The paper was dirty and the handwriting poor and shaky. It was pushed under my door some time in the afternoon between two and four." My words produced blank looks all around.

"But why go when it could have come from anybody?" Adele asked. "You're so naive, Victoria."

"It promised ... news ... of my father ... Ouch," I said, as my ankle twinged sharply.

"We must let her rest," George said. "I promise we'll search, but if there was a note, it seems that it's vanished."

There was tenderness in his look. I hadn't realized how much I'd longed for tenderness. Warmth flowed through my body and I smiled back, held onto his hand, then closed my eyes, as the throb in my ankle sent up even sharper stabs of pain.

"I expect you're wishing now you'd never set

foot on that boat from America, like the rest of us," I heard Adele say sharply. "A fine Christmas this is going to be, with two invalids in the house. It's unfair to Tommy."

I summoned up my last ounce of strength. "Believe me, even if I'd known beforehand that *you* were waiting for me at this end, I'd still have come. I have no regrets."

I opened my eyes and caught George's amused glance as he told Adele that it was time for them all to leave me. I was in Mrs. Ackroyd's efficient, if not especially kind, care. When I'd taken the sleeping draught, she too went out, and I lay back on the pillows and closed my eyes.

Sophie had claimed the White Lady had been there. How right she'd been to sense her presence. For I believed it was she who had saved me. I didn't care if no one would believe me. I would never tell anyone, anyway, not even Sophie. But I hadn't imagined that blast of coldness that had saved my life, taking me out of the direct line of the chandelier.

Perhaps Sophie's blaming the White Lady for my near-fatal accident was an attempt to shift suspicion from herself. She was the one who prowled about the house, knew it well, regularly visited the medieval hall. She could have loosened the chandelier and faked that note, somehow concealed it afterwards. Adele had said that Sophie knew right away where the noise had come from. Of course, because she had laid

A Bitter Legacy

the trap. Nor could anyone pretend that Sophie saw things as everyone else did. Perhaps she was doing it for her beloved George's sake. Only for him would she risk displeasing the White Lady. Perhaps it had been Sophie all along. . . .

Despite the blankets and quilt piled over me, I shuddered. If only I could talk over my fears with someone, but I doubted George would listen to accusations against his sister, and there was no one else I could turn to. Before I could pursue these thoughts anymore, the bitter drink Mrs. Ackroyd had given me worked. I fell asleep but not before murmuring, "Thank you, Leonie, and thank the White Lady for me," into my pillow.

When I awoke, it was mid-morning the next day. Pale sunlight filled the room, sparkling the snow that edged the windowpanes. Rosie sat in the corner, a pile of mending in the basket at her feet, while beside me, true to his word, sat George. I was pleased to see him. He was wearing his jauntiest clothes, and his necktie was pinned with a gold pin, its head a small, luminous pearl.

"I hope you're not going to make a habit of this, Vicky," he said with mock severity, after ensuring that I was feeling better, and reassuring me that my mother's condition hadn't worsened. "Not that I mind spending time with you to pass your convalescence. It pleases me to be with you."

"I'm glad you can spare the time, when you have such important business to attend to."

"What could be more important than you?"

"I was thinking of the accident at the mine. I was intending to ask you last night how the clearing up had gone and how the injured fared."

"Hardly cheering talk for an invalid," he protested.

"Truly, it will help me recover faster. The fate of those poor men has been on my mind."

"You're too tender, I've told you. They get paid for their work, and they know the dangers involved. In fact, the shaft's already been cleared and production is under way again already. I shan't stand to lose much money."

"What of the dead and injured?"

"By luck not many were killed. They can be easily replaced, and no one else was seriously hurt. They're all back at work, bar one."

I frowned. "I can't help thinking about those men who shouted at us. They seemed so honest. Could they have a real grievance, one you don't know about? Adele's husband was killed near the mine. Possibly they're not as safe as you've been led to believe."

The good humor left George's face, and he asked Rosie to leave the room. She shot me a glance I couldn't read as she went.

When she'd gone, he said gravely, "You shouldn't discuss family business in front of the servants. You know how they gossip and

A Bitter Legacy

that's how lies are spread. But I assure you, Vicky, Uncle Samuel and I know our business. We're not fools."

"I know you do, but it occurred to me that the manager, Brown, might be duping you. Suppose he takes the money for repairs but buys inferior goods and pockets the difference?"

"Impossible. Did you think this up yourself?"

Instinctively, I knew I had to protect Jem—and Jasper. "I've had many long hours by myself to think."

"My clever girl," he said, patting my hand. "But this is a man's work, a man's world. Believe me, no one could get away with cheating George Lansdowne. What can I say to reassure you?" He went on when he saw doubt in my eyes, "Look, either Samuel or I check and place the orders personally. We know our suppliers by their first names. One or the other of us actually visits the places to see that the loads tally and that work is being carried out."

"So Brown . . . He couldn't be doing anything without your knowledge?" I said, my voice low because my heart was heavy. Jasper had been right. George misunderstood.

"I'm sorry, Vicky, I know you're trying to help, but it's not necessary."

"But what happens to the family when a man dies for—for whatever reason? Or is injured?" I persisted.

"Ah, now I understand you. I'm afraid there's

nothing we can do. We're not a charity after all. No work, no pay. But we do help out when we can. Trouble is, sometimes men become embittered and lay the blame on the wrong shoulders when they themselves should be more careful. Oh, you'd be surprised what silly risks they take, especially with dynamite. They try to cut corners in order to get more bonuses. But I can't be there all hours of the day and night nannying them, can I?"

My gloom lifted immediately. "No, I understand, and thank you, George. I think I see now why those men behaved as they did." It was Jasper, I thought, who'd been tricked by the likes of Jem, spinning him a hard luck story. He'd taken me in, too.

"And I understand you. You have a kind and generous heart. A fine thing in a woman . . ."

We talked of other matters, until I began to tire, and he left me to sleep. I felt as if one burden had been lifted from me—the suspicion cast at George—only to be replaced by another. Had Jem deceived Jasper with his twisted version of events, or had Jasper bribed him to spread false stories to turn me against my cousin?

I seemed to sink into a strange lethargy while my ankle slowly healed, despite George's attentions, and I didn't know why. The note that had made me hurry to my near-death was never found. My mother's health did not improve;

A Bitter Legacy

if anything, she seemed slightly worse. There was no news whatever of Jasper, and any questions that I raised about my father or William were always met with shaking heads and "I don't know."

I was making no progress at all, and even less in the matter of my own future and how I would pay to keep the Hall. Yet I could not rouse myself to take any action.

Dully, I moved through the days, and hardly minded that George watched over me constantly, as if I were a child who might hurt herself through her own carelessness. The fact that we were trapped together in the house by the weather, so that Adele and I and Great-uncle Samuel were constantly sniping at one another, did not help, either. And then it was Christmas.

The weather had just entered a milder, sunnier spell which had melted some of the snow, although shaded hollows were still full, and all the roads were passable. I'd asked Rosie to ask the carrier to fetch me gifts to be laid beside the decorated Christmas tree, in the new tradition. Even though it was from duty rather than pleasure, I addressed the labels to Great-uncle Samuel and Adele. I reserved my real joy at giving for George and Tommy.

The day began pleasantly enough, with a visit to church. It was my first outing since my trip to Whitby weeks before, and I drank in the faces, voices, color and life, and entered into the singing wholeheartedly. Then we returned to the Hall and tried to practise "good will to all men," but in a family like ours that was well nigh impossible.

That evening, after the gifts had been opened and a vast meal consumed, carolers came to the door. Following Lansdowne tradition, the lamps were extinguished, and only one candle was left burning in the big bay window with the curtains drawn back.

It was sitting there in the near darkness that the feelings I'd been holding back all day began to flood through me. Whether it was the sweetness of the voices raised in holy song that caught at my throat, or whether I was reacting to the effort of smiling and being polite all day, I don't know. But my heart at that moment was where it truly belonged, upstairs with my mother, who didn't know that today was Christmas, who perhaps might never see another.

In the darkness I let the tears flow, tears for my mother, whose future was so uncertain, and for myself and the end of my dream. Because I knew that, although I'd spent my first Christmas at Lansdowne Hall, and that my dream had come true, it was meaningless without her. All those winters we'd struggled through together, none had been so bitter as this. I vowed there and then that if my mother recovered, I'd give up the Hall, sell it, renounce it, if that was what she wanted.

It was a vow that cost me dear. I still passionately wanted my inheritance, and it was like a sickness twisting inside me. Yet I'd give it up, if my mother asked, if only she'd recover.

Chapter Seven

"I wish you could tell me what you think. I know I haven't always followed your advice in the past, but this time I really don't know what to do."

I looked down at my mother's beloved face, her pale skin waxy in the candlelight. She'd lost weight in the last couple of days since Christmas, despite careful feeding. Her cheekbones protruded sharply, and her hair was thin and lank against the crisp white cotton of the pillow. Yet I still pretended that she could hear me, in some far-off place.

"It's not that sudden, now that I think about it," I mused out loud. "We have spent a great deal of time together, and he always speaks so highly of me and takes such tender care of me. When he touches me, it's not . . . unpleasant. But is what I feel true love?"

I picked up her hand. "You could tell me what true love is. You followed your husband to America because you loved and believed in him. You defied Grandfather and left your family, you thought then, forever. Would I be that brave and abandon you for George? But you'd never treat me the way your father treated you, and that's why I can't consider getting engaged, or married eventually, until you're better."

Earlier that evening after dinner, George had not accompanied Great-uncle Samuel to the library to smoke cigars and to drink brandy and port. Instead, he had asked me to walk outside with him. When he'd helped me on with my cloak, his hands had lingered on my shoulders, and he'd put my arm through his as we strolled outside.

The night was clear, with a light sparkling frost, and our footsteps rang on the frosted paving stones, and our breaths plumed in front of us. The black sky was encrusted with brightly twinkling stars from horizon to horizon, undiluted by a moon or city lamplight.

"It's a beautiful night, isn't it, Vicky?" George asked, but I knew he was looking at me, not the scenery. "Sometimes, in the summer, we see the Northern Lights, the aurora borealis. I would like to show you those. I would like to know that the two of us can walk together whenever we like, through the years."

I felt my cheeks go hot and I avoided meeting his eyes. "I hope we'll always be friends, George."

"You know I mean something more than friends. Vicky, look at me, please. I've been a bachelor for a long time, taken my pleasures here and there, but now that I've met you no other woman can compare to you." Gradually, he was drawing me closer. I held my breath. "Dearest cousin, we can be granted a dispensation in a moment. I'm asking you to marry me."

"George, I—I don't know what I think."

"Perhaps I can help you make up your mind," he said softly.

With practiced ease, he slid his arms around me and touched his lips to my face in kisses as light as the touch of a moth's wing. Then his arms tightened as he placed his mouth over mine, and I was held close to his body. I felt warm and alive, and tentatively began to respond, putting my hands on his waist. This was what a real kiss should be, I told myself. Henry under the mistletoe had been a boy, his lips soft and damp. George's lips were firm and dry.

Then, reluctantly, he released me, murmuring, "Ah, I shouldn't go too fast, but you tempt me."

"George, I do like you, very, very much," I

said breathlessly. "It's just that, with my mother so ill, I can't make any promises about the future. I—"

"Sssh." He laid a finger on my mouth and traced the outline of my lips so that my skin tingled. "I understand. All I want you to do for now is accept me as your protector, the one you rely on, and to tell me that I can woo you. Tell me, may I hope for that?"

I nodded and said in a low voice, "Yes, of course. Your suit is not rejected. Far from it . . ."

Now I told my mother, "I think George would make a good husband, don't you? He always tries to please me, and he works so hard. He spends hours, sometimes days, away from the house. It does make me feel—I don't know how to describe it—very good to know he cares for me. The trouble is marrying George would solve all our problems. Then I would have all the money in the world to run the Hall. Our future would be assured. How can I agree to marry him unless I am sure it's because of him alone?"

I felt that I was an adult at last, thinking with a more mature mind, examining the consequences before I rushed headlong into a situation I could not back out of.

"Mama, did you hear me?"

She'd stirred, as she often did when I talked to her, and her lips moved. It sounded, again as it often did, as if she was calling her husband, my father, Spenser. Yet again, it could just have been a deep sigh. I bent my head, depressed by the death of sudden hope.

After a while, I continued, "However, it's not my first proposal, if you can call Jasper's ridiculous suggestion a proposal. It's funny how an inheritance can suddenly make my hand in marriage an attractive proposition. Or am I being cynical? George talks as if come spring a whole horde of suitors will be beating a path to my door. If he's right, perhaps I should wait and see. At least George knows how to make me laugh, whereas Jasper only brings me grief.

"Everything George has told me about his business—and now he's being very open—is totally convincing. So Jasper has either been duped or is duping me."

I sighed. I was back to that circular argument again.

"Perhaps Jasper will be at Sir Gransby's dance on New Year's night? I shall be going, Mama, as George insists. It's the Lansdownes' first official social engagement since Grandfather died. Sophie refuses to come, naturally, and says she will care for you, and I know you would want me to go. My ankle is almost completely better, and I am looking forward to the dancing, though I wish you could be there, too. I don't know how the guests will treat me, whether they'll whisper behind my back or insult me to my face. I don't care. I shall enjoy myself. Oh, why aren't you well!"

A Bitter Legacy

I shook her hand in frustration, trying to rouse her. But she lay as still as a corpse, breathing shallowly, her pulse weak and slow beneath my fingers.

"Yes, I'll miss you tomorrow, Mama, but at least I'll be away from this place. I never thought I'd say that, but the Hall's beginning to feel like a prison. Sometimes I can hardly breathe, and the atmosphere oppresses me.

"When I look out of the window, the countryside is bleak, bare, and barren. You never told me it would be like this, but I am trying to love it, just as much as you did. Because it's going to be our home, just like I promised. I know when you recover you'll want to stay here as much as I do, though I haven't forgotten the promise I made to you on Christmas Day. So, only you can persuade me to leave. I vow I will not be driven away, by lies, cruel words, or fear!"

The New Year's ball at Sir Gransby's mansion, the only one larger than ours in the district, was an annual event, I had been told. George had persuaded me that I should go, explaining that it was my social duty, as heiress to Albert Lansdowne. Besides, he wanted to show me off, he said as his final argument, his hand lingering caressingly on mine.

Adele had watched this little exchange with a bitter expression. Her open hostility these days embraced George as well as me, but he had shrugged it aside.

But another example of her anger came one night a few days before the ball.

"How will you be getting to the Ball?" George asked Adele. "There will only be room for Vicky, Rosie, and myself in our carriage, along with our finery."

"Don't trouble yourself about me!" she snapped, smoothing on her gloves, ready to leave the house, "Redvers has already offered to escort me."

"Redvers still, is it? Isn't he keeping you dangling too long? At least he didn't drop you when he heard the disappointing news about the will."

Adele surprised me by rejoining calmly and without her usual rage, before she left, "Redvers is a good man, and when he chooses to ask me to marry him, I shall say yes."

"I thought as much," George said when she'd gone. "I wondered when she would admit it. Well, Vicky, there's one of us off your hands." He grinned teasingly.

I was looking forward to meeting Mr. Redvers. I wanted to be reassured that Tommy's possible new father would be kind to him.

That had been one of those rare occasions when all three of us were in the same room together. Adele was definitely avoiding me when she could. I had no idea if her legal consultations about me had brought her any satisfaction, though her sour expression told me they hadn't.

Rosie was as excited as I was about the dance. She would accompany me as my maid, and had spent hours working on my best gown to bring it up to scratch. It was my most recent Boston purchase, and she was sure I would outshine everyone else there.

"You look beautiful, miss," she said the evening of the dance, applying the hot tongs again to my hair. Rosie had decided that my hair would be pulled smoothly away from my face and then cascade in ringlets and curls over my shoulders, decorated at the side of my head with a taffeta flower set on a comb. "Just lately you've looked . . . Well, it's not surprising that you're not blooming like when you first arrived at the Hall."

"I suppose a murderous ghost, a dousing in the river, a chandelier falling on me, and my mother's illness have all played their part in that," I said drily. "Not to mention that my financial future is still uncertain."

She nodded. "I said to Ned t'other day, my Miss Victoria needs good news, and he agreed with me that maybe the new year will mean a fresh start." She caught my eye. "Perhaps you'll meet your future husband tonight. There'll be a fine gathering of the best folk from hereabouts."

It was on the tip of my tongue to take Rosie

into my confidence and tell her of George's proposal of marriage, but I could not, even though I longed to tell someone. I had promised myself that I must wait till my mother recovered, and she should be the first to hear, and so it must be.

"Aye, and then perhaps we could have a wedding this year. A wedding would brighten this old place up," Rosie continued with her train of thought, setting the final touches to my toilette. "As I said to our Ned, Miss Victoria would make a lovely bride, and I could dress her hair. Yes, I'd like a wedding soon."

Now it was my turn to catch her eye and raise my brows. She flushed and became quiet, then began to pack away all the implements that were necessary to tidy me again after our journey.

Then, when I thought she was about to leave, she suddenly approached me and bent down to whisper in my ear, "You needn't be afraid, Miss Victoria, after all the accidents that have happened to you. Someone is watching over you, only I can't say more than that."

She hurried out of the room before I could ask her what she meant. I knew she had meant to cheer me, but instead she had made me uneasy. Someone watching me? Hadn't I felt in the few months I'd been at Lansdowne Hall, that unseen eyes were watching my every move, that they would pry into my thoughts if they could, for some evil intent of their own?

A Bitter Legacy

Now I wondered how far I could trust Rosie. She might think that she was acting in my best interests, innocently believing whoever— had what? I stood up and began pacing the room. Was Rosie open to bribery? I doubted it, but she would be open to promises that I would be protected. Or perhaps she had just observed George's tender regard for me. "Someone is watching over you . . ." That was the way Sophie referred to Leonie and the White Lady. But Rosie didn't believe in ghosts. Far from setting my mind at rest, she'd set it actively whirling again.

Sir Gransby's graceful Palladian mansion was some eight miles away, and for a mile of that we were following the boundary of Lansdowne property. I'd seen Sir Gransby's house in the distance when out riding with George. How long ago that seemed now. The gardens were elegantly landscaped, and there were terraces and a formal parterre, as well as a small lake. It was without doubt the most beautiful house and grounds in the district, and I could well understand how my grandfather had coveted it and hoped to marry one of his daughters into the Gransby family. I was curious to meet the man my mother had rejected, even though she had not told him directly.

The carriage lamps cast a welcome light along our route. Rosie and I had George for company, with Ned driving us, while Adele rode ahead with Elise and her escort, Mr. Redvers, in his coach.

Redvers had not been at all as I expected. He was in his forties, his hair thin and gray, his moustache a darker color. He was of medium height and build with a quiet, almost stolid manner. They were an ill-assorted pair, and I wasn't surprised that Adele treated him in the same haughty manner she treated me. But he did not even flinch, let alone answer back.

I thought she was obviously after his money, while he was after her youth and beauty. So perhaps they would suit each other very well. But what of Tommy? He'd been allowed to wait up to watch us leave in all our finery, and Mr. Redvers had barely spoken to the boy, merely patting him on the head in passing. Yet Tommy had seemed quite at ease with him and not in the least frightened of him.

Sir Gransby's main assembly room was a blaze of light and a mass of bright colors, like a summer garden in the depths of winter. The beautiful dresses and the cheerful chatter of the guests lifted my spirits, and I felt a little more like my old self, able to forget my cares, fears, and fancies. At George's side I renewed those few acquaintanceships I'd already formed and met a bewildering number of new people, who'd only been names to me till then. I was presented to Sir Gransby and his wife early on. While they were charmingly polite and inquired about my mother, I found that the question they and everyone else were most keenly interested in was what my intentions were concerning my inheritance.

When I told them that I was going to take up residence, I received many astonished looks, and braced myself, shoulders squared, for battle. To my wonderment, no one tried to persuade me otherwise, and I received offers of support, though no outright help. It wasn't until George left me for a few moments and I stood alone, watching Adele in the midst of an admiring crowd, keeping well away from me, that I realized his presence had protected me. I detected that the veiled looks in my direction held pity and curiosity. In return, I held my head all the more proudly, determined to show that, whatever they may have held against Albert Smith, later Lansdowne, self-made man, it meant nothing to me. But not one remark was made against my mother or father, and for that I was glad.

After supper the dancing began, and George claimed the first one. "I've looked forward to this moment," he said. "You dance even better than I'd hoped, and you look so pretty. All the other girls pale by comparison. Did you like the corsage I sent you?"

"It's lovely." I looked down at the scented flowers attached to my dress. "Thank you, and thank you for persuading me to come."

"I hope always to be able to make you happy, Vicky dearest."

I blushed. "Just go on being my friend then, please."

He held me a little closer. "You know I want more than that. I had hoped that tonight I could make an announcement. Ah, I can see that you're shaking your head. How disappointing. Very well. But don't keep me waiting too long. I want to know you're mine, and I want the world to know it, too." His hand tightened on my waist and I felt an answering tingle. I wondered if later he might kiss me again, and whether that might weaken my resolve.

Even as I smiled happily at George, and allowed him to hold me close, I sensed that something had changed, something was different. Quickly, I glanced around the room, but saw nothing. Yet I was sure I had not imagined it. George took the liberty of my turned head to brush his fingers against the bare skin of my neck.

We danced together several more times, but there were other partners for us, too, though I soon discovered that George was by far the best dancer. The other men were pleasant to talk to, however, including Adele's suitor. Mr. Redvers walked me solidly through a waltz, while Adele was relegated to watching us with barely suppressed fury, and she snatched him away again

A Bitter Legacy

before the music had barely ended.

I was left stranded for a moment in the crush, and it was then that a new hand descended, feather light yet insistent, on my arm. It was Jasper. As I looked into his eyes, my heart began to race. Was I afraid of him, I asked myself, so afraid that my body reacted beyond my control?

"Will you dance with me?" he asked, and took hold of me before I could answer.

Irritated and feeling insecure, I said sharply, "I didn't know you were here."

He regarded me steadily. "You only had eyes for George Lansdowne. Perhaps that's the reason you did not see me."

Now I knew what I had sensed: Jasper's entry into the room. He had been watching George and me dance together. A wave of unreasoning anger took hold of me that I should be so sensitive to his presence. Why, the last time I had seen him he had told me to marry him, then kissed me, and had ridden away, without bothering to contact me again. How dare he try to interfere with my life and plans?

"And why shouldn't I? George has only my best interests at heart, which is more than can be said for you. You spread lies and confusion."

"No, not lies. I told you there were two sides. At some point you are going to have to decide which side you are on—the right side or the wrong side?"

"How can I decide when you refuse to tell me anything? You—you keep your thoughts completely hidden from me."

He was holding me firmly, as if expecting me to attempt to escape, moving with easy masculine grace, and our bodies fitted perfectly together. His dove-gray suit was, as always, of immaculate cut. His hair curled over the collar, and his clean-shaven chin made him look distinctly different in this setting of heavily bewhiskered gentlemen. I looked for that faintest of scars and found it.

He was silent for a moment, then said gravely, "I have to be sure I can depend on you. Perhaps I shall have to take that risk, and soon. Yet I cannot forget you are a Lansdowne."

"My name is Victoria Hunter, and I'm proud of it," I said, seething.

He gave a slight nod, then bewilderingly changed the subject. "I see your ankle has completely healed."

"Yes, almost. How did you know about that?" I asked.

"Ned promised to keep an eye on you for me. He has to fetch supplies, doesn't he? That's when we meet."

He'd cut the ground out from under my feet. Rosie's words earlier, the whispered conversations with Ned. Was there no one I could rely on? "I do not like being spied on," I retorted wildly.

A Bitter Legacy

He grimaced. "Not spying, I assure you. However, I do believe that your life might be in danger. Ned told me everything that happened that day. He also told me he's sure no strangers were seen around the Hall. Therefore—"

"It was an accident. There has been a series of unfortunate mishaps, nothing more." I didn't want to believe him. I did not want to confront my own fears. "What's more, you were entirely wrong about George. Jem has been using you for his own ends." I told him what George had said.

Jasper didn't immediately answer, but scanned the room with his keen, quick gaze from under his dark brows. "It was too convenient," he said at last. "That chandelier has been hanging there hundreds of years, yet it chose to fall on you. And what about the disappearing note?"

"Why do you take such relish in frightening me?" I asked, wishing the dance would end, so that I would not have to listen to him, but I was trapped.

"If that's the only way to make you see sense, then let me frighten you some more. Your mother's illness, how real is that? Has she shown any sign of recovery?"

I gasped. "What are you suggesting?"

"Victoria! Come away from this—this vermin." George pushed his arm between Jasper and myself, forcing us apart. Heads immediately began to turn in our direction. "Who let you in?" he said fiercely to Jasper, who matched his glare of cold hostility.

"I could hardly refuse to dance with him," I rejoined quickly. "It would give rise to gossip."

"I forbid it," George said, taking my arm.

"You don't have the right to tell her what to do," Jasper said challengingly.

"Indeed I do," George said loudly, so that the people around us could hear. "Tonight I intend asking Victoria to be my wife, and she's already indicated she won't turn me down."

"If this is true, then it seems you have made your choice already and the wrong one," Jasper said to me, his black brows drawn together, his eyes not cold, but disappointed. That I could not bear.

Desperately, I looked from one to the other. Had I already chosen? I had just now been denying everything Jasper had told me, and yet. . . .

"George, perhaps you should listen to what Jasper has to say," I pleaded, keeping myself positioned between the two men. I had no doubt that at any moment they would once more try to settle their differences physically.

"Victoria"—George's voice was icy—"after my repeated warnings, you still insist on listening to a man who is a cheat, a rogue, and a liar. But when you are my wife I shall make sure you pay attention to my words."

A Bitter Legacy

Jasper stiffened. I saw his hands clench into fists. I clung to his arm, saying I don't know what, and then suddenly there was silence. The music had stopped, and Sir Gransby was calling for everyone's attention. In the hubbub George gripped my hand tightly in the crook of his arm and edged me away from Jasper. I cast one last look at him, and caught such a bleak expression on his face that my heart nearly broke. I had let him down, I had made the wrong choice. But what other choice, in the circumstances, could I make?

"There's a storm blowing up from the sea, and snow on its way. I advise all of you who can to leave now," Sir Gransby informed us. "Those of you who wish to may, of course, remain here tonight."

"Blizzard," I heard George mutter under his breath.

"George, should we stay? I'll find Rosie and—"

"No," he said, not looking at me. "We can easily outrun the storm. You prepare yourself, while I fetch the carriage."

I held him back. "What about Adele?"

"Redvers will take care of her," he said impatiently. "Hurry now. I'll meet you in the front of the house."

In the confusion it took me a moment to find Rosie. When I did, she shook her head at my instructions to get ready. "But, Miss Victoria, they say it'll be a real blizzard. You don't know these parts, I do. We should stay here."

"Master George says we'll outrun the storm." Then, remembering that she was Jasper's spy, I said shortly, "You can stay here. I'm going."

She set her mouth in a thin line at that and quickly collected our things and helped me on with my cloak.

When we hurried outside, the wind was already howling and shrieking with the force of a tornado, and stinging sleet was cutting through the air. There was a melee of horses and carriages, but I heard George call to us from the edge of the crowd.

"We're ready," I told him. "Where's Ned?"

"In a drunken stupor," he said disgustedly. "I saw him sleeping it off in the stable. But I can handle these horses better than he can. Get in."

I saw Rosie open her mouth to protest on Ned's behalf, but she thought better of it. I relented and asked her if she wanted to stay with Ned, but she shook her head. "I'll not leave you," she said.

George fussed over us, insisting that I sit on the more comfortable side of the coach, and wrapped us in blankets, saying he would be kept warm by the effort of driving. Then he swiftly maneuvered his way free of the other carriages and down the driveway.

When we turned onto the open road, away from the protection of Sir Gransby's parkland,

A Bitter Legacy

the full force of the storm hit us, and the carriage began to sway alarmingly. Each fresh buffet from the squalling wind seemed to be the one that would topple us on our side.

Rosie and I clung to each other, unable to talk for the roar and noise of the elements. In my mind lay the fear that at any moment the sleet could turn to snow. If that happened, we might lose the road or fall into a drift. Then, without help, lost on the moors, we would freeze to death.

Suddenly the carriage lurched almost on its side. We both screamed, and clung to whatever we could. We were going even faster now. George had whipped up the horses in his desperate attempt to beat the arrival of the snow. Then another fear hit me. Had the horses bolted? We were being flung violently from one side to the other, without respite, and I was sure my shoulder was badly bruised from being tossed repeatedly against the door. Then, my stomach lurched, and I was floating through thin air, falling, falling through cold wetness. The door had given way under my weight.

I landed with such a thump that all the breath was knocked from my body. I gasped, fighting dizziness and nausea. When I dared open my eyes, all was blackness streaked with gray. The blizzard was on us. But I looked in vain for the light of our carriage. Surely George had heard my scream? Unless, of course, I was right and the horses had bolted, in in which case he would be unable to get them under control for some time.

I struggled to my feet and began to follow in the wheel tracks, glad that at least Rosie had escaped harm and had not fallen out as well. If only I hadn't quarrelled with her, tonight of all nights, I might have heeded her advice and stayed at Sir Gransby's. As it was, the three of us had been in acute danger. If only George had not decided to try and get us home. Now, I had to reach our coach.

However, by the time I'd walked only a short distance, the snow was already filling in the tracks, and I had to search hard to find my way, occasionally stumbling over frozen mud buried in the show. On either side, too, was the unrelenting moor without the benefit of sheltering hedges. I was completely at the mercy of the elements.

I don't know how long I'd been struggling, desperate to try and catch up with the carriage, perhaps five minutes, perhaps ten, when I thought I heard a horse snort behind me. I whirled, receiving a stinging slap in the face from the wind, and shielded my eyes until I could see a dark outline. For a moment all kinds of fantasies chased through my mind, stories of phantoms and devil riders. I was greatly relieved to hear a man's voice call out, "Who's there? Wait and I'll be with you."

A Bitter Legacy

My heart sang with gratitude for my deliverance. He reined in his horse, leaned down toward me—and I came face-to-face with Jasper.

"What the devil are you doing out here, Victoria?" he said, grasping me by the arm to help me up. My foot found the stirrup and then I positioned myself in front of him, taking hold of the horse's mane to steady myself.

"What happened?" he asked, and I told him, shouting to be heard above the raging storm. I watched the expression on his face settle into that grim, determined look I'd seen too many times before. "Strange, the door springing open like that. Did you fasten it securely?"

"George made doubly sure," I told him and, as his lips tightened, I knew the direction of his thoughts and my heart sank. "Oh, no, you're wrong. George was careful!"

"George again. It always comes back to George," he said thoughtfully. "Unless someone else is . . ." Maddeningly, he didn't conclude his thought, but asked instead where Ned was, and I told him that, too.

"I don't believe it," he said flatly. "Do you?"

And I had to agree. It sounded most unlike Ned to neglect his horses. Humans he might, but not his animals for the sake of a few beers. Again I could see the direction of his thoughts. Someone had deliberately incapacitated Ned so that a less experienced driver, in this case George, would be forced to take the reins, leading to disaster. Except that George had been able to keep the carriage upright.

It would have to be someone at Sir Gransby's, someone who would know our plan to return home. I cast a glance at Jasper's set jaw. It would have been easy for him to arrange the whole incident.

"I hope Rosie and George reach home safely," I said. "We must keep a look out for them just in case, though. But if they do reach the Hall, George is sure to send out a search party right away."

Jasper nodded, but, before he could reply, the storm increased its intensity, hurling the freezing snow into every crevice of our clothes, and making my eyes water so that I could see nothing. At any moment I expected the horse to refuse to go forward, or Jasper to tell me that we were completely lost.

We plodded on, hoping against hope that the blizzard would soon abate, putting every physical effort into combating the cold and the wind. And, although I kept a careful watch, I saw no sign of a coach, either returning or overturned.

When I thought I could bear no more of this white, shrieking hell, Jasper put his lips close to my ear, and said, "I'm sorry, Vicky, but I think we've missed the road somewhere."

A Bitter Legacy

I gripped the mane that much tighter with my ice-encased gloves.

"What should we do? Go back?" I was yelling to make myself heard.

"No, we'd never make it. We'd better take shelter. I'm sure I know where we are now. That's how I knew we'd lost the road. There's a shepherd's hut near here."

How could he see anything in this howling nightmare? And as I asked myself that question, another followed. How had he happened to come along the road at just the right moment so that he found me? It couldn't be luck. And hadn't I seen him leave the ballroom immediately after Sir Gransby made his speech? So shouldn't he have been ahead of us, not behind? Unless, of course, he'd been delayed by incapacitating Ned....

At the moment, bundled up in his arms, there was nothing I could do, except fear that, rather than being rescued, I was trapped. I already knew that Jasper hated my family, perhaps with good reason, and wanted the Hall for himself. I had already half suspected that he might have had something to do with my falling into the river when again he just "chanced along" and saved me. And it was Jasper who was constantly trying to blacken George's character. Everything fitted more neatly into place than ever.

Perhaps he *had* left William alone to die....

By "near" I had thought Jasper meant a few yards away. Instead, without perceptibly changing our direction, the horse walked wearily on, sometimes lurching when he stepped on unseen dangers beneath the snow, sometimes sliding on hidden ice.

Time soon ceased to have meaning and, whatever his designs on me, I hunched against Jasper, feeling the creeping lethargy of the numbing cold, exhausted and deafened by the storm. Now and then Jasper would rouse himself and order me to move, and each time it became harder to do so. My heart went out to the brave animal who carried us, because his strength must surely be almost used up.

Then, when I thought I really could not endure another second, we stopped, and there was the hut, small, square, and built roughly of stone, with a slate roof. My heart sank. We would surely die in there.

But there was enough room for Jasper, me, and the horse, and a fire was laid ready in the open hearth, along with lighting materials. Jasper soon had both it and the oil lamp lit, while I scooped up snow into the billy can to heat for hot water. There were some dry biscuits and a twist of tea on a shelf. I made the tea while Jasper rubbed down the horse, and left it munching hay on the far side of the one room.

We settled down on small stools in front

of the fire. I no longer cared about my fine ball gown, completely muddied and torn. Unceremoniously, I unlaced my boots, glad that I'd had time to change out of my slippers, and stretched my toes out to dry. They stung and tingled into life as my blood began to flow. I felt drowsy and comfortable and surprisingly warm, my fears temporarily removed by these ordinary activities. I smiled.

"What is it?" Jasper asked.

"I was just thinking if Boston society could see me now . . ." And then we were both laughing, a welcome release of tension. "What is this place?"

"Shepherds use these huts which are scattered all over, and they always leave them ready for use." He looked across at me, and asked abruptly, "Do you really intend to marry George?"

"He proposed to me a few days ago. I said I had to wait till Mama was better before I could give him an answer," I replied evasively.

"You must not marry him." Jasper's face was clearly delineated by the firelight, so familiar now.

"I suppose you hate to think that your last chance of getting your hands on the Hall would be gone if I married George. You think you can persuade Miss Hunter, but never Mrs. Lansdowne."

He shook his head. "I've several reasons for advising you against accepting him, one of them being that I've already told you what he is—irresponsible, cruel, and heavily in debt, too, by all accounts. He'd have to sell the mines to buy the Hall. By marrying you, he gets it without losing his income."

"You make him sound so cold and calculating. But is that because it's you who has that kind of mind, not George?" I pointed out. "Perhaps he does not indulge in secret meetings, in spying, in following people."

Jasper did not flinch, but he did not like what I said, and he retaliated with, "Is that why you've never accused *him* of marrying you for your inheritance?"

"No, it's because he has nothing to gain by it. It'd be a drain on his finances. Oh, he'd keep it in the family but . . . Anyway, he's been nothing but generous and helpful to me. My only ally."

Jasper scowled. "What can I do to persuade you? You make me take extreme measures, and I've already warned you your life may be in danger."

"Yes, and half an hour later it is. What am I to make of that? What were you doing on that road? That's not the way to your lodgings. A self-fulfilling prophecy, all planned by you!" My earlier fear returned, and my hands trembled, and when Jasper got up, I instinctively flinched.

He put more wood on the fire and poked it

until it was blazing brightly. When he sat down again, stretching his long legs in front of him, he was calm again.

"Yes, I was following you," he admitted. "However, I did not arrange for you to fall out of the carriage. Someone else did that. I'm sure you'll agree now that it was no accident. Either George or it could be someone else. I will accept that as yet we have no hard evidence with which to accuse George Lansdowne. When Ned recovers, he might have the information we need."

"We?"

His face hardened. "Yes, 'we.' You and I, your mother, and all the people who want to see justice done and rewards given where rewards are due."

"You warned me from the moment we met, as if you knew what would happen. Why now? How did you know?"

"The things that have happened to you, the attempts on your life, are just the final touches in a far-reaching design. I couldn't return before. Albert Lansdowne made sure of that. As soon as I heard he was dead, I laid my own plans."

"All for a house?" I said.

"More than a house, a home, a dream, the family name. Isn't that the way you see it, too?" His voice was soft, hypnotic, drawing from me my deepest thoughts and fears. "Vicky, it's not just the Hall at stake, but a way to keep the past from speaking. I wish I could tell you more, but

I don't know the answers yet myself nor did Caroline."

"How did you know the way I felt?" I asked, strangely moved. "Yes, I have thought these things, alone in the dead of night. But in the cold light of day I refuse to accept them. And yet, there is always that strange feeling lurking inside the Hall. Sometimes I dread going back there when I've been away from it, and all the time it's as if the place is waiting, waiting . . ."

When I raised my eyes to his, I found that he was looking at me intently. Something in his eyes demanded to be met, and it spoke to the depths of my being.

"No," I said weakly, as he reached for me.

"I asked you to marry me once . . ." he began, and those words thankfully released me from the spell he was weaving.

"Yes, the moment you thought possessing the Hall was impossible was the moment you wanted me!"

He looked surprised. "Nevertheless, I thought you understood—"

"I understand nothing about you."

In one swift movement he was kneeling in front of me, his brows drawn darkly together. "Then I'll have to explain. You're mine, Vicky, we both know it. That's why you can't marry George, or anyone else." He grasped my shoulders, more roughly than tenderly, while my heart hammered in my chest.

A Bitter Legacy

"What do you want of me?" I cried. "Leave me alone. There's no room for you in my life, in my future."

Shadows leaped madly on the walls, the room spun, as his arms encircled me, holding me close to him, and when his mouth came down on mine, I could hardly breathe. I knew it was inevitable that he would kiss me. What I hadn't bargained for was my own reaction, as his lips sent fire coursing through my body. Then he released me.

"You know you're mine," he muttered, his eyes glittering. "Whether either of us want it, that's how it is. However much we might want to fight it, we cannot."

I closed my eyes, dizzy from fatigue and emotion, not knowing what was going to happen next, wanting his arms around me, his kisses, knowing that I should not. But he did not touch me again, and when I opened my eyes, I saw Jasper was rolling up his jacket.

"We're both overtired," he said, his voice still husky. He avoided looking at me. "You sleep here in front of the fire and use this jacket as a pillow, and your cloak as a blanket. I've got my own. I'll keep watch for the storm to stop. You can sleep now. I won't harm you."

Warily, I lay down, sure that I would not even be able to close my eyes. But the passionate outburst had drained my final reserves of strength, and I fell asleep in an instant.

At some point in the night, I awoke. There was an uncanny silence, and I thought at first I was dreaming. Then I realized that the storm had abated at last, and thought that that was why I'd awakened. As I gradually came to, I heard the faint sound of breathing. Raising my head slightly, painfully because of my stiff neck, I saw Jasper's large frame sprawled against the flanks of his horse, which was now lying down, its muzzle resting on the ground, its lower lip drooping. Jasper was sleeping soundly, the horse dozing. It lifted an eyelid in acknowledgement of my movement.

It was then that I knew something else had awakened me. There was a sharp pain in my cheekbone, and quietly, I began to rearrange Jasper's jacket, thinking that one of the metal buttons had been cutting into my face. But in the soft red glow of the embers from the fire, I saw that it wasn't a button laying on top of the jacket. It was a piece of silver jewelry that had worked its way loose from an inner pocket.

I picked it up, admiring the fine chain and the delicate chasing work on the case itself, worn smooth. I turned it over in my hands. This was a treasured keepsake. Something Jasper kept close to him at all times, wherever he went.

I turned it over again, then could no longer control my curiosity. It most likely contained photographs of his mother and father, or perhaps his Aunt Leonie. But I had to know. My

A Bitter Legacy

fingers trembled as I fumbled with the catch, then it sprang open easily, as it must have done a thousand times or more for Jasper. I had to know, though, if some other woman's likeness was in there. Some other woman who had captured his heart.

I found myself staring at—myself. It was a newspaper photograph, taken a year ago in Boston, which had appeared in the social pages. I'd been one of a group of young women, but Jasper had cut out only my face. Now I knew how he'd recognized me in the graveyard at Seadale, even though I looked much older than that academy graduate.

I lay still for a while, holding the locket in my hand, puzzling over the man who lay just a few feet away. True to his word, he hadn't harmed me, but what now? All I could think of was the fire he'd lit in my body when he seized me and told me I was his. Being at last honest with myself, I knew that that fire had been there all along, and he'd just brought it blazing to life.

I dozed for a while, and the next thing I knew Jasper's hand was on my shoulder, shaking me awake, and I could see faint chinks of light. In the confusion of straightening my clothes and stretching my protesting muscles, I slipped the locket back into his jacket pocket.

"When you're ready," Jasper instructed quietly, "there'll be some hot tea. Then I'll dampen the fire and take you home. It's dawn now, and shouldn't take more than an hour."

While Jasper attended to food and water for the horse, I tried to comb my thick, chestnut hair, then gave up and braided it in a thick plait over my shoulder. I intended to wash my face quickly in the snow, and stepped outside.

I was confronted by breathtaking beauty. Snow, a foot deep or more, unbroken except by the scarring of tiny birds' feet, stretched pure and sparkling to the horizon. The air was quite still, and the sky was a hazy yellow, with the sun just beginning to show below a dark cloudy streak. Each twig of a nearby bush carried its individual load of snow and, as I lifted a handful of clean snow to my face, a robin landed on a nearby wall and broke into a heart-rending song.

A hand rested on my shoulder. "Ready?" Jasper asked quietly.

I nodded. It was like a new beginning, a rebirth. Now it was time to return to the Hall, and start everything afresh, this time with my eyes wide open.

Chapter Eight

During our journey back to Lansdowne Hall Jasper was punctiliously polite. He did not ride with me, but walked in front, not even leading his horse by the rein. He expected us to follow him and we did. In my ruined ball gown I felt the cold, but the sun, when it rose fully, brought a little warmth. I managed to arrange myself so that both modesty and comfort were served.

Although the countryside looked like a featureless expanse of white, Jasper seemed to know exactly where he was going and, after some time, I saw a cottage beside a stand of trees, smoke coming from its chimney, then some more dwellings, and at last the whole of Holmby Village in the dale to our right. Five minutes or so later and I saw the gateposts of the

Hall, and then the familiar outline of the roof. Emotion balled up in my chest like a lead fist and I halted the horse. After a few steps, Jasper realized what I had done and turned back.

"What is it?" he asked, his eyes still warily distant.

"I have to go down there, and people will be asking questions. George . . . What am I going to tell them? That I spent the night alone in a hut with you? George will never forgive you. As for me—"

"I don't intend to come with you. It will be easier for you if you say you found shelter somewhere and that an early traveler helped you the last part of the way. That's close enough to the truth, and coming back along the ridge means no one could have recognised me."

"But I want you to come with me," I heard myself saying to my astonishment. When he didn't answer immediately, I went on, "I want you to see my mother. She—"

"Of course," he said swiftly. "I'd like nothing better. It had occurred to me . . . Vicky, how much do you, does anyone, know about her mystery illness?"

"Nothing. Dr. Cooper has examined her many times, and has consulted with top physicians in York, but no one has any idea what's wrong with her. Nor is it a rare North American disease, as someone tried to suggest," I added drily. "I've never heard of such a thing."

A Bitter Legacy

"Then I must see her. Are you ready to do battle?"

I nodded. "Quite ready."

"Then the story is that I happened to be the early traveler who came across you on the way."

When we arrived at the great front door, all pandemonium was let loose. George had been searching for me frantically; some men were still out. He had not been able to halt the runaway carriage for some time, and had decided it would be safer to finish the journey, then return on horseback.

"But I would not let him," Sophie said. We were standing in the hallway, George, Great-uncle Samuel, and Sophie lined up on one side, myself and Jasper on the other.

"None of us would," Great-uncle Samuel declared testily. "Madness to go out in that blizzard. Wouldn't have got five yards."

"But as soon as the storm ended, I organized a search," George said, staring coldly at Jasper. "Where was the hut you sheltered in?"

"I don't know," I said, feeling suddenly tired. "I think I managed to walk a mile or two but it was off the road, I discovered this morning. I must bathe and change. I feel like a scarecrow."

"You look like one," came Adele's voice, as she swept in through the door, looking as beautiful as she had the night before. "Redvers has just brought me back but he has appointments to attend so he's not coming in. And what are you doing here?" She addressed Jasper sharply, in her usual manner, but with my new way of observing, I saw that she moved closer to him and gave him all her attention. As she had done the previous times they'd been together. Her eyes ate Jasper hungrily, albeit very guardedly, while her tongue lashed him. Jasper appeared not to notice.

Sophie excitedly told Adele the full story of my adventure while George spoke quietly with Great-uncle Samuel in the background, then he interrupted his sister.

"Ned will be punished for his negligence," he stated. "I've examined the carriage, but have found no damage and no sign of tampering. It was a terrible accident, though I shall never forgive myself. Vicky, why are you still here? You should be bathing and resting."

"Yes, I should. But I'll visit my mother first."

"I'll come with you to pay my respects. My horse is lame, by the way," Jasper informed George casually. "I may have to stay the night."

As we walked up the stairs, I felt all eyes below on us and then, when we reached the landing, feverish conversation resumed, but I could not hear what was being said.

Mrs. Ackroyd was with my mother and, in answer to my enquiry, she said, "Much as usual." Her small eyes darted from one to the other of us. "I couldn't get her to drink this morning. Maybe she will from you, miss."

A Bitter Legacy

I held my mother's hand, whispered to her that I was home, kissed her forehead, and waited for an answering sign, but there was none. I turned round and was taken aback by the gray pallor of Jasper's face. Of course, the last time he'd seen her she'd been bright and well.

"Has she been like this the whole time?" he asked in a low voice. He came forward and took her hand. I saw her through his eyes, the sunken cheeks, her hair now graying, her body wasting away. I read the fear on his face. He thought she was going to die.

Briskly I moved to the door. "I must wash . . . rest . . . I'll leave you . . ." I said thickly, then hurried out, unable to bear that look on his face.

Rosie hurried to me as soon as she learned I was back. "I've not slept a wink," she said. "I kept seeing you falling out of that door, and me not able to do a thing to save you. I shall have nightmares about it for the rest of my days. I'm that glad to see you back safe and sound."

Her happiness at my return was so genuine that I forgave her for spying on me for Jasper.

"Lucky that Mr. Thornley happened by just then," she said at last, when I had scrubbed the last of the dirt from my body and was dressed in fresh, warm clothes. "I suppose you could say he saved your life."

"You know perfectly well that there was more than luck involved. I know what you and Ned have been up to. What made you do it, Rosie?

Was it Mr. Thornley's gold, or did Ned whisper sweet words of love into your ear?"

She started and colored as if I'd slapped her. "Not for money, no. Not for Ned, either, though I do love him, that's true, and where's the harm in that? No, I did it for you, Miss Victoria. He said someone wanted to harm you and he could stop them."

She went to the door, clearly hurt.

"All right, Rosie, I believe you. Mr. Thornley can be a very persuasive man." She was almost out the door, her straight back softening slightly, when I delayed her again. "Rosie, do you think we should send for Dr. Cooper again. To see Mama, I mean?"

I couldn't stand the pity in her eyes. "You can send if you want, though he'll have plenty to do in this weather. I don't think it'd make much difference to your ma, one way or t'other."

So she, too, thought my mother was going to die. I wished that I could return to yesterday's innocence and hope, but it was all gone. I saw the world how it was now, not how I wanted it to be. I lay on my bed and abandoned myself to the grief that, buoyed up by those false hopes, I'd held back until now. Unless she recovered very soon, my mother would waste away.

When I awoke much later, I was aware that someone was in the room with me. George was standing at the window, his back to me. He heard me stir and came to stand by the bed.

A Bitter Legacy

"What a terrible ordeal you've been through," he said softly. "Yet you are as beautiful as ever. What are you going to do now?"

"What do you mean, 'do now?'"

He sat on the edge of the bed and took my hand in his. "Do you think I could miss the unhappiness in your eyes? Your time at Lansdowne Hall has brought you fear and pain. I'm afraid that you're planning to leave after all."

That roused me. I sat up. "Leave? Oh, no. This is my home now, how many times have I told you that? Nothing can change my mind."

A strange expression crossed his face. "I'm very... moved to hear you say that," he said, even more softly than before. "But then, I should have expected it. You're a brave girl, even though a foolish one."

"George, let go my hand! You're hurting me."

He sighed and let go. "I'm just so happy to have you returned to me. When they stopped me searching for you last night, I—I feared I would never see you again. Vicky, you must promise me now that you will marry me, and soon."

I heard the urgency in his voice. I knew I should say yes, here and now, when I owed him so much. Without him my life would have been intolerable and he clearly loved me. I opened my mouth to speak, but the words I heard in my mind stopped me: Jasper's voice saying, "You're mine. You're mine."

I prevaricated. "But what do Adele and Sophie think about us getting married?"

"I don't care what they think, and neither should you. Adele is practically engaged to that bore Redvers, because he has money enough to keep her happy, and Sophie naturally wants whatever I want to make me happy. As for Uncle Samuel . . . Well, he won't be living here with us, will he?" He smiled his usual merry smile. "You see, whatever objection you raise I can answer. And when your mother's better, she can live with us, of course."

I had to smile back. "In that case I'll give you my answer as soon as I can. Will tomorrow do?"

In answer he took my face in his hands and kissed me on the lips. "I think I know what your answer is going to be, and you've made me a very happy man. Will I see you at dinner tonight?"

"Yes, I'll be down. Will Mr. Thornley be there, or has he left already?"

His lips tightened. "I made it perfectly clear that I would not have that man under this roof, yet I discovered only just now that Adele has allowed him to stay over the stables again, on the pretext that his horse is lame. We have a stableful of horses, and I would rather he took one of them than have him near us—near you—for a moment longer than necessary. Vicky, I want to know what passed between the two of you this morning."

A Bitter Legacy

I knew I could not lie to George, and was glad that I could truthfully answer. "Very little. He hardly spoke at all, except to ask about my mother."

He stood up, biting his lip. "Thornley's mind is poisoned against us, the Lansdownes—and that includes you too, Vicky. He blamed your grandfather for what happened to his own father, and has always felt that he was due a share of our good fortune because his aunt married into our family. That's why he killed William. Never forget that fact, Victoria. But rest assured, once I can announce to the world that you are my fiancée, he won't trouble you again."

When George had gone, I bowed my head and tried to think. I was sure that both men believed their version of the truth, just as I was sure that both of them were wrong. A third party had been at work, and had been at work since before I was born, maligning my father, leaving William to die, perhaps even tipping Aunt Caroline into that unreal world she inhabited. And now that third party was at work again, and I was the target. Perhaps I should be glad that my mother was in a coma; she was safe there.

Mrs. Randall had created one of her best meals for dinner that night. The souffle melted in the mouth, the meat was tender, the dessert a perfection of sweetness, but I barely touched my food. My appetite had deserted me. Adele was at her most vivacious, talking nonstop throughout, drawing George into her games of wit, and even coaxing a smile from Sophie. But I could only think of Jasper, alone in the room over the stable, and wonder what he was doing and thinking. I had also begun to fear for Ned, too, and whatever punishment George might serve out to him.

As soon as I could, I escaped upstairs. I needed to be alone, to examine my tangled thoughts. I had discovered, while sitting at dinner and toying with my food, that I was in the fierce and painful grip of an emotion, and that emotion was love. I loved Jasper Thornley.

That knowledge made me tremble. I strode up and down the room, possessed of a fearful burning energy. I didn't bother to undress; I could never hope to sleep. Instead, I relived every moment that we'd spent together, recalled every word he'd spoken, over and over again. Most of all I remembered his clear gray eyes. They were what I'd noticed most when we first met. Since then I'd seen them colorless with anger, or a stormy gray like the sky when deeply moved, or even a gentle blue-gray, like the surface of the sea in summer, when he smiled.

Worse, I had discovered in myself a sudden jealousy of Adele. All this time, I had thought she hated him, yet it was Adele who arranged for a room for him to sleep in—both times—and it was Adele who was free to come and go as she pleased, to spend time with him. Could they be working together to deceive me? No, I could not believe that. I did not know what I believed, only that I loved him.

At last I could stand it no longer and, to put my restlessness to good use, went to sit with my mother, dismissing Elise.

I forced myself to sit down, and sat bolt upright by her bed, staring unseeingly at the pattern of lovers' knots of red roses on cream wallpaper. At last I whispered, "It's true, Mama, I love him." A thought struck me. "Of course, he's already asked me to marry him. I could hold him to that." But, no, I knew I could not, not when it was Lansdowne Hall he loved, not me. All the same, I dwelt foolishly for a while on a possible future of Jasper suddenly discovering how much he'd come to love his devoted bride, but the intense joy of fantasy was short-lived.

"Falling in love is supposed to be the happiest moment of your life, but for me it's the most miserable," I continued. "And what about George? If I married him, he would never be more than second best, and one day he'd realize it. No, I couldn't chain us both to such a future. I shall have to tell him I cannot marry him."

Feverishly, I got to my feet and began to pace again, the only way I could find relief from the violence of the emotions that boiled inside me. I had to tell George that my answer would be no. I looked at the clock on the mantelshelf. It was barely two in the morning and I would have to wait until nearly eight, then I'd catch him at the stables, where he exercised his horse, whatever the weather.

My thoughts returned to Jasper and the way he called me his. It was at that very moment, I now saw, that the truth had begun to stir in me. It was true. I was his, my one and only true love. Once his lips had touched mine, I'd become his willing captive, never to be free. He must have seen it in my eyes before I'd known. And in the course of twenty-four hours, I now felt that I'd always loved him, through eternity, in other lives and other places. How deep and hidden had been my emotions, now touched into life.

It wasn't a tender, sweet love I felt, rather an uncompromising force that ruled every part of my being. Only when I was with Jasper did I feel truly complete. His kisses, too, had been less loving endearments, more driven and desperate. That was understandable. There could be no future for us. Too much lay between his family and mine.

Still, I loved Jasper Thornley. That was the one fact that I kept returning to. And he carried my photograph in his locket. But that meant nothing, only that he could use it to identify me, identify his victim. If only my head would rule my heart. . . . At last, tired out, I feel asleep holding my mother's hand. Any change in her condition and I would know it.

A Bitter Legacy

I made my way down to the stable yard carefully the next morning, avoiding the main stairs, and no one saw me. My heart was thumping heavily as I crossed the yard which had been scraped clear of its snow. The sound of cheerful whistling led me to one of the stalls, and I saw George saddling up his horse himself. Had Ned already been dismissed? I waited until he came out, leading his horse. He gave a start when he saw me, then smiled. "So early, Vicky. Can this be a lovers' tryst?" he asked happily.

"I—are we quite private here, George? Where's Ned?"

"Preparing feed in the barn. He's sulking after the dressing down I've given him. Why so solemn, Vicky?"

"I've been thinking all night, trying to decide the best way to tell you, but . . . I really am very fond of you, you must believe that."

He became very still, the smile leaving his face. "I don't think I'm going to like this," he said slowly.

"I—I've reached my decision. Much as I honor and respect you, I—can't marry you."

George was shaking his head in disbelief. "I didn't expect you to love me necessarily, but I never thought you'd throw away the chance of marrying me and securing your inheritance, even if you didn't love me." He looked long into my eyes and found his answer there. "So, it's true, you really mean it. Vicky, I advise you to think again and think hard. If you mean this, you don't know what you've done."

"Oh, George, I really am very sorry, but so would you be if we married and I didn't—"

But he was mounting up and rode past me at great speed, so that I had to jump aside. I held my hand to my throat. What did he mean? "You don't know what you've done." Those words sounded threatening—or had he just been letting his feelings go? I shaded my eyes against the rising sun to watch the retreating figure on horseback... and a dark shadow interposed itself. "Ned?" I called, unable to make out who it was at first because of the dazzle, and then I saw it was Jasper. It was clear from his expression that he had heard every word.

"Vicky," he said, and stretched out his hand toward me, but I could not bear to read the triumph in his eyes. I turned on my heel and ran from the yard.

All that morning I kept to my room. I heard George's return, his voice raised in anger echoing through the house, and I waited, half dreading, half expecting that he would seek me out and try to change my mind, but he didn't come. Instead, Rosie brought me my luncheon on a tray.

"Mrs. Randall made this up for you," she said, still speaking stiffly to me, indicating that we weren't quite friends yet. "She overheard Master George telling Miss Sophie you'd turned him

A Bitter Legacy

down and thought you'd want to keep out of the way."

"She's right. Is he very angry still? I'm sorry if I've made trouble for other people. And Ned, what news of him? Is he to be dismissed?"

"He's to go without a reference," she told me. "He's hardly spoken a word to anyone. Master George was in a terrible rage with him. And now, no one dare go near him."

"I'm sorry, Rosie. What will you do? Can I give him a reference?"

"Won't mean anything round these parts. Reckon he'll have to go down south. When he's settled, he'll send for me. But—thank you, miss." She tried to grin, but all her sparkle was gone.

I ate the food, thought I wasn't hungry despite having missed breakfast, to please Mrs. Randell for the trouble she'd taken. Then I sat, staring unseeingly at the book on my lap. An ominous quiet had settled over the Hall. I tried holding my breath, listening for the slightest sound, but there was none. My hands were cold with foreboding. I could not shake off a sense of doom.

Yet at the same time, in a hidden part of me, I felt an enormous sense of relief. I had been flattered and warmed by George's attentive wooing, but I had felt no answering thrill of passion. Every time he had talked about how it would be when I was his wife I had felt as if doors were closing, barriers coming down, instead of the excitement of horizons opening and a glorious future lying ahead. Now, with my new way of looking at people, I couldn't help sensing that he didn't love me at all, that his lovemaking was practiced show. His anger was because I hadn't fallen in with his plans.

It would have been convenient for us to have married, but I was sure that given time he would soon cool down and then realize what a lucky escape he had had. For now, I would wait out the storm, then face them all at dinner.

The light tap at my door made me jump, but boldly I went to open it. It was Elise, with a message from Adele, summoning me to the drawing room.

She was standing beside the piano, one hand resting on its top, wearing a fancy new gown with a highly exaggerated bustle and decorated with ribbon bows and much braid. She looked like a beautiful piece of porcelain waiting for a portrait painter to arrive, such was the artfulness of her pose.

She beckoned me over and pointed to some framed photographs on top of the piano. "What do you think of these?" she asked. "I've brought them from my room. I had them framed in York. Expensive, but worth it, don't you think?"

What did she want? "They're good, yes. Tommy looks very handsome in his sailor suit, and you're posing as a shepherdess. But who's this?

A Bitter Legacy

Not Grandfather Albert?"

She let out a peal of laughter. "That was my husband, Mr. Roberts."

I picked up the photograph and looked at it closely. It revealed a gaunt face with receding hair, made up for by a long beard and thick muttonchop whiskers. Beside him, Mr. Redvers looked young and bounding with energy.

"I can see what you're thinking and, no, I didn't love my first husband. He was chosen for me by Father because he was a major shareholder in the Great Western Railway, and that meant cheaper freight for our minerals and coal. He was a very proper gentleman. But we managed well together, and I was not unhappy, and he loved Tommy, though fortunately Tommy was only two when he died so he didn't miss him for long. Why he had to poke around these infernal mines I . . .

"Well, no more of that. This is what I wanted you to know. He left me independent, and with Father's settlement I'm well off. However, if I receive another proposal, and I very much expect I will and soon, I shall say yes. It's the only way for a woman to be, to take her position in society, as a wife and future mother.

"Now George tells me you've turned him down and he's asked me to intercede on his behalf. Speaking honestly, I have no interest in your well-being or your marital position. If you want to remain a spinster, that's up to you. What I can't understand is why you're throwing away your only chance of getting everything you want at once—both finance for the Hall, and the Landsdowne name."

I shook my head. "I can't do it. George deserves—"

"Who cares what George deserves? If he wants you, that should be enough. You can always work out an arrangement later on that's satisfactory to both of you. Won't you reconsider? No, I thought not." She frowned. "You're playing some new game, one I don't understand—yet. But I will. I can read you like a book, Victoria. You have absolutely no finesse, no subtlety whatsoever."

"Now look here," I began angrily, "I've had enough of your insults. I would rather make my feelings plain than hide them behind a simpering smile, or manipulate with soft words. I—"

"Yes, that's just it." she said icily. "You think you're that little bit better. Well, let me tell you, your rough American ways will get you nowhere here. Already you're the laughingstock of the county. Honestly, I'm ashamed to have to claim you as kin."

My face flamed. It couldn't be true! I had thought my presence at Sir Gransby's Ball had been a great success. And then I saw her purpose. She'd been waiting to strike, waiting to spit her venom at me all this time, and she

A Bitter Legacy

thought she'd found my weak spot; in fact, she very nearly had. Controlling myself, I said, almost keeping the tremor from my voice, "Not as ashamed as I am—now." I held up my hand as she straightened that already ramrod-stiff back of hers ready to hurl the next jibe, "If you've made your point, I'll go. I have more important things to do than argue with you."

Suddenly she relaxed and her eyes narrowed calculatingly. "Perhaps it's the money you've been after all along. Yes, that's it. Your obstinacy is just a ploy to push the price of the Hall up, strike the better bargain. You've decided on the money, without the bother of a husband attached. In which case, when I marry, sell to *my* husband. I'll make sure he outbids everyone else."

"No," I said firmly. "I won't sell to you and your new husband, whether it's Mr. Redvers or someone else. You've got it all wrong, after all. Give it up, Adele. The house is mine and it will never be yours. It was your father's will, after all, just as it has been all along, in every sense of the word. Blame him for setting us against each other. Why not? I do."

She went pale with anger. "I'd like to shake some sense into you. You're doing this just to spite me, all of us, you've just admitted as much. Take care your revenge doesn't rebound on you, though!" She turned her back on me and picked up the picture of Tommy, studying it, dismissing me. I made my way to the door, but she stopped me, my hand on the knob, by saying, "You never knew your father, did you? I suppose I should pity you for that."

"I want neither your pity nor your sympathy, and I don't believe you feel them, either. Stop goading me, Adele, you'll never win."

Still with her back to me, her neck a graceful curve of creamy skin, her golden curls shining almost with an inner radiance of their own, she said, "I said I supposed I *should* pity you, not that I did. Of course, you know you look just like your father. Another reason it's impossible to accept you as a Lansdowne, possessing Lansdowne Hall." Now she turned back to me, her face a perfect and composed oval again, as if we were holding polite afternoon conversation.

"So I've been told. My mother only has one sketch of him, as a very young man."

"Then you've never seen Aunt Caroline's portraits? She used to be a good artist, once upon a time. Her room was always full of the smell of paint, though I don't expect you remember. Oh, what's the use." She gave an impatient sigh. "You share none of our heritage, you simply don't belong, yet you're too pigheaded to admit it. You may as well blunder on until the bitter end. Well, I've done as George insisted, and it was as unpleasant as I expected. I see no point in our talking any further. I promised Tommy I'd—"

A Bitter Legacy

"Wait a moment, Adele. Where are Aunt Caroline's portraits now? Are they with her in Rosebank?"

"They don't allow them anything in that place." She gave a delicate shudder, as false as her bitter smile. "I have no idea. Her things would be in the attic, if they're anywhere. I was only seven when they took her away, moaning and crying, as if she were about to be tortured."

I swallowed hard and left the room. In my turn, I supposed I should pity Adele, who had endured many painful sights and lived through much grief—except that I didn't. Nor did I feel anything but gratitude that she and I were poles apart in thought, in looks, in speech. No wonder she couldn't understand me and never would.

I could not forget the portraits of my father that she had mentioned, however, and while I was taking care of my mother, washing and feeding her, I remembered practically the last thing she'd said to me—that she had a surprise for me among the things she'd found in the attic. I'd already been up there, of course, but I'd only searched her trunk. There were many boxes which, in my anxiety, I'd not even looked at. I decided to have a further search, especially for canvases.

With my hand on the door behind which lay the stairs to the attics, Sophie caught up with me. "I've been looking for you," she said reproachfully. "How could you, Victoria? You've hurt George. Now you can never be my friend again."

"He would be much unhappier in the end if I'd said yes. We weren't meant for each other," I told her. "Did you want us to marry?"

She cocked her head on one side, her face more glisteningly pale than usual, sickly too against the mustard-yellow of her dress. "Nobody could ever love George more than I do. He takes care of me. He always has. If he married you, he'd still take care of me. Now I must take care of him. You've broken his heart." She bit her lip and her eyes were moist. "George is hurting and it's your fault."

"Sophie, listen to me, please. He's only hurting because I've spoiled his plans. You'll see, in a couple of days he'll be his old self again. I know he didn't love me."

"He told me he did, only now he hates you. And I hate you, too, because you're not even sorry for what you've done. But I'll make you sorry, I will, I will." She sounded like a petulant child.

"Sophie, you're upset. In a couple of days you'll be glad that everything is just as it was, and you'll forgive me."

"I'm going to make things better for George," she muttered, staring at me fixedly with a strange light in her eyes, and for the first time I felt a little afraid of her and her

A Bitter Legacy

unpredictable nature. I could see that I was not going to change her mind, or that she would easily forgive me, so I lifted the latch on the old wooden door.

"Where are you going?" Sophie asked.

"I'm looking for Aunt Caroline's paintings. Do you know if there are any in the attic? Adele said there might be."

She didn't reply, so that at first I thought she was being deliberately difficult. Just as I began to move away though, she nodded her head vigorously. "Oh, yes, they're up there, or they used to be. I used to play with them when I was a child—pictures of my imaginary friends. She didn't like me in her room. I had to go in when she wasn't there. When she became sick, I took them away and played with them up there, where no one could see and stop me." Then, in one of her quick changes of mood, the old Sophie was speaking again. "Of course I haven't looked at them for years. You'll like them. She was a very good artist." She patted my arm. "I expect you're right, Vicky. George will be happy again soon. I must help him to be, mustn't I?"

Even though she'd returned to normal, I was glad to be away from her, and away from Adele's sharp despising words. I felt shaky and emotionally drained, and needed this time alone to browse and to recover.

The attic seemed to be in more disarray than I remembered from my last visit. This time I made my search methodical, particularly looking for canvases. At last, my hands grimy with dust, my hair damp with perspiration, I found them, wrapped in brown paper and tucked away behind an old chest of drawers. They were unframed, some canvas, some board and beginning to warp, and mainly watercolors. There were also many charcoal sketches on paper, and they all bore the initials *CL* in the corner. I passed quickly over the landscapes, though they were good, and skipped through the portraits, which included all the family, young and old, though I intended to study them all at a later date. Today, it was my father I sought.

I recognised him immediately. There were two sketches, one of the head only, the other of him standing with his hand resting on the globe, which I knew stood in the library. I drank in his open, regular features, his strong neck and shoulders, the broad grin, and the springy curls which I'd inherited. This was a man radiating strength and purpose. This man would not have run willingly from anything, from even the foulest of accusations.

I must have still been feeling shaky, because I sat on the edge of a broken chair by the window and cried for this man I had never been allowed to know. No wonder my mother had given up everything in order to find him. I realized that for all these years I'd harbored a tiny grudge against her. She could have stayed at

A Bitter Legacy

Lansdowne Hall and I could have been brought up in splendor and luxury, the apple of my grandfather's eye. Now this tiny grudge was gone, replaced with the conviction that she had done the right thing—and the conviction that I, too, must put all my resources into tracing him. Because I now had resources. This Hall and its lands were my resource. . . .

At last I stood up. From the angle of light I guessed it to be late afternoon. Soon it would be twilight. I could not wait for this winter to end. I took the two sketches of my father and went to the door, but it would not yield to my hand.

I pushed and shoved with all my might, but still it would not budge. I threw my whole weight against it, but it was useless. It appeared to have jammed. And yet it couldn't have. I knew that it was set loosely in its frame. A horrible suspicion entered my mind. I knelt and peered through the keyhole. The key was gone. Next I examined the door itself, but the hinges were on the other side. There was no escape.

"Whoever's playing this stupid prank open the door now," I commanded, but it remained obstinately closed. I laid my ear against the door, but I could hear nothing. There was no use shouting, because with this door and the one at the bottom of the stairs, no one would hear me.

The windows were both sashes and securely nailed shut. I remembered now hearing Gandy comment that he'd done that because they were loose and their rattling was disturbing the servants asleep in their rooms nearby. Unfortunately the servants' quarters were reached by a separate set of back stairs. Still, if the worst came to worst, I could bang against the wall when it was their bedtime—as long as they didn't think I was the White Lady.

My only conclusion was that anyone would know that with the door locked I had no escape route. My only hope was to attract someone's attention through the windows.

Down below I could just see part of the stable yard and the long row of stalls beyond, a horse's head looking out over a half door. Ned came into view, carrying a bucket, heading for the stalls. I shouted and knocked against a windowpane as hard as I could. He stopped, looked round, and I redoubled my efforts. "Up here," I yelled. "Please, Ned, look up!"

Instead, he suddenly dropped the bucket and began to run in the direction of the house, and was soon lost to view. I could not believe that he had heard me, because he had not seen me. What was happening down there?

I redoubled my efforts, shouting until I was hoarse. Then Ned came into view again, running down the yard, followed by others. I knew I had to break the glass, and looked round for a suitable object. If need be, perhaps I could splinter the wood around the pane of glass. I quickly found what I wanted, a child's cricket bat. I lifted it over my shoulders, muscles tensed for the first blow—and then I became aware of an acrid smell. I paused and sniffed. The atmosphere in the attic had definitely become mustier since I'd entered. In the next instant I knew it wasn't age and dust I was smelling, but smoke! Landsdowne Hall was on fire, and I was caught on the topmost floor, without any way out, while down below everyone would be too preoccupied to hear me.

I didn't waste any more time but hefted the bat and struck at the window. The glass shattered reassuringly and cool, clear air entered, but the wood was not even dented. Again and again I beat at it, until splinters flew around me, while the smoke was growing thicker by the minute, its bitter reek catching at my throat and making me cough. I could hear distant shouts, catch glimpses of frenzied activity, but everyone was too busy to look up at the attic windows. My only hope was that Sophie would remember I had come up and think that I might still be here, several hours later.

Unless she had locked me in herself to punish me for hurting George. Would she have set the fire, too, for the same reason? I could not believe that of her. But she might see the fire as an added bonus in her plan. And I had not told Adele outright that I was coming to the attic.

I had to find a way out! I dropped the bat and desperately began to rummage again. This time I found something more useful, a rigid metal lever. As I attacked the window once more, gouging at the wood to release it from nails and catches, my thoughts turned to the others in the household and I prayed that my mother and Tommy in particular were safe.

At last the sash yielded and I was leaning out, breathing in gulps of cold air. Now I had to work out a route down and in the next instant I saw Jasper on the sloping roof to my left, making his way across, crabwise, and then, as I watched heart in mouth, lowering himself down to a stone ledge a foot wide that ran below the window.

"Climb out," he ordered, speaking for the first time. "Don't look down. I'll hold you."

I did not think twice. Carefully, I climbed out, turning to face the wall, by which time he'd edged along enough to grab my arm.

"Now move as I do. It's not far and there's plenty to hold onto."

I obeyed him unthinkingly, and he was right. The old house had projections of stone decoration and guttering in plenty. All the time his hand was on me, and I concentrated on this, rather than the fact that fifty feet below was cold, hard ground.

At last we reached the roof, and Jasper helped me scramble up, then held me close

A Bitter Legacy

until the shudders that trembled through my body ceased. Finally he said, "The fire is under control, but we'd best hurry in case it breaks out again. I'll help you across the tiles."

I crawled face down across the steep pitch of the roof, past a tower of chimneys, Jasper behind me, steadying me again with his hand, urging me on with a calm voice. Not long after we were on the iron fire escape that led down from the servants' quarters, and climbing down the back of the house to the stable yard. By now my clothes were torn and dirty, my hair wild around my shoulders. Jasper's shirt, too, was badly ripped and his grazed knuckles were bleeding. A haze of smoke hung in the air, and people were still running to and fro with buckets of water.

"How bad is the fire?" I asked, leading him to the pump and washing his hand under the clean water.

"It's been contained already and hasn't spread further than the east wing. The entrance hall and stairs are badly damaged, too. It started in the butler's pantry. Vicky, it was deliberate. There was a pile of rags soaked in turpentine."

"But why?"

"Can't you guess?"

I looked away. It was one thing to allow these thoughts into my mind, another to speak them aloud. "I must see the damage for myself. I must go."

"Listen to me." He held me fast by the shoulders, his eyes compelling me to pay attention. "This fire must have been set to kill you. It's the only explanation that makes sense. You know that's why I stayed, to keep an eye on you."

"Then, yes. Someone intended to frighten me. And, yes, I was locked in." He started when he heard that, his face like thunder. "But the fire wasn't intended for me. If it was, the fire would've been started upstairs, wouldn't it?"

Jasper's frown deepened and he let go. "I hadn't thought of that. But locked in? Vicky, you must have been terrified."

I said more gently. "I was. Thank you for coming to rescue me. Without you . . . But we can talk later. Let me go to see how Mama is."

"She's safe. She's been taken to the gamekeeper's cottage." He began to walk with me. "You have Sophie to thank, too. She remembered you'd gone to the attic. I couldn't get along the landing because of the heat and smoke. I thought that was why you didn't come down, because you couldn't come through, which is why I climbed up the back."

"Yet she was angry with me for hurting George!" I suddenly halted. "I can imagine her locking me in, then later regretting it. You're right, though, she could have meant me harm. Adele, too. We quarrelled earlier today. It was she who told me there were drawings of my

A Bitter Legacy

father in the attic. It could have been her plan to trap me up there. Then there's Great-uncle Samuel. He's always trying to get rid of me. Sophie might have told him where I was. This morning I rejected George—and then there's you, too. Perhaps you wanted to frighten me just a little bit."

His jaw tightened and his eyes became wintry. "I thought you trusted me now."

"So did I," I said dully. "But it was you yourself who warned me to trust no one. And now I don't."

I took my chance at freedom and ran around to the front of the house. Smoke oozed lazily from several windows on the ground floor and first floors, and the stonework was blackened, the wood framing the windows smoldered. But the roof was intact and the west wing apparently unscathed.

George, Great-uncle Samuel, and Sophie were grouped near the front door, while Rosie and Mrs. Randell were busy sorting through belongings laid on the drive. Mrs. Randell hugged me wordlessly, then assured me my mother was well, before turning back to her task. Rosie and I walked to one side.

"Thank the Lord you're safe," she said. "Miss Sophie said you were in the attic, but no one believed her at first till Mr. Thornley—"

"I know. He rescued me. Rosie, is it true the fire was no accident?"

"It's true! Mary was passing the butler's pantry when *whoosh*, flames came gushing out. She was terrified, near screamed the place down. We worked as fast as we could, but the flames spread. It was terrible. But no one's hurt, beyond little scrapes and bruises."

We stood for a moment in silent thanksgiving. Then I was amazed to see Adele coming out of the front door. The beautiful dress I'd seen her in earlier was grimey and ragged, completely unrecognizable, and she carried a bucket in one hand. Her hair was tangled on her shoulders, but her head was held as high as ever. She glanced at me, then ignored me, striding over to Mrs. Randell and giving her instructions.

"Yes," Rosie said, following my gaze. "Mrs. Roberts was the bravest of them all. She carried Tommy out herself, then went back in to help me with your mama, all the time carrying water, smothering flames with blankets." She could not hide the admiration in her voice, and I shook my head at this new picture of Adele. This Dresden shepherdess had risked her clothes and her looks to save both people and her beloved Hall. She could not have started the fire.

"I must thank Sophie," I said. "Without her I wouldn't be here. I'm thankful the damage isn't too severe."

"It'll cost a pretty penny to put right though."

"Yes, and who's going to pay for it?" But her words had given a lift to my spirits rather than

A Bitter Legacy

dampening them further. Perhaps the fire had been started, not to kill me, but to *force* me to sell.

I was about to join Sophie, but Rosie put a detaining hand on my arm. She was holding something out in the palm of her hand. "What should I do with this, Miss Vicky? I found it under your mama's mattress. I didn't know what it was, so I thought I'd better bring it. We had such a todo carrying her out all wrapped up in blankets I forgot about it. Is it one of Dr. Cooper's remedies, do you think? I can't say as I remember seeing it before."

It was a small glass vial stoppered with cork, containing a pale yellow liquid. My spine tingled with sudden prescience. This was no potion of Dr. Cooper's. What did this have to do with my mother's illness?

Chapter Nine

"What is that?"

Jasper had followed me. At first I closed my hand over the vial, but then reluctantly opened my fist. My mother was my first priority, and if Jasper could help, I would let him. I handed it to him. "Rosie found this in Mama's bed. Neither of us has seen it before, and I know that it does not contain one of Dr. Cooper's remedies. The bottle is wrong, and it has no label."

Jasper examined it, and as he turned it over, I saw again the raw scrape on his knuckles, still oozing blood, but it appeared not to pain him. "Rosie, is there anyone who might have left some local remedy?"

"Not as I know of, Mr. Thornley."

A Bitter Legacy

When he looked up, I could see he'd had the same thought as me, that the contents of this small bottle might have more to do with the cause of my mother's illness than with its cure.

"I'd like to take this to a pharmacist, find out what's in it. We should talk to Mrs. Ackroyd, too, see what she knows. In fact," he went on, "it might be best if just you two do all the nursing from now on. If only there was some way we could keep your mother away from the Hall, Vicky."

As he spoke, understanding dawned on Rosie's face, but she managed to stifle her gasp of indignation. Easily and naturally, I entered into further conspiracy with Jasper, and he knew now that I would take his warnings seriously at last. If I had little regard for myself, I would do all in my power to protect my mother.

I left Jasper with Rosie and approached the group who had gradually assembled while we'd been conferring, as if we were forming two opposing factions. Indeed, they'd been formed long ago. Adele, a woolen shawl in a paisley pattern over her torn and blackened clothes, held her head as high as ever. Great-uncle Samuel, his face purple and red with cold, a little unsteady on his feet, so that I almost felt sorry for him, fixed his small, rheumy eyes on me, and I recoiled once more from the coldness in them. If he wasn't going to change, why should I?

"We must tell George. I don't know what George is going to say," I heard Sophie muttering over and over to herself, as she rubbed her hands agitatedly up and down her arms to keep warm. Her eyes glittered with overexcitement, and her face was quite white. Mrs. Ackroyd was at her side, her sloe eyes watching me maliciously.

"There's probably no point in it, but I'll give you the opportunity of confession anyway by asking which one of you locked me in the attic, expecting to frighten me? Perhaps you also set fire to the house—my house—either to stop me from having my inheritance, or to add to my money troubles."

Adele made a sound of annoyance. "No one locked you in. You probably jammed the door or locked it by mistake. Incompetent, as always."

"Probably locked herself in on purpose, threw the key away. Getting sympathy. Stuff and nonsense! Absolute outrage!" Great-uncle Samuel scoffed.

Sophie suddenly flung her arms around my neck and hugged me. "I didn't want you to die," she said intensely, "That's why I told Jasper where you were, but the White Lady wants you gone. She did it!"

"Sophie, stop that ridiculous nonsense and let Victoria go!" Adele ordered. "Once and for all, there is no ghost, and I for one will not stand for these accusations."

"It was you who told me about the pictures of my father in the attic," I reminded her. "Why do you think I was up there? I even managed to save one. Look."

I held out the drawing, which had been tucked up my sleeve. Great-uncle Samuel snorted and shook his head, while Sophie touched it lovingly.

Adele, however, opened and closed her mouth in anger, finally settling for, "Mrs. Ackroyd, take Sophie away and make sure she rests. Take her to the kitchen and Mrs. Randell with you."

"Now, Victoria," she said, when they'd gone, without Sophie complaining about being treated like a child. Indeed, she seemed to enjoy it. "We must put everything else aside and discuss what is to be done about the Hall. There is fire damage to assess, and as trustees Uncle Samuel and I think—"

"You will have enough rooms," I told her. "I'm moving to the gamekeeper's cottage, and I would like Rosie to stay with me, too. I don't want my mother moved again. The shock may prove fatal." Inspiration and a faint ray of hope since the discovery of that vial made me add, "She has been looking very poorly these last few days." If our suspicions were correct, and the contents of the bottle were some kind of poison, I would prefer our enemy to think they were succeeding, which would give us time to nurse her back to health in secret.

Adele looked pleased. "Good. I did not like having her and Tommy under the same roof, in case the infection spread. As for the house—"

Again I interrupted. "We must get it cleaned up, and then estimates for repairs. It's only a matter of six weeks or so until I turn twenty-one. Then I will see about putting the Hall to rights."

Adele gave an astonished laugh. "Repairs cost money," she said.

"Men won't work for nothing," Great-uncle Samuel said, moving closer. "Admit it, girl, your position's hopeless. You've lost!"

Now it was time for me to stick my chin into the air. "On the contrary, I am just beginning to scent success," I said, before turning on my heel and stalking away. There was a part of me that wanted nothing more than to give up the Hall and get myself and my mother as far away from it as I could, but I could not allow the Lansdownes to think they'd won!

Jasper watched me stride by, a sardonic smile on his face. I thought he might stop me or call me back to tell me that I was making a fool of myself, but he let me go without comment. It was only afterwards that I realized I had never thanked him properly for, once again, saving my life. Instead, I had included him in my net of suspicion.

A Bitter Legacy

* * *

Fortunately the gamekeeper's cottage was large enough to accommodate my mother, Rosie, and me, being originally a rambling farmhouse built of the local stone. Even more important, the Barneses welcomed me when I explained the situation, and said I must stay as long as I wanted.

As I went upstairs to check on my mother, I couldn't help a small smile. How long ago it seemed now when we were in Seadale and I'd complained that I would never understand the local dialect, and that the landlady had disliked me. Now I had no problem understanding the speech and I could also read in the gamekeeper's and his wife's brusque, no-nonsense manner the underlying compassion and interest that was there.

Ned had carried my mother on a makeshift stretcher with the stable lad, and they were drinking tea in the kitchen downstairs. Rosie soon arrived, having stayed behind to pack our bags, and then it only took a brief hour to settle in. It was twilight by then, and she went downstairs to confer with Ned, who had been told by George only that morning that he must be gone from Lansdowne Hall that day.

I stood by the window, looking at the squat shape of Lansdowne Hall half a mile away. It was a dull gray in the winter light, and its windows were dark and blank, repelling the inquisitive gaze, revealing nothing of the secrets I knew lay within.

To me, it was no longer a gilded palace. Instead, a miasma of evil now hung over the place. It was no good telling myself that it was only stones and mortar, that it was those who lived inside who were evil. The two were now inextricably linked for me. I could not look at the Hall without thinking of the thwarted wishes of a murderer. I was sad for only two of its inhabitants, Tommy and the White Lady, although she would no doubt survive this as she had all past upheavals. I wished I could close the place up and leave it to her. As it was, the Hall was now repugnant to me. No longer the focus of my dreams for the future, but a repository of all that I hated—selfish greed and ruthless lust for power, revenge. My own included.

In the next two days, my feelings remained the same. My brave words to Great-uncle Samuel were not a lie, however. I would not hand the Hall over without a struggle, and even then not to any of my family. There was Jasper's offer, of course, and any number of others. I secretly sent word to Mr. Pontefract to draw up a likely list of candidates to be ready for my twenty-first birthday. Though, of course, my final decision still depended on my mother, and all my attention was now focused on her.

A Bitter Legacy

Rosie's and my vigilance in preparing my mother's food and watching her at all times was soon rewarded. Mrs. Randell still sent over her special broths, brought direct from the kitchens in a straw-lined box to keep them warm. But, Rosie and I disposed of them and substituted our own concoctions. Not that I suspected Mrs. Randell for one minute, but there were too many opportunities for the food to be tampered with on the way, and I wanted to keep our experiment quiet. If it was a poison, the poisoner might be driven to desperate measures if the would-be killer thought he or she were being thwarted and might attempt to finish my mother off.

Although Rosie was missing Ned and was anxious for their future, so that her good-natured face had lost its usual glow, she was much cheered by our immediate signs of success. Within forty-eight hours my mother began to improve. Color crept almost perceptibly back into her face, and her withered flesh seemed to fill out before our eyes. We redoubled our efforts to stimulate her circulation and to feed her.

"I wouldn't have believed it, never have believed it," Rosie said, shaking her head in happy bewilderment. "When I think that all this time she was . . . Why, if I got my hands on that person—"

I laughed. "You'd have to beat me to it!" I

said, suddenly realizing that the last time I'd laughed with genuine happiness had been a very long time ago. There was a gulf between myself then and now. "Nothing is clear, Rosie, except that Dr. Cooper's original diagnosis was correct after all. She wasn't really ill, but deeply asleep—in a coma."

"Shouldn't we send for him now?"

"I'd rather no one knew she was recovering yet. Nor do I want to leave her side for a moment. I want to be here when she wakes."

"Aye, but we'll both need our sleep," practical Rosie pointed out. "We'll take turns on the truckle bed over there. I wonder when Mr. Thornley will have news for us?"

"Soon, I hope."

Rosie nodded, casting me a sharp glance. "Let's hope he comes in person, too."

I kept silent. Since our quarrel we had become friends again, forming a new bond where we were more honest with each other. And yet, I did not want to discuss Jasper with her. I knew she would plead his case to me, and I still needed to keep an open mind, even though my love for him was like a firebrand being twisted painfully inside my chest. Thinking of him set my skin burning with a fever to have him near me, to touch him, to have him touch me. But I must not think of him. He was still keeping something back from me, and until I knew his true purpose, I could not reveal my love.

A Bitter Legacy

On the third day in our new home, I woke to find that my mother's heartbeat was strong and vital, her breathing like normal sleep, and she had even muttered, her eyeballs clearly moving under their lids as she dreamed. But my joy was short-lived as I saw a visitor on his way to the cottage. The Hall was only half a mile away, but already it was another world, one I was glad to be free of, and I wanted no reminders of the past. The sight of George on his high-stepping stallion, whipping at the foliage with his riding crop, quickly dampened my delight.

I left Rosie guarding my mother and went out in front of the house. Mr. Barnes, the gamekeeper, was chopping wood a short distance off, the blows of his axe echoing through the trees. He greeted his master with a wave, then went back to his work, while I stood in the clearing, looking up at George who did not deign to dismount.

"I have not forgiven you yet, Victoria," he said, and I looked away from the hurt in his normally merry brown eyes, "But I don't take my responsibility as nominal head of the family lightly, so I have come to see that you and your mother are comfortable here."

"As comfortable as we can be under the circumstances."

"You have chosen your own place of exile," he said. "You can return to the Hall at any time.

The damage is not that great, and it has been cleaned."

"You misunderstand me. I was referring to my mother's condition. I think to move her at the moment would be a grave mistake."

"Ah, I see." He bowed his head for a moment. "You see, your welfare is still important to me. If there's anything I can do . . . Send for a doctor. I'll bear the expense. You shouldn't have to worry about the fees at a time like this."

"Thank you, George, but there's nothing Dr. Cooper can do now," I said, and I had not lied.

"Vicky, are you sure you won't change your mind? Even in your present predicament, you are still more attractive to me than any of our English misses hereabouts. No? Then I'll take my leave. I can see you want to return to Alexandra. Remember, send for me any time. I'll do anything to help. I'll even pay for the repairs at the Hall."

When he'd gone, I stood with my back against the inside of the front door, my eyes closed, trembling with emotion. How easy it would be to heed his words of comfort, to sink into his supportive arms. No harsh demanding lips, like Jasper's, but soft relaxing comfort. But I had to be strong, and I had to be fair. George must be one of my suspects, too.

Later that day Ned brought me a hastily written letter from Jasper. While Ned sat in the

A Bitter Legacy

kitchen in his stockinged feet, Rosie teasing and fussing over him and Mrs. Barnes listening with amusement, I took the letter to read alone in the little-used front parlor. The sight of his bold, strong handwriting on my first letter from him affected me deeply, so that at first I held the paper to my lips and closed my eyes, imagining that he was there in person for the moment.

Then I fixed my eyes to the page and read: "The vial contains a powerful and toxic vegetable extract from the tropics in a highly concentrated form. It is known to produce paralysis when administered in minute quantities, and death from any dosage greater than a droplet every twenty-four hours. It is both expensive and rare. With Ned's help—he is now working for me—I'll try to find out who bought it. Yours ever, Jasper Thornley."

I wrote a brief note, thanking him and telling him that all was well. Ned would give color and life to my words for him.

"Yours ever . . ." If only that could be true. I walked outside among the trees for a while, a thick shawl around my shoulders, and my boots crunching in the pockets of snow caught against bushes or thick tussocks of grass. I thought one minute of Jasper writing to me, of when he would next visit me, the next minute of the exotic poison that had nearly killed my mother. It had been made to look like a degenerative illness, given in tiny, but perhaps increasing doses as her body became tolerant of it.

In great detail I went over every moment since she had become ill, barely registering Ned's taking his leave. I arrived at the inescapable conclusion that, as my relatives had proved such poor visitors to my mother's sickroom, either Mrs. Ackroyd or Elise had administered the poison. I was certain of it as I remembered that Adele had only stepped inside the room once and had not even approached the bed. Nor had Great-uncle Samuel who had harrumphed from midway across the room on the couple of occasions he'd looked in on my mother. George and Sophie had both held her hand, but again had not visited more than a handful of times. Rosie, of course, I eliminated. It was possible that Mrs. Ackroyd or Elise had only been following someone else's orders.

"Come quickly!" It was Rosie calling from an upper window. "It's a miracle. Your mother's awake!"

I ran up the stairs two at a time, not caring who might have overheard the good news, and rushed to the bedside. My mother's eyes were open, and, when I seized her hand, they focused on me, but she didn't speak. Was it possible that she no longer knew me? Who could tell what happened to the mind and memories during such a long sleep? No, not sleep, something darker than that.

A Bitter Legacy

Then she smiled sweetly, and said weakly, "Vicky, my love, good news. Your father is alive." Then she sighed and fell asleep again, but this time quite naturally. Rosie and I fell into each other's arms, unable to control our tears and broad grins of happiness.

"Whose bedroom is this? I don't recognize the wallpaper. And is it today you went to Whitby or yesterday now? I can't seem to remember."

Having awakened again that evening, my mother wanted to talk.

"Mama, prepare yourself. You've been ill for a long time. A very long time." I didn't know how much I should tell her all at once, though common sense told me the sooner she knew the truth, the sooner she would adjust.

"Is it November or later than that? And where are we?" She struggled to sit up straighter, and Rosie and I helped her while she smiled, a faint trace of her former smile. "I'm weak and helpless," she said. "My arms feel like water. You'll have to feed me. I do feel hungry. That's a good sign, isn't it? And you must tell me everything. Was it pneumonia I had? That must be it. I've been isolated from the Hall so that no one else will become ill."

"I'll go down t' kitchen and fetch you some soup," Rosie said at a glance from me.

When we were alone, I began to tell my mother everything, as gently as I could, watching for signs of shock. "Christmas has come and gone already, and it's January now. There was a small fire at the Hall, so you were brought here to the gamekeeper's cottage for safety, and Rosie and I are nursing you. You've been lucky, in fact, because you've missed the worst of the winter. There has been such ice and snow, and even a blizzard on New Year's. I went to Sir Gransby's ball, but that's the only time I've left you."

She nodded. "Yes, that makes sense. I knew it must have been longer than a day. It was like a dreamless darkness, thick and impenetrable, in a long dark tunnel where even I didn't exist. I can't describe it any better. No wonder I feel so weak. It must have been a very severe illness."

I didn't want to tell her yet about the poisonous liquid someone had been giving her, or about the "accidents" that had happened to me, though I would have to soon. Instead, I told her, "You had a mysterious illness. All the doctors have been scratching their heads."

She smiled again. "Well, you can tell them I'll be back on my feet in no time, especially now that at last we have some way of tracing your father. But of course! You will have been doing that anyway. What news do you have, darling Vicky? I wish I had been able to share your excitement with you. Oh . . ." She saw the expression on my face. "Bad news? He's been confirmed dead? Yet I was so sure he would be alive..."

"Mama, I don't know what you're talking about. How can we trace my father?" I asked, as gently as I could, fearful that her mind might have been damaged in some way.

She looked bewildered. "Didn't George tell you?" I shook my head, feeling a thrill of fear mixed with surging hope.

"I found Spenser's journal, right at the bottom of my last box in the attic. I had no hope that it would have survived. Indeed I was sure it would have been destroyed.

"But I began to hope when I discovered how many of my possessions had been saved. I don't know by whom—Caroline perhaps—when I had expected my father would have ordered everything removed, in his anger. But it was all there, my childhood books and trinkets, correspondence with old friends, my efforts at embroidery, my collection of dried wildflowers, and my sketches—though I was sadly lacking in talent—as well as old clothes and costume jewelery, mementos, and keepsakes. Then there it was, Spenser's journal."

She closed her eyes, still smiling, as if to savor that moment of happy discovery all over again.

"It was bound in fine leather and as good as new. It was a record, in his own hand, of his great journey of exploration, continuing with his travels in Europe and his arrival here. There were funny drawings in the margins, maps. Oh, it was like hearing his voice speaking to me all over again. I, well, I didn't tell you immediately because I wanted to keep it to myself for a little while. I didn't want anyone else to know what I had found, because I didn't want to hear those insults all over again. But I was so looking forward to giving it to you, a treasure from your father so that you could begin to get to know him a little. The day you went to Whitby I was on the final pages and intended to give it to you that evening, as a present. And then . . .

"And then, on the very last page, I saw he'd written in a hurried scrawl and at an angle, and not in his usual color of ink. It was as if he was using the book as a notepad. There was the name of a boat, *Island Queen*, and a time. I puzzled over this for some while, then finally remembered that this ship sailed regularly from these parts to the Carribbean."

I avidly drank in everything she told me, even though she had to pause periodically to get her breath. Rosie now returned and, even though I was longing to hear the rest, I felt my mother should eat and drink first. As she did, I told Rosie what I'd learned so far, and she made gratifying exclamations and asked more questions, finally saying, "Where's your father's book now?"

"I don't know. I didn't find it in the attic.

Mama, did you hide it?"

She'd finished her light meal, and settled back on the pillows again, her face pale in the lamplight, but at last there was some healthy color in her cheeks.

Now she frowned. "I don't remember. Let me see. Ah, yes. Then George came to find me. He said he urgently wanted to discuss your future, but I showed him what I'd found first, and after some thought, he said he thought he remembered that ship and it carried Lansdowne cargo to the West Indies. Now we can trace back the records for the ship. There was also an agent we dealt with there. Great-uncle Samuel will remember his name."

I put aside for now the question why George had not revealed this conversation to me, and pointed out, "But if my father's still alive, why didn't he write to anyone?"

"He could be suffering from amnesia. I've read about it. George thought it a strong possibility." She frowned again. "He didn't tell you?"

"No, and I've been through the attic myself, but I didn't see a journal like you describe. Though the second time I went up, it did look as though the room had been searched, only, of course, that could have been someone fetching something of their own."

"Mmm. It must've slipped George's mind." Her attention turned elsewhere. "I think he wants to marry you."

"He did ask me, but I've rejected him. I didn't

love him." I said bluntly.

She looked sad. "How you've grown up, and I've missed it because of my . . . What did you call it, mysterious illness? I do wonder what caused it."

"You haven't told her?" Rosie asked. "I reckon you should, especially now Mr. Thornley's told you what was in that bottle. Mrs. Hunter'll get better faster if she knows what did it."

I hesitated. How many shocks could she bear? Gently, I told her the truth, and when I'd finished, she lay back on her pillows, her eyes closed.

At last she spoke, "Is it possible for someone to hate so much?"

"No, Mama. We think my inheritance is the cause of it all. Someone intends that the Hall shall never be mine. With you ill, they probably expected me to give up and sell."

"We? And did you change your mind?"

"Jasper and me. And, no, not yet. But now, finish telling us exactly what happened on the day you fell ill. How long did George stay?"

"About twenty minutes, and then I began to pack up, putting on one side those items I intended to keep. I missed lunch, and so Mrs. Ackroyd brought me a cup of tea. After I drank it, I got pins and needles in my legs. I tried to stand up and that's all I remember."

"Your first dose must have been in that cup of

A Bitter Legacy

tea. Mrs. Ackroyd could have put it in, but was it her own idea or was she following someone else's instructions?"

"You and Jasper really think—"

"I didn't agree with him for a long time, but now I think that even setting fire to the Hall—yes, that was deliberate, too." I watched her face for signs of fatigue, but if anything she seemed to grow stronger.

"But what purpose would arson serve?"

"To give me more money problems, to scare me, I think. I should question Mrs. Ackroyd."

"No, Vicky, I forbid it. If you're right, you'd be placing yourself in great danger."

I bit my lip, then smiled. It was a long time since someone had told me what I could or could not do that I felt I should obey. It was both smothering and heart-warming. "That's exactly what Jasper would say."

"You've mentioned Jasper quite a few times," she observed shrewdly. "Do I take it you no longer suspect him of murdering my brother—" She broke off and looked at me in horror. "Could it have started so long ago?" she whispered. "And if not Jasper, then who was it? And whoever it was felt the Hall was within their grasp until Father's will this—no, last year. Then the lies spread about Spenser were all to remove each contender. Father's use of his will, promising here, threatening there, kept each of them alive till the new threat appeared. Us. But

Adele was a child at the time, only Samuel was . . ."

We gripped each other's hands, trembling with shock and indignation. "Then perhaps Jasper . . ." my mother began.

"No. You were right and I was wrong about him. He may only be helping us for reasons of his own, pretending to sympathize with us, and at the moment it's more to his advantage to aid us. All the same I'm tending to believe him," I assured her.

"I'm glad, because I always trusted and liked him. And I'm glad you rejected George's offer of marriage, even though it probably means being unable to keep the Hall. It shows you still have a heart, you're still my daughter. For a while I was afraid you were changing, that that place had cast its spell over you, but not so."

"I know. I would allow nothing to stand in my way. That was the Lansdowne in me. But if you could throw off your heritage for what was right, so could I."

Soon after she went to sleep again, worn out at last by everything she'd learned. I knew we'd go over it all again, in much greater detail. As she slept, so did Rosie, and I thought long about what my mother had said, drawing all the threads so neatly together, that all the pain, the misery, the death, was the result of one twisted mind, planning and plotting over the years. I was filled with revulsion at such cold-

A Bitter Legacy

blooded behavior. Had my grandfather known or guessed, and was that why he'd given me the Hall, in order to lure the evildoer out into the open once and for all?

I resented being staked out like a piece of helpless bait. Yet I also had a sneaking regard for my grandfather's foresight, and, of course, for choosing *me* as his instrument.

I came to a decision. I wrote yet another letter to Jasper, telling him first of my mother's recovery and also her discovery about my father, thanking him again for the information he'd sent.

I then wrote: "I've decided to sell the Hall, for a reasonable price. Mr. Pontefract assures me I can do this now, even though my twenty-first birthday is not till the end of March. I would like you, too, to be there, and will let you know the time and date of the announcement, once I have examined all the bids. The Hall was never meant for me, I can see that now.

"I'm going away after that, with my mother. She's determined to find my father, and I feel I should go with her."

I knew he'd understand that I was telling him that there could be nothing between us in the future. I would give the letter to Rosie when she woke up. She would find a way to get it to Ned.

The next day I put on my mantle and walked

that dreaded half-mile to the Hall. As I drew closer, I could see where the brickwork needed restoration, and the woodwork needed protection. I could also see where the new architecture had been added and did not blend with the old. It looked ugly to me now. I walked up the front steps as if I was entering a gaol rather than my ancestral home.

John, the footman, let me in, and I went straight to the library where Great-uncle Samuel, sure enough, was dozing off in an easy chair. On the great mahogany desk lay heaps of papers, and there were all the trappings of an office—the inkwells, the pens, the paper knife, and paperweights, even a small pair of weighing scales to judge the postage costs. But there was an air of neglect. No work had been done here for some time. But what did I care? Not a fig, any longer.

"Where's George?" I demanded. "He has something of mine—of my mother's."

"Eh? What?" He started awake, and the newspaper that had rested across his chest when he fell asleep, rustled to the floor. "George? Utter nonsense. What've you got he'd want?"

"My father's journal. I was tidying my mother's papers and, well, anyway, I saw a reference to it. She found it with her belongings in the attic. Or perhaps you have it now."

"Never heard of it." All the same, he got clumsily to his feet. "Can't you leave an old man in peace? Barging in here, accusations of theft. Shame on you. No relative of mine."

"That makes me very happy," I countered, moving toward the desk. "So you deny you've seen my father's journal?"

Swiftly, despite his arthritis, he intercepted me before I could read any papers, lowering his head at me like a stag at bay.

"Don't believe he ever wrote one. Don't believe he traveled further than across the North Atlantic. Braggart and a liar, Spenser Hunter, everyone knew."

I turned on my heel and marched out of the room, not sure that I could control my anger. I went in search of George, but he was away from the Hall. I climbed the turning staircase to Tommy's room and was surprised by a rare scene there. Adele was kneeling on the floor, regardless of her dress, tossing a ball to Tommy who, laughing, would catch it and toss it back. Once, when it went wide, Maire picked it up, and Adele swiped it from her crossly, saying, "You're not playing," but the black moment was soon gone. Maire raised her eyes to the ceiling and, in doing so, caught sight of me. She started to rise from her chair, and I went in.

"Oh, it's you," Adele said, sitting back on a low stool. "I thought you were living in a servant's cottage now." Implying, naturally, that that was where I belonged. I ignored the expected dig.

"Until—if my mother recovers, yes. Hello, Tommy!" He'd run to me and clasped my knees, looking up for a kiss, which I gladly gave. We talked for a few moments, then I asked Adele, "I'm looking for my father's missing journal. My mother thinks that it may hold a clue to his whereabouts. Have you seen it? It's beautifully bound in maroon Morroccan leather, with gold lettering."

"I'd rather you didn't spend too long in here. Tommy's come to no harm as yet, but until we know what's wrong with your mother, I don't want to risk it. Tommy, come here and leave your Aunt Victoria alone!"

Reluctantly, he went to her and leaned on her lap.

"Journal did you say? I've never heard of one, let alone seen such a book. Anyway, I thought your father was dead."

"My mother always believed he was alive."

"Oh, well, if she couldn't accept the inevitable, that's her own fault." Adele's tone was bored.

"Such sympathy! Still, that's what I've come to expect from you. If you see George, tell him I'm looking for it, will you? Good-bye, Maire. Give Tommy a kiss from me."

"Sure an' I'll be glad to, and if I see the pretty book I'll be sure to let you know—"

A Bitter Legacy

"Maire, stop prattling and fetch Tommy's tea. It's five minutes late already."

Maire gave me her ravishing smile, no longer going brick-red at Adele's taunts, and I left them.

I had little hope of the journal turning up now. At first I'd thought that George must have taken it, and everything pointed to him. But Great-uncle Samuel had just now revealed that he knew the contents of the journal, otherwise why refer to my father's explorations. Adele, of course, was the great dissembler, distracting me with her remarks about Tommy, and so I could not yet rule her out. I did not see Sophie, though I looked for her. She would hear that I'd visited, and if she knew the whereabouts of the book, she would surely bring it to me. Unless, of course, it was she who was the guilty party.

It seemed that I was no nearer to uncovering the face of my enemy. I would have to be extra vigilant from now on.

January became February, and still we were held in the grip of winter. Snow flurries arrived on icy winds, the sky was leaden and gray, and the trees showed no sign of life.

Now that I'd made the decision to leave the waiting became increasingly tiresome. I wanted to be free of the place and the Lansdownes, but wait was all I could do. Then Jasper paid an unexpected visit, his horse picking its way carefully over the thin layer of snow that covered the ground. He'd chosen a day when the sun had at last broken through, and the sky was the bright blue of speedwells, the air clear if cold.

My heart flipped at the sight of him as he entered the cottage, even though he had been constantly in my thoughts. Had I really believed he would stay away? Or was it wrong to hope again, that somehow we could be together? He wore a jacket and trousers of deepest charcoal-gray with a white silk shirt, which emphasized his glossy black hair. He carried some primroses.

"I know a sheltered spot where these grow. When they're out, you know winter's nearly over. It's a pity you're leaving and won't be able to see the moors in summer. They can be the most beautiful place on earth," he said, handing the flowers to me.

"Or the most hostile and forbidding," I reminded him, then sniffed the sweet, delicate scent of an English spring from the orange centers of the golden yellow petals.

We stood awkwardly together for a moment. I had been in his arms, his lips on mine, and claimed as his own. My body and heart had responded to him, and to talk of anything else seemed pointless. And yet what could we say to each other? I had not taken the hand he held out. As far as he knew, I still suspected him,

A Bitter Legacy

and I'd told him I was leaving Yorkshire with my mother. For his part, he still stubbornly refused to share his innermost thoughts and dreams. I saw suddenly that the gulf between us was unbridgeable, and I didn't know if I could bear it.

"I haven't been able to trace who bought that rare drug yet. I am visiting each apothecary myself, and now that I've employed Ned, he's helping me," Jasper said, his voice low.

"Is it expensive?" I asked. "Not only do you have the cost of paying Ned, but also conducting my search—our search. Although it's pointless of me to ask. Our money is all gone, every penny of our savings, and Grandfather never even left my mother a cent. We've been living on *their* charity, and now Mr. Pontefract has somehow managed to advance us a few pounds. But when I've disposed of the Hall, I'll be glad to pay you. I don't like being in anyone's debt."

"Spoken like a true daughter of North America," Jasper said, struggling with some emotion I could not identify. "But I don't require payment. This is for me as much as for you, remember."

"I would remember that better if you would explain yourself."

"What better purpose could I have than to clear my name and finally discover who was responsible for Will's death?"

"True, except that I know you have another,

hidden goal, which you refuse to tell me."

I held my breath and waited, but he did not reply. He moved to the parlor window and looked out. My heart filled with pain.

"That's only your opinion," he said, his back to me, blocking out the light. "But I do have some important information for you. The fire at Lansdowne Hall was started by an outsider. It was Jem's brother."

"Oh, no!" I gasped. "What will happen to him? How was he found out?"

Jasper shook his head. "Someone informed on him, someone with an old score to settle, we think. Fortunately Jem's brother has no family. Deportation is a possible punishment, preferable in my view to imprisonment here. And though I can't condone the man's act, he had his reasons."

I shuddered. "If only he had waited. I've been talking to George about the conditions, and I'm sure they will improve. I—"

He swung round, his face grim. "Too late. Jem's littlest one died two weeks ago. It just didn't have the strength to survive the winter. The man was desperate."

My eyes filled with tears. "A child is dead? Oh, Jasper, is there anything I can do? I know he was wrong to blame my family, and to start the fire, but not too much damage has been done."

"No? When you could have died yourself?

A Bitter Legacy

But don't fret, I shall speak up for him at the trial. Now, I have one further point to make. I was very worried when I read your letter. One last time I ask you to drop the idea and sell to me now. Otherwise, you're still in danger, you know."

I swallowed, my throat raw from holding back my emotion, and when I spoke my voice was husky. "I have made my decision, and my mother agrees with it. There's no more to be said. Now, let me take you upstairs to Mama. You will be delighted by the change in her."

Quickly, I led the way, effectively silencing Jasper, and avoided being alone with him. I could no longer explain why I would not sell to him. My feelings were quite irrational on this point. It was as if I'd backed myself into a corner, and nothing and no one could make me budge—not even him.

After that day I alternated between fretting impatience for the date I had set when I would reveal the fate of the Hall, and deep despair that the man I loved was lost to me. The only brightness was my mother's speedy recovery. While we kept her progress secret, she exercised by walking about her room, and within weeks she looked just like her former self, though there were times when she deeply regretted those months lost from her life.

"I daresay in some ways it has been a good

thing. You've had to shoulder such responsibility, and make decisions without me. You're quite grown up now. But I wish you could have had a little longer before having to face the world alone. And are you sure you want to sell the Hall, Vicky? You're not doing it only to please me, are you?"

I looked out of the window to where I could just catch a glimpse of the Hall through the palest rime of green shoots, yellow catkins, and new leaves on the trees. Nothing stirred inside me. My heart was dead.

"I told myself that I wanted it for *your* sake, stubbornly ignoring the fact that your feelings for the Hall had changed long ago. But it was for my sake, really. I wanted to play the grand lady and have everyone curtsy to me, for a change." I tried a playful smile. "And why not? That would still be fun. However, there is too much unhappiness here, and the past will always cast its ugly pall over us. Grandfather has won after all."

"I've been thinking about Father's will over and over again, and I know you'll say I'm only trying to see the best in him, and avoiding the harsh truth. But I really do believe that bequeathing the Hall to you was in part a gesture of reconciliation toward me. He could never ask for my forgiveness, because he could never admit he was wrong. All the same, I'm still curious as to why he kept the income from you."

A Bitter Legacy

"Mama, I'm going to surprise you yet again. I agree with you, in part. I don't hate Grandfather any longer. And I believe the terms of his will were either to make me reveal who has committed the evil here or to use me as a lure. The former I hope."

I did not reveal to my mother that that was exactly the way in which I planned to use her, though without endangering her, of course. Once the family and senior servants were assembled in the library, I would arrange for Rosie to bring her in. Surely then the guilty person would come forward. It was inconceivable to me that he or she would not. That person, I was sure, would be guilty of everything else, too.

At last the day arrived. I dressed in a skirt Rosie and I had made from one of the new paper patterns in a magazine. A subdued purplish brown tartan with a hint of green, it brought out the highlights in my chestnut hair. I wore a white high-necked blouse and fitted jacket with flaring peplum to which I pinned the silver-and-pearl christening brooch my mother had given me. She also had a new navy-blue gown, trimmed with plum, that accentuated the clear blue of her eyes. Rosie's new outfit was a striking emerald-green and she spent a long time fussing over my hair.

"You're very talented you know, Rosie. You could become a top ladies' maid anywhere," my mother said.

"Depends on our Ned," Rosie pointed out. "Where he lands a new job. Would you like me to do your hair, too?"

"Do let her, Mama. I'll go on ahead with Ned to make sure all is well, and you can come with Rosie and Mr. Barnes."

The tension had communicated itself even to my usually calm mother. "Yes, why not?" she agreed, her cheeks flushed with excitement, and I went down to the kitchen to fetch Ned, who was gossipping with Mrs. Barnes while he waited.

We stepped out into the first day of spring. The air was soft on my cheek, the sky was a gentle blue, and there were signs of new life everywhere. When I pointed this out to Ned, he said, in his dour Yorkshire way, "Aye, but we'll likely get more snow and ice, always do. Sometimes there's snow even in May. But the summer, ah, that's when you'll miss the best of it, when the bees are in the gorse and the breeze is mild as a lamb's breath."

I was reminded sharply of my last conversation with Jasper and kept silent the rest of the way.

Everyone except Jasper was assembled in the library. Mr. Pontefract, resplendent in black with a gold watch chain, was already positioned behind the library desk where he'd laid his papers amongst the clutter that had accumulated there and had still not been dealt with.

A Bitter Legacy

Adele, in strident peacock-blue, looked pale and tense. She said curtly, "So you've seen sense at last, though why we have to go through this charade, I don't know. I hope you'll be accepting Redvers' offer."

"No, no. Of course she'll be selling our home to George, won't you, Vicky dear?" I was shocked by the change in Sophie over the last month. She looked unwell and her hair was pulled back unbecomingly. She slumped in her chair as if too tired to move.

"Shut up! I don't care." But Adele's tensely tapping fingers betrayed that she did.

"Course she's selling to George, about time, too. Dowry big enough to get a husband to control her. Best thing," Great-uncle Samuel grunted, and we all looked at George.

Only George looked as if he really didn't care, standing by the French windows looking out, whistling under his breath, ignoring us.

Mrs. Ackroyd and Mr. Gandy entered and took up positions by the wall.

"May we start now?" Adele demanded.

"We're waiting for the others, I believe?" Mr. Pontefract looked at me, and I nodded, then stood up, gaining everyone's attention, and went to stand by the great desk.

"I've instructed Mr. Pontefract to act as official witness, too, so while we wait I want you to listen to what I have to say. It's my belief that my father is still alive. I know he went to South America, not Boston, on a ship carrying

Lansdowne cargo for the West Indies. It's my opinion, too, that he was forced to take this action by someone in this room who spread lies about him."

I now had George's attention. He watched me with a half-smile on his face, still whistling, only soundlessly. Adele tutted and muttered under her breath, while it was left to Great-uncle Samuel to bluster, "How should we know?"

I grimaced in disgust. "One of you knew that his pride wouldn't allow him to tolerate the lies and rumors about him and he'd want to clear his name. Was it you, Uncle Samuel, you and Grandfather who pushed him to the edge? Or did you have something to do with it, George? Adele and Sophie were surely too young, I know."

"What're these ridiculous questions about?" George spoke up at last. "Your father's been dead for years. Everyone knows that."

"Where's the journal, George? The one you stole from my mother when she became ill."

"I don't know what you're talking about. You're making this all up in some bid to hurt us. I can understand how difficult it must be for you to swallow your pride and hand the Hall over but, dammit, Vicky, there's no need for hysterics."

He was still smiling and, as always, so convincing.

A Bitter Legacy

"We—we have an agent in the West Indies, don't we? Someone who can verify . . ." I looked to the door, willing my mother to appear now. So far, I had achieved nothing. "Great-uncle Samuel, surely you have reports in those records you refuse to show me?"

"I—I . . . You're above yourself, my girl," he stuttered, and that gave me strength to continue.

"Not me. Someone else in this room, who has attempted to kill me several times, and my mother, too. Because that was the plan—to increase the dosage of a deadly poison and kill her."

Great-uncle Samuel went purple, and Adele protested, her hands plucking at the air, "What warped accusations!"

With relief, I saw the door open and Rosie appear. "Here's my mother now. She'll want answers, too."

I enjoyed the gasps of shock as the two women entered. I only felt sorry for Mr. Pontefract, now quite bewildered and overcome at the sight of her.

Everyone was talking at once, but then another figure appeared in the doorway and, as he had done once before, Jasper silenced them. "I can take it from here, Victoria. I know who bought the drug that poisoned your mother. I also have a signed deposition from Mr. Brown, the mines manager, stating that Samuel and George have been systematically cooking the books and letting the mines rot, regardless of other people's lives. Furthermore . . ." He had to raise his voice to be heard over the babble of outraged voices, though I noticed that Great-uncle Samuel had at last given way, subsiding like a collapsed balloon. George, though, looked as insouciant as ever.

"Furthermore, it was George Lansdowne who not only tried to kill your mother, and arranged the 'accidents' to frighten you, Vicky, but it was he who left William to die that day, not me!"

Chapter Ten

I expected George to explode into action, to offer explanations, refutations. To my surprise, he stood quietly, smiling. Then I saw his calculating eyes. He always thought before he spoke. But was that so that he could make up falsehoods? Could Jasper's accusation be true, or was he bluffing?

"Well, George, what's your answer?" Jasper prodded. "You can't deny you bought that drug. I have witnesses. You wanted to stop Mrs. Hunter from looking for her husband, didn't you, when she told you what she had discovered in her husband's journal—which you've now probably destroyed."

George shrugged. "I don't know what drug you're talking about. Mr. Pontefract, will you please bring some order to these proceedings or I for one shall walk out."

"I've brought Ned with me and one or two other strong men," Jasper said grimly. "You'll not escape this time."

"I think I can see the drift of things," Mr. Pontefract said unhappily. "But before we continue, a chair for Mrs. Hunter."

I had not noticed, so intent was I on George and Jasper, that my mother had gone white and was clinging to the desk for support. Rosie quickly fetched her a chair, and she sank into it, then my attention reverted to George and Jasper, once more facing each other, ready for battle.

"I was referring to a toxic vegetable extract from the tropics which you bought from an apothecary three months ago. I have the receipt here, signed by you."

"Ah, that. Yes, I bought it for using on pests and vermin on the grounds. They've been ruining the shooting. It was misplaced, now I can see it was stolen. Someone else must've been giving it to Vicky's mother. And I must say, I resent these accusations. Poking around in other people's private lives, too. Just the sort of thing I'd expect someone like you to get up to," George said bitingly.

Jasper grinned, an awesome sight. "You mean I'm not a gentleman like you? I'm glad to hear it. However, if you won't admit to harming

Alexandra, you can't wriggle out of your shameful behavior at the mines."

George tutted and waved his hand, turning his head away, as if to say the mines and their miners were unimportant. It was at that moment that I knew with utter certainty that Jasper had been right all along. George was uncaring, neglectful, possibly even corrupt in his administration of our family's source of wealth. Why then had Grandfather left them to him? Had he been party to the crime, too? Yet I'd not heard a word spoken against him by the miners.

"You and Samuel have over the years consistently been pocketing more than your share of the profits from the mines, and then falsifying the accounts. That's why you couldn't let Victoria read any of the records, in case she spotted that money was short for the upkeep of the house."

Everyone in the library was silent, looking to George for his answer. Lazily, he moved to the fireplace and leaned against the mantelshelf. "I'd laugh if that weren't such a serious accusation. How much did you pay Brown to bribe him to say that? And how did we manage this alleged cheating under Uncle Albert's nose?"

"Easy to conceal at a low level. A bit here, a bit there. Once Albert had his stroke, you increased the scale of your activities. He was too ill to prove or to put a stop to it, but he knew something was wrong. Then you moved your business away from Mr. Pontefract to a questionable solicitor in York, so that Mr. Pontefract would be blinkered, too. As for Brown, no money was necessary. He didn't require bribing, though that's what he's used to from you."

Still no one else spoke, while George looked down at his boots, then flung up his head in an angrily dramatic way, and strode into the center of the room. "I'm tired of this charade. It's about time you were ejected from this house once and for all!"

"You mean you want to fight again?" Jasper began to strip off his jacket. "Only this time you won't be able to cheat. Too many onlookers. You've always been first class at concealing your evil."

My heart filled with dread. George had beaten Jasper once, and perhaps it was true that he had cheated, and perhaps he would do it again. I could not bear the idea of Jasper being hurt, and I made a move to step forward and intercede, but I was held back by Ned.

As the two men traded insults, general uproar broke out, with Adele moaning and wringing her hands and saying, "Oh the scandal, the shame, what will Redvers say?" Great-uncle Samuel buried his head in his hands, and Sophie tried to persuade George to stop, but instead he gave her his coat to hold. There was general dismay on the rest of the company's faces.

A Bitter Legacy

Ned said to me in an undertone, "If you care for him, leave him to it."

"But George might hurt him."

"Never! Master Jasper's all sinew and muscle. Only trouble is, he hasn't the killer instinct. That's where I could help him out." There was a disturbing gleam in his eye. "Oh, yes, there's plenty I could tell about your pretty cousin and his cruelties, things I've not even told Rosie."

"Why didn't you speak up or find work elsewhere?"

"Who'd take my word, a servant, against his? As for work elsewhere, I couldn't abandon the horses to him, could I? Then Rosie came."

Before I could answer, there was a sudden loud banging, and silence ensued.

"Enough, gentlemen, please. There will be no fighting here," Mr. Pontefract ordered. "Else the proceedings are null and void." He glared in particular at Jasper.

At last, reluctantly, Jasper accepted his ruling with a curt nod.

Once again I was filled with dread, but this time it was that George would escape punishment. But even as I thought it, Jasper spoke, "Tell us, George, about Victoria's father and how you spread the rumors that made him leave. How did you trick him onto the Lansdowne's ship, though? That was the clever move. And after that, did you have him killed, or is he alive and imprisoned somewhere, in case he might be useful to you one day? Did you ever stop to think what suffering you were causing? No, I don't believe you did."

George rubbed his chin, breathing heavily, and I could tell his mind was working furiously.

But then Great-uncle Samuel, his head still held in his hands, groaned, and said, "Yes, he's alive!" as if giving up a great burden. "And God forgive us for what we've done."

George's composure immediately deserted him. Angrily, he turned on the old man, who shrank back in his chair, fending off a blow that never came. George glared icily at him, his expression utterly changed. Gone was the merry affectionate pose. In its place was something quite the opposite. "So Hunter's alive. What would have been the point of telling Victoria or her mother? The man's ill with a fever, has no memory of what's happened, and might not survive. Why raise their hopes only to dash them again?" George asked callously.

I moved closer to my mother, and we clasped hands in horror. It was too much to contemplate. My father was still alive, but in what dreadful condition? My mother closed her eyes, and I saw a tear roll down her cheek.

Now that George was cornered and talking, Jasper pressed into the attack again. "Mrs. Ackroyd swears that you paid her well to give that drug to Vicky's mother. What about that?"

A Bitter Legacy

Jasper asked quietly. I looked at Mrs. Ackroyd, but her face was as stony as ever.

"She—she's lying to save her own skin," George stuttered, showing the pressure he was under for the first time. "Thornley, this is a waste of—"

"Then let's talk about William's death. When we went to see Caroline in the asylum, her first thought was of his death, and she referred to 'the other one.' She can only have meant the other young man of the house. You, George."

George shook his head. "Those are your hard facts? I purchased a drug, but if I could, then so could others. And a madwoman thinks of murder. Is that so strange?"

"He's right, Thornley," Mr. Pontefract said reluctantly. "He can twist everything you've said so far and throw it right back at you. Speculation's not enough."

I had to speak up. "My mother remembers clearly what my father wrote in his journal—the name of the ship and the time of sailing."

Mr. Pontefract shook his head. "But where is the journal as evidence?"

I frowned, desperately cudgeling my brains, but then Jasper sprang another blow. "Then how about this. Ned says that on the night of the blizzard you deliberately tampered with that carriage door, so Vicky would fall out, and then knocked him out, so that you could drive the carriage."

Sophie looked on wide-eyed with fear, but George began to laugh quietly, confident again. "Is that it? Ned holds a grudge against me because I lashed out at him once or twice in a temper, and now I've turned him out without a reference."

"What about the other two attempts on my life—being left to drown and the chandelier falling on me?" I asked. How could I make sure that George would not get away with his crimes and be allowed to go free? Jasper, however, did not look worried, which reassured me.

"Then read this," Jasper said, and the deceptive mildness of his voice made me look at him sharply as he handed a paper to George. "That's the official judgement that the contract you forced the miners to sign was illegal. Your manager, Brown, rather than go to gaol as party to that fraud, has told us that for years you and your Uncle Samuel have deliberately allowed the Lansdowne businesses to decay till the safety standards were so low that there are fifty percent more accidents there than elsewhere. You see, Brown responded to reasoning, especially when I pointed out that when this news became general knowledge, all those people who had suffered injury or the loss of a loved one would come for him first."

"You!" Adele jumped up, pointing a finger at George. "It's your fault that Mr. Roberts was killed. He was my father's choice, not mine,

A Bitter Legacy

but he was *my* husband and Tommy's father. But for you, he would be alive."

"Adele, an accident is an accident," George said shortly. "Railways are notorious for them."

"Not if they're properly maintained!" She turned to Jasper. "I can help you. The night Victoria was nearly crushed by that chandelier, I saw George coming from the hall carrying tools. Later, I saw him take and conceal the note she had in her hand, asking her to come to the medieval hall. I didn't say anything at the time because she wasn't badly hurt, and it was in my best interests if Victoria didn't inherit. I thought he only wanted to frighten her."

"Is it true, George? Did you really do all that? How clever you are, cleverer than all of us." Sophie's eyes were moist with sickening adulation. "But you should have known you couldn't disturb the White Lady's home. She's been working against you ever since. You must have seen—"

"Shut up!" George's tone was vicious, but it didn't alter her adoring expression. Then he recovered his control, saying, "Of course Adele is making all that up. She never fell out of love with you, Thornley. You didn't know that, did you? She was just a little girl following you and Will about, but she's always had a soft spot for you and now she's trying to please you again."

Judging by the stunned expression on his face, Jasper had never known. While Adele rounded furiously on George, I met Jasper's eyes, and this time it was me who steadied him.

Then suddenly Great-uncle Samuel silenced us all. "Why don't you tell them everything and have done with it, George? Thornley won't rest till he's hounded out the truth, and, who knows, he has the right of it. I told you we'd be discovered sooner or later. I told you—"

"Be quiet!" George once again turned on the old man, but it was too late. Mr. Pontefract was writing down Samuel's words, and George looked isolated as more words fell out of the old man's mouth, each one condemning George and himself further and confirming Jasper's every accusation.

At last George interrupted, as if he could no longer bear his uncle's dull delivery, and wanted to show off his own cleverness at the vile deeds he'd performed in secret over the years.

"Albert never cared for me, like he never cared for my father, his brother, Robert," he began. "And I knew that he'd never give me anything, especially when my father and mother died in the cholera epidemic that summer they insisted on going to London. Everyone talked about William, and then Jasper, never me. I wanted to do things to make him notice me, but he refused to. I knew he hated Spenser Hunter because he wanted his daughter to marry someone else, so I spread the lies about him, hid the message he

A Bitter Legacy

left behind, tore up his letters from the West Indies till he became ill.

"I thought Albert would be pleased, but when Alexandra ran away to America and I told him what I'd done, he beat me instead of thanking me. He told me to be like William, and William was given a new horse for his birthday. So I told him Spenser was dead, and he had to live with that guilty secret for the rest of his life. He never could bring himself to tell anyone."

George paused, not looking at any of us, his face almost emotionless, but I could detect still that tinge of pride in his work. "I followed William and Jasper that day, hoping William would let me ride his new horse. When they separated to race back to the Hall, I went after William. He was thrown. A curlew flew up from its nest in the grass and made the horse rear in fright. The most experienced of horsemen would have been unseated. He lay on the ground, heavily winded, perhaps slightly stunned. His eyes were closed when I went over to take a look at him.

"So I picked up a stone. Something made me do it. I didn't plan it that way. But the opportunity was too good to miss. I needed to destroy him so that I could live. He opened his eyes just before I hit him, and I think he said, 'Why?' I had to hit him twice to finish him off."

Adele made a loud sound of disgust and turned her back on him, while I tightly gripped my mother's hand. I could see she was in deep shock, and I hoped for once she would not find it in her heart to forgive someone their trespasses against her. Only Sophie still regarded George with affection, and I knew that she had already forgiven him. I stole a glance at Jasper. There was a kind of relief on his face. At last he knew how his friend had died.

"I thought that surely then Albert would turn to me, but, no, he married again. Your Aunt Leonie, Jasper, and they had Adele. He doted on them both, was madly, possessively, in love with his new wife. Now there was someone else to stand between me and what I considered ought to be mine, the power and money of the Lansdownes. I knew I was the only one who'd be able to handle and use them. But I also knew I'd have to find a different route to get them, so I worked hard at becoming indispensible in running our businesses. Albert was mean and hardly gave Samuel and me any money, so together we devised our schemes."

He actually laughed then. "For years we lived two lives, with all the pleasures and excitements you only dream of. Isn't that right, Samuel?" He prodded his accomplice, who nodded obediently, and I saw how it had been between the two of them. Samuel, weak and malleable and without a family of his own, devoted to his own comforts, had been reeled in then shaped by George to his

A Bitter Legacy

own ends until he was in too deep to escape. Finally bribed and befuddled on port wine and brandy.

"What did you do to Caroline?" my mother demanded.

He waved a hand airily. "I didn't have to do anything. She was already nervous. I just played a few tricks on her memory so that she couldn't trust herself anymore, and that was that. You know, hiding things then replacing them, making things creak in the night. You know how fanciful she was.

"It was almost too easy and simple to drop hints to Albert that she'd be better off out of his sight. After William's death she was a reproach to him. After long years in that place, she has no idea whether she's mad or not, so I go along every now and then to confuse her a little more, and remind her it was Thornley she saw with blood on his coat returning to the Hall, not me. I had told her it was rabbit's blood on my coat when I returned from killing William, but I could tell she didn't believe me when they brought William's body home.

"You know, I thought the same tricks would work on Vicky, but she was a more worthy opponent." He actually looked at me with admiration! My skin crawled with loathing. How nearly he'd ensnared me! How could I have enjoyed the touch of his hands, his lips! I felt deeply ashamed.

"But whatever I did made no difference. I bought a foreign bird from a traveling circus, remembering how William's horse was startled, and it worked until she was saved by Thornley. Then I set the trap in the medieval hall. I swear she was standing right underneath the chandelier, but somehow she escaped. You should never have survived, Vicky. And to live through that blizzard, what stamina!

"Finally, I arranged to have her locked in the attic, intending to come upstairs later and arrange another accident. But the fire was started, and I thought for once things were going my way—until you interfered. I've you to thank for that, Thornley!"

Suddenly he swung a powerful blow at Jasper, who quickly deflected it, then drove his own fist against George's chin, sending him flying into a chair. It broke into splinters, depositing him on the floor. He glared at Jasper in fury, wiping blood from his lip. There was a glint of great satisfaction on Jasper's face.

Sophie flew to George's side, cradling his head in her hands, but he pushed her away roughly. "If you hadn't interfered and told Thornley Victoria was in the attic, she'd've suffocated."

"But, George, I didn't know." Sophie was in tears.

"Ah, well, and perhaps I was pleased that she lived. I always hoped there might be another chance for me. What say you, Vicky? You were fond of me at one time, and I think I could have put up with the yoke of marriage for you, for a while at least until the pleasure grew stale and we looked elsewhere. Now you'll never know what you missed. We could have sold everything, traveled the world together." Was he mocking me now?

"Sell everything? Sell the Hall? Travel?" Sophie cried. "But what about me?"

"Well, I wouldn't've taken you with me, that's for sure," he said callously. "Let's be truthful for once. You wouldn't have been much use to me once I was married and had everything I ever wanted at last."

In a blur of movement Sophie leapt away from him, letting his head fall to the floor, and before anyone could move she was standing over him again. She had snatched the letter opener from the desk, and thrust it into him, sobbing with terrible abandon the whole time. Then she flung herself on top of him, kissing him and calling his name. It wasn't till Jasper prised her away from her brother that we saw the blood and knew he was dead, killed by the one person who'd loved him the most.

I asked the driver to halt the hired carriage at the gates of Lansdowne Hall. I took one last look at the home I'd dreamed of possessing, and which now I was leaving, probably never to see again.

Even so, I'd resented even having to stay there just two more nights, so that we could organize our departure. Our luggage was piled high and tied securely. We had left nothing behind, and had added very little extra to what we'd had when we'd arrived. A few keepsakes that meant something to my mother, some books and drawings—especially those of my father—that she'd selected from her past. I had nothing, except a gift from Tommy.

My heart wrenched at the thought of him. I hadn't realized how hard it would be to leave him. I wanted to grab him and take him with me. He'd asked when we'd see each other again and I hadn't known the answer to that, but Maire had stepped in. "Ah," she'd said with her sunny smile, "Not many a one can see the future, that's for sure. But I have the second sight, and I say, you'll see each other again soon. Now, come and see what's for your tea." And she'd winked to me over his head.

But nothing else wrenched my heart. "All the ghosts are laid to rest now," I said to my mother who sat next to me. "The atmosphere of menace has gone. It's just a house, and one I never came to love after all. I am sorry. This must be doubly hard for you, a second parting."

"Not hard at all. I have too much to look forward to. And remember that you've changed, with nothing to fear any longer, rather than the house," she pointed out sensibly.

A Bitter Legacy

"Perhaps," I said. "Shall we go on now? Are you ready?"

She nodded. "Ready," she answered, and asked the driver to carry on.

I closed my eyes for a brief moment and wished the White Lady farewell. At least she should be at peace now. But would she miss Sophie, or would *her* troubled spirit not be missed?

"Mama, what will happen to Sophie?"

She sighed. "She knows what she's done and is sorry for it. I think that eventually she'll be placed in an institution like Rosebank, for her punishment. She's never really grown up, has she? When she had George to protect her, she was safe, but could she live outside of the Hall alone? I think not."

"She always made me feel uneasy. I was never quite sure what she'd do or say next. Great-uncle Samuel, on the other hand, was entirely predictable."

"I have to admit never being as fond of my Uncle Samuel as I should have been. He was always curmudgeonly and never liked children. Not that I ever dreamed he could . . . He has been falling over himself to help now, telling every scrap of information he can remember." My mother went on, "Without George, he too is a broken man."

"I know I should forgive them only I can't, nor will I ever, I think."

"We both need time to recover, Vicky dearest." Then her face was suddenly suffused with joy. "Now we can begin our hunt for Spenser. I'm sure I can nurse him back to health. I never felt he was dead, which was why I could never marry anyone else. Maybe one day you'll experience the happiness that comes from the true bond between a man and a woman. That's what I hope and pray for you."

I looked away. I already knew what she meant. My soul was bound forever to Jasper Thornley, but our paths were going to separate us. Since George's death I'd seen him several times alone, but he'd made no attempt to speak to me about anything except practical matters. Indeed, he'd treated me very gently, as if I'd been ill in some way, and was only now convalescing. Not once had he said, "See, I told you it was this way." Not once had he pointed out that George was everything he'd said, and worse.

I could not rid myself of my sense of shame at having believed George. Perhaps if Jasper had taken hold of me, kissed me as he had before, it would have wiped all trace of George's touch away. But he behaved correctly, almost formally, and the sad thought came to me that, of course, now he could. I was no longer an important adversary to be won over to his side. The war had been won, and he'd won it.

So we made our slow way down from the moor's edge into the valley and through Holmby

A Bitter Legacy

Village, over the pretty river and past the rows of stone houses, and through the woods. We admired the fresh new leaves, the hint of spring flowers, and concentrated our talk ever on the future, not on the past. Soon, we arrived in Whitby, where we'd arranged to stay in a fine new hotel above the esplanade in order to finish our business. Mr. Pontefract had arranged some money to be paid to us from the estate, and we were able to live in style and enjoy the very finest of luxuries. We were able to hire a ladies maid, too. Rosie had not come with us, as she had decided to look for employment so she could be with Ned once they married, which they planned to do very soon. I missed Rosie, but I did not feel I'd left her behind.

It was pleasant at the hotel to watch the other guests and residents, to take part in their conversations, even to spend a little time exploring the pleasant sights of the town. We also had a steady stream of visitors since the events had been reported in the newspaper and our move to Whitby was noted in the social column. People I'd met briefly at Sir Gransby's, and others who remembered my mother from twenty years ago came to see us. From all, we received good will and sympathy. And if occasionally we were followed by a sensation seeker, we ignored them.

As for our business, my mother had two pressing items. The first was sending letters, seeking out people who had recently returned from the West Indies, or who had business in that part of the world. We haunted the telegraph office, waiting for replies from America, finding what information we could about my father. There was also Aunt Caroline, and I went with my mother to visit her sometimes. As they sat together for long hours, my mother was sure that Caroline began to show some improvement, though she still reacted fearfully to any change in her routine or environment.

My mother explained to her most carefully what had actually taken place when William died, and claimed that her sister understood and accepted the truth. However, Aunt Caroline was liable to become easily confused and, while neither of us despaired that perhaps one day she could live outside an institution, we knew that she would always need regular nursing care.

I had only one pressing item to attend to. What to do with my inheritance, the Hall itself. The day I had designated as the day for arranging the future of the Hall had, of course, been taken over by other events, which was what I'd hoped. But if they hadn't, I had fully intended to announce my choice from the list of interested purchasers that Mr. Pontefract had provided me with.

Now I spent many hours wandering the town, especially haunting the site of the ruined Abbey, which rapidly became my favorite spot. I stared at the gray sea under lightening blue skies, listening to the raucous calls of seagulls, ponder-

A Bitter Legacy

ing the best course of action to take. I didn't want the Hall. The question was who should have it? I could simply leave it up to Mr. Pontefract as my agent to contact a suitable purchaser. Yet, I felt that the Hall was my responsibility and that I must decide myself who its next owner should be. I was reluctant after all to sever all ties with my heritage so completely.

Jasper had offered to buy it from me several times, though he hadn't mentioned it since that terrible day in the library. Since we'd moved to Whitby, he hadn't come to see us at all. Over two weeks had gone by and not a word. I nursed the hurt to myself. It was too raw to tell even my mother. All the same, it wasn't only pique that made me decide not to sell the Hall to him after all. I remembered everything that I'd heard, that Jasper worked for a French vineyard, that his family had been bankrupted by mine, that his father was ill. How could he possibly pay for the Hall? To buy it would surely mean plunging himself into terrible debt, and I didn't want to be a party to that. With George out of the way, now Jasper would probably not care so much about possessing it himself.

These were the reasons I gave myself, anyway, but underneath my rationalizations was an entirely unreasonable thought, one I could not consciously acknowledge.

My mother knew that I was wrestling with this problem, and tactfully left me to it. She said she would support whatever decision I made, and was delighted that I no longer wanted to live there. In the end, the solution was simple. I sent a message to Adele.

We sat in the hotel lounge, and I ordered afternoon tea. Outside, rain was lashing down, obscuring the view through the windows. Inside the volume of noise was high as Whitby society met and compared notes, and threw an occasional eye in our direction, too. Adele was as beautiful as ever, completely unruffled by the squally showers through which she'd traveled to get here. She sat stiff-backed, her hands folded in her lap, her blue eyes cool.

"Tommy is hardly aware of anything," she said in reply to my query. "And I want it to stay that way. I'll not send him to boarding school to be bullied when the other boys learn about his family, as they doubtlessly will. Rupert agrees he'll learn better with a tutor at home."

"Rupert? Is that Mr. Redvers?"

"We're unofficially engaged," she said. "We plan on an autumn wedding. I see no reason to mourn for George any longer than that. I see no reason to mourn for him at all, but one must observe the proprieties..." She paused while we were served, and I considered that that was how we differed. The proprieties were something I didn't care about at all. Then she went on, "I expect you heard that Uncle Samuel has gone, too ashamed to stay in Yorkshire. At least he left his affairs in order. He's renounced all claims on everything. I doubt we'll see him again. Once everything's settled and sold and shared between us—George left no will, as you know—you'll have the money you need to run the Hall."

She took a sip of tea, bit delicately into a crumbly Viennese pastry, and wiped her fingers on her napkin. Then she fixed me with her bright blue gaze. "But you surely know all this already."

I nodded. "Mr. Pontefract has been in regular contact with me, and I learned about the money this very morning."

"Then why did you invite me here?"

"Because I told the truth when I left two weeks ago. I'm not coming back," I said. "And because I've decided you should have Lansdowne Hall."

The color came and went in her cheeks. "I can't accept gifts of that sort. Not something for nothing. Not from you," she said, her chin high.

I knew it cost her to say that, because she'd shown how fiercely she loved the Hall, and never more so than when she fought the flames, regardless of her personal safety.

"And I have no intention of just handing it over. You've told me what I needed to know, that you'll be marrying Mr. Redvers. Get him to make me a fair offer. He can buy it as a wedding present to you." I drank some tea while she digested the twist in her fortunes. "You and I will never get along, but I know you'll care for the place. Then, from time to time, we could visit, Mama and me, to see Tommy, if you agree."

She inclined her head stiffly in agreement. "I'll take it. As you say, we cannot be friends, but I am the rightful heiress."

I let that go—for now. "Adele, is it true that you once cared for Jasper Thornley? I'll swear that he didn't know until George announced it."

"Even I suffered from puppy love. Have you been talking about me with Jasper behind my back?" she asked suspiciously.

"No, I haven't seen him. Have you?"

"Ah, you're wondering if he's showing interest in me now. Victoria, don't deny it, your emotions are always written quite vulgarly all over your face."

"Why should I care if he is trying to get you to jilt Redvers?"

Her smile was cold and calculating. "You'll know the answer soon enough. If you're too stupid not to know already, then you don't deserve to be told."

"I don't understand you, as you intended. But there's one last thing I want to tell you. There is a ghost at Lansdowne Hall. The White Lady exists, just as Sophie always said. I know. I've felt her presence."

"Not you, too. Sounds to me as if you've left the Hall just in time." But I could tell she was piqued. She didn't want me to be marked as special in any way.

"Yes, it was she who saved me from the chandelier. Remember what George said? It should have killed me. So you see, perhaps I am the right heiress after all."

"Superstitious rubbish," she countered, searching for her gloves, quite obviously peeved. If only she could have been gracious, just for once, but, no, and so I could not resist one last gibe.

"It's right for you to have the Hall, pragmatic and modern as you are. But that's not why I'm doing it."

"What do you mean? Was it your mother's idea all along?"

"No. I'm doing it for the best thing you've ever done—Tommy. You'll be keeping it in trust for him."

My twenty-first birthday dawned a delicate spring day with a breath of the promise of warmth in the air. Large puffy white clouds sailed through a blue sky, and a few early daffodils were out in the town's gardens. I opened my eyes to my mother's cheerful greeting as she poured me hot chocolate brought by the chambermaid. I couldn't resist hugging her, as I thought how nearly I might have been alone for this birthday.

There was an air of suppressed excitement about her as she returned my hug, then sat down on the edge of the bed.

"You've let me sleep in," I complained. "It's after nine already."

"A birthday treat for you," she said. "I've ordered breakfast to be taken in our room. Jane is setting it out next door now. Here's your present from me. But before you open it, remember what this day was to have meant to you. Do you have any regrets?"

"None at all," I said, allowing only a fleeting thought of Jasper to cross my mind. "May I open your present now?"

"I'm longing to see your face when you do. Oh, you have many more, a basket of goodies from Mrs. Randell, a mysterious shape from Rosie and Ned, something from Tommy and Adele, and a lovely posy of flowers from Mr. Pontefract. But I wanted you to have mine first. Is that selfish of me?"

I laughed as I pulled off the wrapping paper. "Not at all! Oh, Mama, it's beautiful!" It was a delicately carved jewelery box, richly inlaid with mother of pearl, and inside the finest jet jewelery Whitby could offer.

I hugged her once more, tears in my eyes, then shooed her from the room so that I could get dressed. I wasn't going to let the fact that there was no gift, no message from Jasper waiting for me, spoil the day. Perhaps there was anyway, and she just hadn't mentioned it.

After breakfast, after admiring the gifts and cards yet again, marveling that Adele had managed to pen a few stiff words of congratulation beside Tommy's careful letters, some back to front, I said, "I must write and thank everyone but we also have to pack, because today we're leaving. What would you like me to do first, Mama?"

"First, I would like you to read this, a telegraph I received this morning, and I've been saving it till last as perhaps the best present of all."

For one absurd moment I thought it might be from Jasper, but it was not. However, the brief kick of disappointment was soon replaced by surging joy. It was from the Pinkerton Agency in America, whom, on the promise of funds from the sale of Lansdowne Hall, my mother had employed to search for my father. The message read: "Spenser Hunter located in Jamaica and set free. Weak and ill but prospects good. Sends his respectful wishes and love to his wife and daughter." Now I knew the reason for her excitement.

"You see? Once we knew where to look, the rest was easy," she said.

"I'm so pleased," I said, once we had calmed down. "For both of us, but especially for you."

She suddenly became very serious, stood up and went to the window, looking out at the glorious spring day. "I am pleased, ecstatic even, and to have been right all these years. But I'm frightened, too. Twenty years we've been apart, and then we had such a brief time together. Oh, if only he'd told me he was going, I would have gone with him. How will it be for us, strangers now, linked only by a name and a memory of love and happiness? But I must go to him—we must. It's only right, and then we shall see. I won't hold him to me, if he doesn't want me ... and there are my feelings, too. I may not love the man he is now."

She swung round. "Remember, Vicky, don't let it happen to you. Don't let your husband slip through your fingers as I did mine. Though, of course, it was George's fault, plotting already. Only a young man, but already evil through and through. You never believed you'd hear me speak ill of anyone, but he had no redeeming features, none at all, and deserved forgiveness from no one."

Later, I completed my chores, while my mother bustled about organizing our packing, to take her mind off our future. First we would be visiting her old friends, and then we would journey to my father. I took the opportunity to slip away, to be on my own one last time and bid farewell to the county of my birth.

I climbed the steps away from the town and wandered through the ruins of the Abbey on the cliff top, looking out to sea, wondering if it

A Bitter Legacy

was true that the old bell from the tower could be heard tolling under the sea as a warning of trouble. Today there were no visitors, and I had the place to myself, and I was glad.

How long ago it seemed, when I'd stood in that little graveyard up the coast by my grandfather's grave. I no longer hated him. I felt close to him because I understood how his pride had caged him, and because I was free now of his influence. I had carried out his purpose, to expose the evildoers. Nor, oddly, did I hate George any longer. I just felt a great emptiness at the thought of him. I also felt that I was on the verge of a great new beginning in life. Why, then, did I feel my heart would break when I left this place?

I thought I heard my name, turned, and there was Jasper, standing only a few feet behind me. I drank him in, as if I was parched for the sight of him, but did not move.

"Did you speak?" I asked. "How did you know I was here?"

He shook his head, coming closer. "No, I didn't say anything. I didn't need to, did I? You knew I was here. Your mother told me I would likely find you here."

I nodded. "I love it up here. I can see for miles, and I feel free." I did not want to look into his insistent gray eyes. He must not see how I felt, but I could not stop myself saying, "Have you come to say good-bye, or did you remember my birthday after all? We haven't seen you for two weeks. My mother was quite concerned about you."

He took one step closer. Now he could just reach out to touch me, if he wanted to. But he didn't. Nor did he smile, but just continued to look at me steadily from those gray eyes that gave so little away until the moment of passion, when they told me everything. But I must not think of that.

"You're angry with me," he said. "I know, because your mother was not in the least concerned. You were. I've been sorting out matters for Jem's family, arranging help for his brother's trial. There has also been business to settle for my father."

"I see. And is it all satisfactorily resolved now? You're on your way back to France?" I turned my back on him and hunched my shoulders. The sun had disappeared behind the clouds gathering over the sea. A spring shower was on its way. How was I going to be able to bear this? Why couldn't he leave me alone?

"But you're right, I should have written to you, sent you a message. However, I . . . Written words seemed inadequate to the task. I needed to see you, to watch your face as we talked, and then the days went by, and it all took longer than I expected. In the end I had to be up at the crack of dawn to be here at all. I heard you were leaving Yorkshire today."

A Bitter Legacy

He was standing right behind me now. I could feel his warm breath on my neck and cheek. My body ached to be held by him. I kept my gaze fixed on the waves crashing and foaming on the rocks below. Why was he telling me all this?

"I also heard that you are selling the Hall to Adele or rather her husband-to-be, Redvers."

So that was why he'd come! It wasn't to see me, but to make one last bid for that wretched pile of stones. Fury swelled in my heart, and I whirled to face him. "And I expect you want to know why I didn't sell it to you! Believe me, I thought about it, but it wasn't for any of the reasons you will no doubt come up with, but because that place is tainted. It needs a fresh start. Adele loves it, but it's for Tommy, for the future. That place is no good for either of us, it would only bring you unhappiness, as it did me. Abandon your search for revenge now against my family, as I have. Give it up."

Slowly, he placed his hands on my arms, warm and heavy. His lips were not far from mine. I only had to stand on tiptoe to reach them. But I could not, must not.

"What reasons do you think that I will come up with, Vicky?"

"Oh, to keep it from you, to stop the Thornleys from winning, on a childish whim—"

"I see. I see that you were right, long ago, when you asked me to explain myself. Now I can. Yes, now I believe I can, especially as you've said what I've longed to hear, that you have no further stomach for revenge. But first, there's something that will explain far better than words."

I did not have to stand on tiptoe as he pulled me gently to him, and wrapped his arms around me. His mouth was on mine, softly sensual at first, and then with growing hunger. I did not care that my bonnet fell off and the wind began to dishevel my hair, or that the first drops of rain were falling, or that someone might see our indecorous behavior. I was swept away to another world, and I never wanted this moment to end.

But then Jasper, laughing, looked up at the sky. "Come, we'd better take shelter, and I'll tell you everything you have a right to know, Vicky my darling, my love."

We found shelter beneath an ancient arch of stone. Holding each other close, it was not cold. Jasper began to talk, of Jem, of the courts, of his father's business, while I nodded, not listening. Instead, I heard his voice saying over and over again, "Vicky, my darling, my love." Dazed with happiness, I leaned my head against his chest and sighed. He leaned down and kissed my cheek.

"I think you love me, too," he said, "Even though you haven't told me."

"Oh, I do, I do." I reached up and touched his face, felt the smooth coolness of his cheek,

A Bitter Legacy

the slight roughness of his chin, ran my hand through his springy black hair. "I knew after Sir Gransby's ball, although I'd denied it before. And you, when did you know?"

"Now I have a confession to make. I fell in love with you, or your image, before we even met. I saw your picture in one of my father's magazines and cut it out."

Ah, yes, I thought, *so that's why you had it in your locket.* And I had thought it was for other reasons.

"There was something about your face, the way you held your head, and I knew I had never fallen in love before, and why my dalliances had not resulted in marriage.

"When Albert Lansdowne died and you were named as heiress, I had two thoughts. Now Will's murderer might make a slip, and I could clear my name, and you needed protection. I saw myself as your savior and you as eternally grateful." He grinned down at me. It was a delight to see him smile, and smile again. "But you had other ideas. You wouldn't be persuaded that by selling the Hall to me, or by marrying me, you would be safe.

"I went to Albert Lansdowne's grave, and there you were. I recognised you immediately. But what did I find? No sweet young girl needing my help, but a self-possessed young woman eaten up with anger, fueled by revenge and a hatred I could understand only too well.

Then I wondered if you were like some of your kin after all. As I got to know the real Victoria Hunter, I was more powerfully attracted to you than by the milksop of my dreams. But could I trust you?"

"So," I stated slowly, "you didn't care at all about the fate of the Hall?"

"Not much. It was your fate and your mother's, of course, that mattered to me. I was certain that George was the evil force, but I was powerless to expose him without any proof."

I removed myself from his hold. "You tried to warn me about George over and over again, yet I—I—" I held my chin up to get the words out. "I even contemplated accepting his proposal. How can you forgive me?"

His eyes seemed to grow darker, and he cupped my face in his hands. "George has always been completely plausible to those whom he finds useful. I was not, therefore he didn't bother to hide his true self from me. Remember, even your grandfather, despite knowing how George tricked your father, never suspected him of anything else until the end when it was too late and he could do nothing about it. You must learn to forgive yourself, Vicky. I have nothing to forgive."

I sighed and closed my eyes, then disengaged myself again from his hands. "Revenge," I said in a low voice, "that was what I thought you wanted. Revenge by possessing the Hall and

A Bitter Legacy

destroying the Lansdownes. But that was what I wanted. How can you love me when . . . How pointless it seems now."

"I saw you struggle with yourself over and over again, and whatever happened, you always chose the right course in the end. Now come here, I have something to ask you."

The shower was nearly over, and a rainbow shimmered across the sea as the sun emerged again. I could hear voices, but still we were alone in our own world. This time, I put my arms around Jasper and held him tightly as we explored each other's mouths in growing ecstasy.

Then he whispered, "Now will you marry me, now that you know it's you I want. Do you trust me?"

My body sang with joy. No wonder Adele hated me. She'd known all along that Jasper was in love with me, that he'd never ask her to be his wife. So I had what she wanted, and she had what I wanted—or used to want. There was no doubt that I had received the better end of the bargain. I also knew the real reason I decided against selling to Jasper. I'd still secretly hoped and longed for this moment, and hadn't wanted the Hall to come between us. But my joy was short-lived.

"Yes," I whispered back, even though a black fist had suddenly closed around my heart, squeezing the life out of it. "I trust you."

And I did, I was sure that my personal fortune held no interest for him. But something else was troubling me now. "I can't marry you, however, Jasper. My mother needs me. My father has been found on the Caribbean island of Jamaica, and I must go with her to help nurse him back to health. You know I'll always love you, and perhaps later we can . . . But I can't be your wife yet."

Now I could not bear it. To find my love and lose him at the same time was insupportable.

I stood on the broad stone terrace in only my gown and wrap, leaning against the balustrade. Above swallows wheeled and screamed their thin scream against a wide, cloudless sky of azure. Around the terrace bloomed roses and honeysuckle and vibrant purple bougainvillea, their heady scents mingling in the warm morning air. Far away, beyond the dark green-blue spires of cypress trees, beyond the expanses of lavender and sunflower fields, beyond the vineyard, I could just see the deeper blue curve of the sea near Nice.

I never tired of this view, seeing it in different moods, at different times of the day, when the colors altered from pastel to stark vibrancy and back again. I even loved the ceaseless rasping of the crickets in the gnarled branches of the silver-leafed olive trees just beyond the house, where there was no grass, just dried-up stalks and dry

A Bitter Legacy

dusty tracks, and the occasional hobbled goat.

Behind me was my home of cool marble floors, the minimum of elegant furniture, long drapes at the shuttered windows matching the delicate colors of the wash walls. In the kitchen Marie-Louise would be warming croissants and hot chocolate for me, and brewing thick black aromatic coffee for the two masters. Outside the kitchen door, in large pots, grew pungent herbs, and using these, Marie-Louise would create wonderful meals.

It seemed impossible but it was true that every second of every day could be filled to the brim with utter happiness.

Jasper stepped out of the French windows to join me, clad only in trousers, showing his chest browned by the sun. He put his arms around me from behind and kissed my neck. "Shameless wife," he said. "Have you forgotten your genteel Boston manners so soon?"

I smiled. "This is another world, one I never dreamed could exist."

"Then you don't miss America? Or Yorkshire?" He pulled back my gown and punctuated his questions with further kisses across my naked shoulder.

"I never shall, as long as you keep kissing me like that. Where you are is my home now."

He was suddenly serious. "I still love my boyhood home, but I could never return there for good."

"Perhaps we'll go back to visit one day together, and I'll see the beauty there that you see." And if I should ever dream of northern skies, well, there was talk of newer and faster ships all the time. We could always visit. But life was about going forward, not back.

"One day but not too soon. We've so much else to explore . . ." His mouth began to send tremors of pleasure through me. With the delicious distraction of his body against mine, separated only by thin cotton, it was awhile before I remembered I had something to tell him.

"I had a letter from Mama this morning, Jasper. She tells me my father is getting better all the time, and they will soon be traveling to Boston. He was delighted with the photographs of our wedding." It had been a whirlwind affair, organized within weeks, with only a few guests, but had been ideal for us. "You still don't regret my sharing the money from the Hall with my mother, do you?"

"For the thousandth time, no. Do we need it anyway?"

I shook my head. Contrary to George's disparaging words, I'd discovered that Jasper's expertise had been highly respected and rewarded by the French, and he and his father now owned their own small vineyard in Provence. My money had been placed in trust for the future of our children, when they came.

A Bitter Legacy

"My father told her that he'd never stopped thinking of her or planning his escape from that disgusting gaol where he'd been thrown on a false charge after George spread lies to the Lansdowne agent on the island that my father had stolen money and was running away. Later, when that agent died, George bribed the corrupt prison governor to keep my father there. You cannot imagine the conditions he lived in, the beatings, kept in chains, often alone for weeks in a hole in the ground. It's a wonder he survived at all, weak as he was, but he was determined. I can't think what barbarous deeds—" I broke off, swept suddenly, as I still was on occasion, back to the bleak nightmare of winter at Lansdowne Hall.

"Ssh, it's all right, darling Vicky." Jasper's hands began to work their magic on me once more, and brought me back to the present.

"I love you," I said simply.

In answer, he picked me up and said, his voice husky, "Come inside, my love . . ."

"But your father . . ."

"Is happy to sit with his newspaper and coffee for half an hour longer. He dotes on you as a daughter, as I knew he would, but I shan't allow him to come between us."

He was teasing, but I remembered how nearly I had lost him in Whitby, until I had remembered my mother's own words earlier that morning, "Don't let the chance of happiness slip by."

So I'd told Jasper yes, and then returned to our rooms to tell my mother my decision. I needn't have worried. She'd been overjoyed, said she'd hoped for this outcome all along, that we were so well suited, and she could arrange for another traveling companion. I also realised, later, after I was married myself, that it was probably easier on my parents if they were alone together at first. But Jasper and I intended to visit them in Boston at Christmas.

Now Jasper picked me up, my squeals of protest stopped by his lips, and carried me back into the cool, bright interior of our bedroom. The darkness lay behind us, ahead lay only the light.

LOVE SPELL

THE MAGIC OF ROMANCE PAST, PRESENT, AND FUTURE....

Dorchester Publishing Co., Inc., the leader in romantic fiction, is pleased to unveil its newest line—Love Spell. Every month, beginning in August 1993, Love Spell will publish one book in each of four categories:

1) *Timeswept Romance*—Modern-day heroines travel to the past to find the men who fulfill their hearts' desires.

2) *Futuristic Romance*—Love on distant worlds where passion is the lifeblood of every man and woman.

3) *Historical Romance*—Full of desire, adventure and intrigue, these stories will thrill readers everywhere.

4) *Contemporary Romance*—With novels by Lori Copeland, Heather Graham, and Jayne Ann Krentz, Love Spell's line of contemporary romance is first-rate.

Exploding with soaring passion and fiery sensuality, Love Spell romances are destined to take you to dazzling new heights of ecstasy.

COMING IN JANUARY!
HISTORICAL ROMANCE
HUNTERS OF THE ICE AGE: YESTERDAY'S DAWN
By Theresa Scott

Named for the massive beast sacred to his people, Mamut has proven his strength and courage time and again. But when it comes to subduing one helpless captive female, he finds himself at a distinct disadvantage. Never has he realized the power of beguiling brown eyes, soft curves and berry-red lips to weaken a man's resolve. He has claimed he will make the stolen woman his slave, but he soon learns he will never enjoy her alluring body unless he can first win her elusive heart.

_51920-8 $4.99 US/$5.99 CAN

A CONTEMPORARY ROMANCE
HIGH VOLTAGE
By Lori Copeland

Laurel Henderson hadn't expected the burden of inheriting her father's farm to fall squarely on her shoulders. And if Sheriff Clay Kerwin can't catch the culprits who are sabotaging her best efforts, her hopes of selling it are dim. Struggling with this new responsibility, Laurel has no time to pursue anything, especially not love. The best she can hope for is an affair with no strings attached. And the virile law officer is the perfect man for the job—until Laurel's scheme backfires. Blind to Clay's feelings and her own, she never dreams their amorous arrangement will lead to the passion she wants to last for a lifetime.

_51923-2 $4.99 US/$5.99 CAN

LOVE SPELL
ATTN: Order Department
Dorchester Publishing Co., Inc.
276 5th Avenue, New York, NY 10001

Please add $1.50 for shipping and handling for the first book and $.35 for each book thereafter. PA., N.Y.S. and N.Y.C. residents, please add appropriate sales tax. No cash, stamps, or C.O.D.s. All orders shipped within 6 weeks via postal service book rate. Canadian orders require $2.00 extra postage and must be paid in U.S. dollars through a U.S. banking facility.

Name_____
Address_____
City _____ State_____Zip_____
I have enclosed $_____in payment for the checked book(s).
Payment <u>must</u> accompany all orders. ☐ Please send a free catalog.

COMING IN JANUARY!
TIMESWEPT ROMANCE

TIME OF THE ROSE
By Bonita Clifton

When the silver-haired cowboy brings Madison Calloway to his run-down ranch, she thinks for sure he is senile. Certain he'll bring harm to himself, Madison follows the man into a thunderstorm and back to the wild days of his youth in the Old West.

The dread of all his enemies and the desire of all the ladies, Colton Chase does not stand a chance against the spunky beauty who has tracked him through time. And after one passion-drenched night, Colt is ready to surrender his heart to the most tempting spitfire anywhere in time.

_51922-4 $4.99 US/$5.99 CAN

A FUTURISTIC ROMANCE

AWAKENINGS
By Saranne Dawson

Fearless and bold, Justan rules his domain with an iron hand, but nothing short of the Dammai's magic will bring his warring people peace. He claims he needs Rozlynd—a bewitching beauty and the last of the Dammai—for her sorcery alone, yet inside him stirs an unexpected yearning to savor the temptress's charms, to sample her sweet innocence. And as her silken spell ensnares him, Justan battles to vanquish a power whose like he has never encountered—the power of Rozlynd's love.

_51921-6 $4.99 US/$5.99 CAN

LOVE SPELL
ATTN: Order Department
Dorchester Publishing Co., Inc.
276 5th Avenue, New York, NY 10001

Please add $1.50 for shipping and handling for the first book and $.35 for each book thereafter. PA., N.Y.S. and N.Y.C. residents, please add appropriate sales tax. No cash, stamps, or C.O.D.s. All orders shipped within 6 weeks via postal service book rate. Canadian orders require $2.00 extra postage and must be paid in U.S. dollars through a U.S. banking facility.

Name_____
Address_____
City _____ State_____Zip_____
I have enclosed $_____in payment for the checked book(s).
Payment <u>must</u> accompany all orders.☐ Please send a free catalog.

COMING IN DECEMBER 1993
FROM LOVE SPELL
FUTURISTIC ROMANCE
NO OTHER LOVE
Flora Speer
Bestselling Author of *A Time To Love Again*

Only Herne sees the woman. To the other explorers of the ruined city she remains unseen, unknown. But after an illicit joining she is gone, and Herne finds he cannot forget his beautiful seductress, or ignore her uncanny resemblance to another member of the exploration party. Determined to unravel the puzzle, Herne begins a seduction of his own—one that will unleash a whirlwind of danger and desire.

_51916-X $4.99 US/$5.99 CAN

TIMESWEPT ROMANCE
LOVE'S TIMELESS DANCE
Vivian Knight-Jenkins

Although the pressure from her company's upcoming show is driving Leeanne Sullivan crazy, she refuses to believe she can be dancing in her studio one minute—and with a seventeenth-century Highlander the next. A liberated woman like Leeanne will have no problem teaching virile Iain MacBride a new step or two, and soon she'll have him begging for lessons in love.

_51917-8 $4.99 US/$5.99 CAN

LOVE SPELL
ATTN: Order Department
Dorchester Publishing Company, Inc.
276 5th Avenue, New York, NY 10001

Please add $1.50 for shipping and handling for the first book and $.35 for each book thereafter. PA., N.Y.S. and N.Y.C. residents, please add appropriate sales tax. No cash, stamps, or C.O.D.s. All orders shipped within 6 weeks via postal service book rate. Canadian orders require $2.00 extra postage and must be paid in U.S. dollars through a U.S. banking facility.

Name_____
Address_____
City _____ State_____ Zip_____
I have enclosed $_____ in payment for the checked book(s). Payment <u>must</u> accompany all orders.☐ Please send a free catalog.

COMING IN DECEMBER 1993
FROM LOVE SPELL
HISTORICAL ROMANCE
THE PASSIONATE REBEL
Helene Lehr

A beautiful American patriot, Gillian Winthrop is horrified to learn that her grandmother means her to wed a traitor to the American Revolution. Her body yearns for Philip Meredith's masterful touch, but she is determined not to give her hand—or any other part of herself—to the handsome Tory, until he convinces her that he too is a passionate rebel.

_51918-6 $4.99 US/$5.99 CAN

CONTEMPORARY ROMANCE
THE TAWNY GOLD MAN
Amii Lorin

Bestselling Author Of More Than 5 Million Books In Print!

Long ago, in a moment of wild, rioting ecstasy, Jud Cammeron vowed to love her always. Now, as Anne Moore looks at her stepbrother, she sees a total stranger, a man who plans to take control of his father's estate and everyone on it. Anne knows things are different—she is a grown woman with a fiance—but something tells her she still belongs to the tawny gold man.

_51919-4 $4.99 US/$5.99 CAN

LOVE SPELL
ATTN: Order Department
Dorchester Publishing Company, Inc.
276 5th Avenue, New York, NY 10001

Please add $1.50 for shipping and handling for the first book and $.35 for each book thereafter. PA., N.Y.S. and N.Y.C. residents, please add appropriate sales tax. No cash, stamps, or C.O.D.s. All orders shipped within 6 weeks via postal service book rate. Canadian orders require $2.00 extra postage and must be paid in U.S. dollars through a U.S. banking facility.

Name _____
Address _____
City _____ State _____ Zip _____
I have enclosed $_____in payment for the checked book(s).
Payment <u>must</u> accompany all orders. ☐ Please send a free catalog.

**Spellbinding historical romantic suspense
exploding with dangerous love!**

LEONA KARR

Obsession. Tara is mesmerized by the stranger's smoldering eyes, captivated by his masterful touch, but the name he whispers in the heat of passion belongs to another. She will create herself in the image of that other woman; she, too, will glitter on stage, and her golden-haired beauty will hold the same sensual lure for the man she adores. But when he takes her to the heights of ecstasy, is it an act of love or the fulfillment of a dark obsession?
_3531-6 $4.50 US/$5.50 CAN

Illusions. For lovely Charlotte Conrad her first Atlantic crossing turns into a nightmare when she learns that she must accompany a total stranger—as his bride. With her father's very life in jeopardy, she has no choice but to submit to the pretense of a lavish wedding trip, complete with whispers of seduction. Caught in a silken web of danger and desire, she knows that the swirling ecstasy of her husband's embrace, like the words of his love, is nothing but an illusion.
_3572-3 $4.50 US/$5.50 CAN

**LEISURE BOOKS
ATTN: Order Department
276 5th Avenue, New York, NY 10001**

Please add $1.50 for shipping and handling for the first book and $.35 for each book thereafter. PA., N.Y.S. and N.Y.C. residents, please add appropriate sales tax. No cash, stamps, or C.O.D.s. All orders shipped within 6 weeks via postal service book rate. Canadian orders require $2.00 extra postage and must be paid in U.S. dollars through a U.S. banking facility.

Name_____
Address_____
City _____ State _____ Zip _____
I have enclosed $_____in payment for the checked book(s).
Payment <u>must</u> accompany all orders. ☐ Please send a free catalog.